"Never worry about
about in
Winston Churchill

This book is dedicated to those who take action when it's needed.
If you enjoy this story, then stick around afterwards, as I have
something pretty awesome to offer you. I'm sure you'll love it.

Scorpion's Vengeance

Scorpion One, Volume 3

Lawrence Hebb

Published by Lawrence Hebb, 2023.

SCORPION'S VENGEANCE

First edition. July 14, 2023.

Copyright © 2023 Lawrence Hebb.

ISBN: 979-8223784920

Written by Lawrence Hebb.

Scorpion's Vengeance
By Lawrence Hebb
(A Scorpion 1 book)

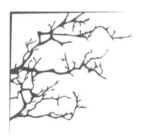

Dedication

This book is dedicated to all those who served, and literally, put their lives on the line so that we can enjoy the freedom we have today.

Acknowledgements.

Before we get into the story I want to take a few minutes to say a big thank you to all the people who made this book possible, mainly those who as soon as Book two was out started asking "when's book three coming"

I also want to say a big thank you to my family who made sure that I had the time to write and do whatever I needed to in order to get the book finished, I hope you enjoy the result as much as I enjoyed writing it.

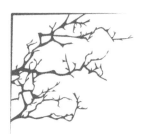

Chapter 1

L ocation London
Time Tuesday 05.30 (local time)

There was a slight chill in the air as she stepped out of the apartment block. The trail from the moisture she exhaled was noticeable. The temperature was in single digits, and probably near to zero celsius. Not surprising considering it was autumn, and winter was closing in.

The first thing she noticed outside (apart from the cold, that is) was the traffic. It was pretty steady at this time in the morning, any later and it would be its usual diabolical situation, it made her glad that the 'tube' (as Londoners affectionately call the London underground rail network) got her to within a few minutes walk of work.

It also meant that instead of having a horrible commute of at least an hour by car. All she had to do was walk to the local underground, or tube station, as the locals called them. That one was known as the 'Elephant and Castle' jump on the Northern line, and ten minutes later. She'd be right outside the Bank of England in one of the world's greatest financial hubs.

But the really great part about the place was, just a quick jog from home was some of London's best attractions. Walk out of the apartment. Take a right on Brook-street, and you're right outside the Imperial war museum, with the massive fourteen-inch guns from the front turret of HMS Warspite. One of Britain's last battleships to be decommissioned after the second world war on full display.

4

Turn right onto Kensington Road and first left onto Horse-ferry road and Lambeth Palace is right there. The official residence of the Archbishop of Canterbury, and a medieval palace in its own right. Head across the bridge and you're right there, in the seat of power. Westminster Palace, better known as the House of Commons, and the House of Lords, Parliament, and all within a quick jog of her place.

There were a few cars about, but most of the traffic was commercial. Trying to make their last deliveries before the six am deadline when delivery trucks need to be out of the urban centres. Giving room for those crazy enough to try getting to work by car. Not that there are many of them in London. Congestion charges make sure of that either only those who live within the limits drive their cars around, or those addicted to their cars and willing to pay the exorbitant charges for using it. The tube is much easier, and safer.

She stopped for a moment, adjusting her beanie. Checked her ponytail. No need to hide any keys. The apartment had one of the latest locks with a four-digit keypad system. It was unbreakable. Then again, the four-digit code she'd programmed would have been easy to break. It was her birthday. Easy to remember and easy for anyone who knew Jane to break into the apartment. If they knew her date of birth, that is!

As soon as everything was ready. She checked and working then she was off, a morning jog. She always planned to start gently as there were a few main streets to cross, and the last couple of years the local council had been converting the pedestrian underpasses to cycleways. At this time of the morning, she could deal with a few maniacal cyclists hell-bent on running anything in their path down.

After the run, it would be a shower, breakfast, and into work by 8 am. That was the plan, the same every morning. She had no idea the change that was going to happen.

At the end of Hercules street she 'hung a right' and started picking up the pace. The next stop would be Lambeth bridge, just alongside Lambeth Palace.

It always puzzled Jane. She worked in the financial world and was used to opulence or wealth. But wasn't the church founded by a poor son of a carpenter? And didn't he teach "The love of money is the root of all evil?" Yet here was a vast Palace, all for the use of one man! Just made little sense to her really, in some ways, she was a traditional 'C of E' as they said in Britain for the Anglican church, but in other ways, she didn't really have too many beliefs, apart from the need to be a basically 'good' person, yet the church seemed to flout its own rules, teaching poverty for its members, but wealth for its hierarchy!

Crossing Lambeth bridge, she turned right, but not the hard right that would take her along the river, and started her run in earnest. Sycamore trees lined the right-hand side of the road. They'd lost about half their leaves so far as the autumn crept in. A street sweeper was slowly making its way down the opposite side of the street. Clearing away the foliage before 'the powers that be' surfaced and took charge of the country for the morning. This was the time when only the lowly paid ruled the streets.

About half a mile further up, she took a right. The House of Lords on her left. The imposing tower where Big Ben rang out was on the other side of the building.

Most tourists think of Big Ben, the most iconic landmark in London as the big clock tower you see on just about every postcard from London. But Big Ben actually is the massive bell inside the tower, and at thirteen tons, it lives up to the name! The tower has another name, the Elizabeth Tower. Named after the present Queen, and in honour of her Diamond Jubilee celebrations.

Reaching the Thames, she turned right again and was just hitting her stride something caught her eye, something floating in the river.

"What the?" was Jane's first thought. "What is that?" She stopped to take a closer look. "Oh my God" she screamed as the thing turned over. Slowly, seemingly reluctantly, as if it didn't want to reveal itself, but now there was no doubt as the gruesome thing stared back through lifeless eyes.

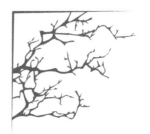

Chapter 2

L ocation Bay of Plenty off the coast of New Zealand
Time. Monday, 0500 (local time) and 12 hours ahead of
London.

"You are aware," Jacko shouted into the headset, "the mission is over. You are aware of that, aren't you?" He tapped Carol, the pilot, on the shoulder as he spoke.

They were at fifty feet, touching two hundred miles an hour, and heading for the coastline. No navigation lights.

"Sorry Captain," Carol almost laughed. "In case you didn't know, you're not supposed to be here. That means I've got to get you outta here with no one knowing you were ever around. Get my drift?" she had a cheeky grin.

'Black ops' or Covert Ops aren't just about getting in without your enemy knowing you're coming. They're just as much about getting out again with no one knowing you've been there! Literally 'keep them guessing and that means the 'exfil' can be just as hairy as the 'infill' and Carol was loving every second, it's rarely she got to push her 'cab' to its limit (and well beyond what the manufacturer said it could do).

Jacko turned back. The rest of the team were busy. Mac, Smithy and Joey all had their weapons stripped and were busy cleaning them. Sandy was poring over the laptop, checking files. From the look on her face, he wasn't even sure it'd registered that they were airborne. Sam and Hene were at the back, slightly dazed looks on their faces, *with what they've just been through, no wonder,'* he thought to himself. He was surprised and encouraged how well they were holding things together.

He keyed his mike again. "How far to our destination?"

"Fifteen minutes until we're over land," Carol replied, "then about forty minutes."

"Bird off the Starboard" the co-pilot spoke the warning. The set of navigation lights seemed to be heading straight for them and coming in really fast. "Closing fast, break right, BREAK RIGHT" the second command was almost a shout as Carol yanked the controls hard right. All Jacko saw was the sky as the aircraft went into the steep turn.

"What the" Mac's reaction was instinctive. He grabbed for the bulkhead, not really necessary as they were all strapped firmly in, "what the hell boss? I'm looking at the bloody ocean!"

"Thank your lucky stars you can still see it and aren't in the bloody stuff," Carol cut in, she glanced at the co-pilot, "thanks for that,"

"Eagle one, this is Eagle's Nest," they all heard the call. It couldn't be a good thing. 'Eagle's nest' was where 'Mildred' was. Someone was changing things, and that was never good.

"One go ahead," Carol replied on the radio.

"Go to channel one,"

Everyone was listening. They were still working through cleaning the weapons. But there was a sense of urgency. Carol had told them at the start that channel one was the scrambler channel. "You know, just in case," she'd said. Now, whoever it was wanted to speak to them without even the professional 'snoops' listening in, that was reserved for only the most important. It didn't bode well for whatever they had to say.

The co-pilot reached out with his left hand, turning a dial on the central console. They heard nothing at first, then a voice came on the line. They'd heard it once before, at the start of the op, but five of the seven recognised it straight away.

"Captain, I presume you can all hear me?" the voice asked. It was female, and from the sound, she was an older middle-aged woman, one used to being in charge.

"Yes, ma'am," Jacko replied, "We're all here,"

"Good," the voice came back, "then I don't have to waste my time repeating myself. Sorry about this, but a formal debriefing will not happen at this stage,"

'Shit', no one said the word. But that's exactly what everyone was thinking. Whatever was going on meant that this op wasn't over, but what the hell can be next?

"We've got so much information," the voice went on, "it's going to take months to put everything together, but some of what we got we've got to get our arses into gear and move on it, and I mean now!"

"Figured that," Joey thought he whispered it, but the 'voice' heard it and cut him off.

"Glad you're with us, Mr Metcalfe, how's the wound?"

"The jacket took the bullets" Jacko silenced Joey with a glare and a finger over his lips. "Just a couple of bruises, that's all. Besides, where there's no sense, there's no feeling, right Joey?" he joked. It brought smiles from the rest of them. Even Joey enjoyed the joke.

"Glad to hear it," Mildred's voice came back. "We're going to need every one of you in this, and that includes the two police with you!" she didn't refer to Sam and Hene by name. She didn't know their names, but that didn't matter.

Sam and Hene had been sitting trying to comprehend what they'd just been through. Police training prepares you for a lot. But what they'd just done was in a different league. Yes, they'd used firearms, and there'd been times when Sam had drawn hers in the line of duty, but this had been a full-fledged firefight where they'd been shooting to kill with every shot, and the team had been absolutely ruthless. What had thrown them was the fact that none of the team seemed too concerned they'd just been in a life or death firefight. The voice mentioning them snapped them back to reality.

"As I said." The voice went on, "we've got to get your arses into gear, otherwise we'll lose the momentum. At the moment, we've got an enemy that's wounded. But from what we can make out, they're a long way from being finished, and if we don't move fast, they're likely to strike back and do it hard!"

"Roger that, ma'am," Jacko cut back in. "What do you need from us?"

"I'm going to need you to deliver a message for me," the voice came back. The helicopter had turned nearly ninety degrees and was heading straight for the Coromandel Peninsula. It was going to be an interesting flight. "The two police, with you, Sam and Hene, isn't it?"

"Yes," both of them confirmed.

"You're still officially with the police," the voice replied. "But as of this moment, you work directly with me. A new task force that the Prime Minister will set up as soon as I've put the paper on the PM's desk, and yes, they've already agreed to it. You'll be working for me on the legal side of things here in New Zealand. At least that's what the papers will say. Reality is you'll be running 'backup' for the team, and just about anything else I can think of,"

Sam and Hene just stared at each other. Sam was a good cop, even got noticed by her bosses, but this was way beyond even her paygrade, whoever it was, clearly had some pull!

And that phrase "that's what the papers will say" kind of bothered her. It made it sound like there was more to things than even Mildred was letting on.

"As for the rest of you," the voice went on. Jacko and Mac. A vehicle's waiting on the tarmac for you. It'll take you to a waiting C130 that'll fly you back to Aussie as soon as you're aboard. From there, you'll board a flight to London. Papers and passports will be given you when you get to Sydney. Should take you about twenty-four hours all told."

Silence. No one knew what to think. Clearly, something was going on. "Might I ask why?" it was Mac asked. No one liked the sound of what was going on.

It took a few moments for the voice to reply, "We need to get the information to Sir Michael, but can't use the normal channels."

"We've got a leak haven't we?" It was Sandy who cut in. "Not just a mole, but one that could blow the whole thing, isn't that right?"

"Whoever it was," the voice came back, "fed your names and details to the ship. That means the entire organization knows who's hunting them! And as far as I know, only three people knew who you were. All three can be accounted for, and they didn't pass the information. So it has to be someone working in the secure comms networks!"

"Holy crap," Joey let out a few more choice words as well, "that means every."

"Every signal we sent, every word we reported back, all got given to them, not only that, but every detail about us. They have, and they probably know that we know!"

"Hence the 'old school' face to face," the voice came back, "and that's where you come in Captain."

Chapter 3

L ocation London

It had been one heck of a day. It felt more like a bloody week. But the watch on her wrist assured her it was only a day. Actually less than that, but that didn't matter. A body turns up in the river right outside the Houses of Parliament and the cops better have answers bloody fast. So far, they had none!

Hell, they couldn't even tell the name of the body they'd found. All they could tell was it was male, in the late twenties and either southern European or Pakistani, maybe even Indian, so far nothing. Nada, zilch. And the whole frigging mess had landed right in Billie's bloody lap! She was pissed off about the whole bloody thing!

"It's the kind that can make a career," her boss, Detective Chief Inspector or DCI Steve Townsend, had told her. What he'd left out was that it can just as easily break a career. And that's why he was avoiding the case it like it was the bubonic plague. It was a poisoned chalice, so he gave it to the cop he liked the least in the department. The one who'd told him to "piss off" at the last Christmas party when he tried seducing her. She'd been ready to drive the point home with a good kick 'right between 'em', but even in his drunken state, he'd seen the sense in backing off. Just he hadn't forgotten, *'this is payback,'* she thought.

The coroner had taken the body away about midday. They'd re-opened the scene as soon as they could, but not before marking everything and going through to the last little detail. Even where the cigarette butts were on the pavement.

Billie, or BJ, as she was sometimes known, was back at the scene. She wanted to see it the way it would have been before anything happened. The only way to get that idea was to 'walk the scene' after everything was put back to 'normal' whatever that was, literally to 'pace everything out' and see what fit where.

"Report says he didn't enter the river here though." She spoke out loud, but to no one in particular. "I wonder where then?"

'*At least I'll have some idea about that when the toxicology report comes back.*' She thought to herself as she reached for her mobile. BJ had been taking pictures of the area. Not that it would arouse any suspicion. It was a popular tourist spot. It's when they're not taking pictures you get worried!

Dialling the number she asked one question, "Any luck?"

"Not so far guv." the voice on the other end came back, a young copper, still a 'probie' with CID. (Criminal Investigation Department) but damn good with computers. "I can't find the sod anywhere"

"Tried the D.V.L.C?"

The D.V.LC stands for Driver Vehicle Licensing Centre, the government body that issues everyone's driving licence. It's also the most extensive database of anyone who's got a licence, or had one in the past. Almost the unofficial identity card that Brits didn't know they had.

"This boy didn't have one," the voice cut back in, "at least none I can find."

"But" she began.

"Everyone's got a licence, right?" He cut her off, "this boy didn't have, and before you ask." He went on, "I've tried customs, passport, and Interpol, just in case, but nothing, Nada, zilch, bloody guy was a ghost!"

"Okay" she was more than a little frustrated, but tried hard not to let it come out, '*count to ten girl*' she was telling herself mentally, *'count to ten'* as she went on with her instructions. "Keep at it, someone has to know this guy, keep digging" she swiped the screen.

This wasn't good. She had a press conference planned for an hour from now, and all she had was a body found in the most public place possible. No identification, no record, no idea if it was an accident or not, and no idea where the bloody thing went into the river.

In London, nothing happens without someone knowing! That's the reality, there are more CCTV cameras in London than any other city on earth. Yet not around where the body was, which was odd, as it was right opposite the Houses of Parliament. The biggest terror target in the United Kingdom. But unless she knew where to look, it was all useless!

The city is fifty miles across, and from the moment you leave the M25 (the London orbital route), every move, every signal, every breath you take is watched by someone or something. BJ knew that someone somewhere would have the answers. Finding them, however, would be like looking for the proverbial needle in a haystack.

What she didn't know was that someone was intentionally trying to hide that 'needle' from her and that someone had the means to hide it.

That's what people were trying to decide right at that moment. MI6 already knew about the body. They got the information from the computer searches that the Met had initiated that they were looking. So far, they'd blocked them without raising too much suspicion. They knew it would not last. Eventually, someone would get frustrated and ask *'Those little shits'* as MI6 were often thought of its opposite number that dealt with internal security, then all hell would break loose, and someone would need to tell the Metropolitan police or Met for short to 'back off'

"What do you think?" the junior case officer asked his superior. He was the one monitoring the radio frequencies, and illegally wiretapping the police officer in charge's phone. "Want me to put a block on the information?"

"Nah," the reply came back. His superior was actually younger than he was, but a university education still got you a good job with the security services. How good you were determined how far you went. "Better flag it and send it on its way upstairs. Let them decide what to do with the whole damned mess!"

It took less than five minutes to transform the whole conversation into a written 'transcription' that could be sent as an email, with a little red flag noting that it was a priority, a name added, the audio file attached to the email and sent on its way. No need to encrypt the file, as it was internal, and MI6 had never been breached. At least not as far as they were aware.

Sir Michael had worked on the whole thing since he first got word about eleven am that morning. Things had been winding up, though it was strange they hadn't heard from the team. "Probably just a precaution," he'd told himself, but part of him didn't totally feel at ease.

A light came on his screen as he was reading a hard copy report. It was Farid Akbari's service record. Farid was the one that had been killed, a blow to the service, and gut-wrenching to him, he knew the family well.

Mohammed Akbari was an Egyptian who'd first come to their attention in the 1980s. Born into a Muslim family, he'd been raised in one of Cairo's most conservative areas. Even went to the great Al Azhar University studied Arabic literature and got a PhD in Islamic studies only to fall foul of the Egyptian authorities in his progressive views.

Egypt had tolerated him for a while. But when he renounced Islam and married a Christian woman. All hell had broken loose, and they'd had to flee.

Farid had been in England at the time, studying Oriental studies at Oxford, compliments of his father having a good friend in the Embassy. Sir Michael was simply 'Mike' then, and was 'officially' the MI6 officer in residence.

They never 'officially' found out what happened to Farid's father. Rumour had it. He was dragged into the street, beaten to a pulp. Then forced to watch while the local firebrand Islamic fundamentalists repeatedly raped and mutilated his wife and Farid's younger sister before they were killed. Then finally he was put out of his misery by a bullet from a police gun. The body disposed of somewhere in the desert. The police hadn't just watched, they'd joined in. It had been done with the blessing of the government! "One less trouble-causer to lead people astray" had been shouted.

Sir Michael knew about it through a mutual friend. The Babba Butros, the assistant to the Coptic Bishop of Cairo, he told Michael all about it, hoping to get Michael to warn the boy not to come home. He'd done a little more than that. Farid had wanted revenge, and Michael had given him a chance to work towards that. The old Arab saying, "The enemy of my enemy is my friend" came back with a vengeance.

'And now he's dead' was all Sir Michael could think, 'and no idea if it's linked to the Islamics, or could it even be the drug barons?' He was really hoping it wasn't linked to the 'mole', but nothing could be ruled out at this stage.

He reached out and touched the screen with his right index finger; the screen came alive with a picture. It was Cairo, the secure room at the Embassy, a call he'd been expecting as soon as he'd sent word of Farid's death.

"Michael," the youngish woman at the other end of the line addressed him. He was still surprised it was a woman in charge in Cairo. He was surprised he had pulled that off, but that was before he took over as director. The Middle East is still a very male-dominated society, and as the 'head of station' Rachel had to deal with a lot of men who thought they were better than her. What they never got was the fact that, if you want to know what the President of Egypt is thinking, you don't talk to his aides, you talk to his wives or mistresses, and that Rachel was very good at. "Thanks for the heads up. Sorry to hear about Farid, any news?"

By 'any news?' he knew exactly what she meant. "How are we affected? Are we in the proverbial?"

"All the above," he replied, "and none as well." He stood and walked over to his coffee machine, a Nespresso machine. There were capsules. 'Ristorante Andretti, he took one, slid open the top and dropped the capsule in. There was already water, the machine's reservoir push of the button and a coffee to rival the best of any cafe was ready. Only then did he continue.

"He's one of us." He went on, "that means all bets are off, but otherwise, we've no-no all we know is he went into the river, but no idea where, or how." He'd ambled back to his desk, slowly sinking into his chair he went on, " what was Farid dealing with?"

"Nothing major, least not as far as I'm aware," Rachel replied, "just doing some tracking of our usual suspects, nothing too high risk. Mainly tracking the money,"

If it caused any alarm, he didn't show it. Then again, Rachel, and just about everyone else in the Embassy knew you don't play poker with Sir Michael. The poker face was out and on the show. That told her to be worried, but didn't show it.

"You think he was a target then?" she asked, trying not to sound too concerned.

"Can't say right now," he replied. "could be many things. We've got a few things going on. They could be connected, but which one? I just don't know!"

"So," it was more a statement than anything, "not an accident then?"

"Hell no," he replied, "not an accident,"

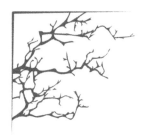

Chapter 4

"Barry," Sir Michael spoke into the intercom, "can you get the car ready? Meet me in the car park," he clicked the mike from 'transmit' to 'receive.'

"Will do sir," the reply came back.

"Thank you" he replied, "I'll be there in about ten minutes" he clicked the intercom off altogether, next he turned the office scrambler off, there were listening devices throughout the building, technically, no one was allowed to use scrambling devices, everything was recorded, even the Director wasn't supposed to use one, officially he stuck to that rule, but some conversations weren't meant to be recorded, it was just too dangerous for the wrong people.

"Heading off?" it was Chambers asking. He was still working, poring over the files they'd got from Sandy in the last transmission, still trying to find the 'needle in the haystack.'

"Yeah," he replied. It felt strange, leaving before a subordinate officer. It wasn't his way normally, but there were things to think through, and that was best done away from here. Away from the distractions of minute by minute updates with ten different operations. There was a mole to catch, and he did not know where to look. Actually, he had an idea, but he needed time to work it out, time to work through the issues.

Closing the door, he activated the silent alarm. That one was linked to the 'control room' in another part of the building. If that went off, the offenders would need to start praying. Getting arrested for 'breaking and entering' would be the least of their worries.

Staying alive would be their top priority, and even that would be doubtful.

The lift was waiting. Michelle, his secretary, always saw to that. She saw to all those kinds of things. Even when he didn't need them, as was the case this evening, there wasn't much chance for exercise in his day. So, making the most of the chance of some exercise, he headed for the stairs and the car park six floors below.

The building has three stairwells. Two on the outside of the building, and used as fire escapes. They're on the plans, but the third is in the middle, and isn't on any plans. It's there as an emergency for if there's ever a 'breach' in their security, that's the one he was using.

The good thing about the inside stairwell is it takes the user directly to the secure underground car park. One that's totally sealed off. Try to get in this one from the outside and you're going to get a nasty shock. Passkey controls allow you to get as far as the guards' checkpoint. Facial recognition by both a human and a computer allows you further in. Fail any of those two and let's just say the parking attendants are the only ones in Britain that carry L85-A2 semi-automatic rifles.

The original L85-A1 was a piece of junk that was first made by the Royal Ordnance depot in the UK. But when Royal Ordnance bought Heckler and Koch, the first thing they did was give the plans over to HK to remodel the L85. The result, the L85-A2, a seriously underrated assault rifle, and ideal for close quarter combat. Also close enough to look like a standard police weapon in the UK, but badass enough to scare the shit out of anyone, fool enough to try their luck.

The car park looked deserted. That is all except for the vehicle that had just started up, and was heading towards the doorway he'd just come out of. His Bentley was on its way. Sir Michael relaxed slightly. It had been a long and damn difficult day, no word from the team in NZ. That was only partly expected. They still had a mole, and from the last intel they'd got, the mole knew they were in NZ. The team had 'gone dark' and he had a good idea why.

He couldn't see the driver, but in a place this secure. There wasn't any question as to whom it would be. Sir Michael made his way to the car. He noticed that 'Barry' was wearing a cap he didn't normally do. Something wasn't right. He closed the door and stepped away.

Out of the shadows stepped another. He felt his arms pinned in two vice-like grips. A voice he recognised spoke through the balaclava that the 'shadow' had pulled over his face. A blunt Scottish accent said, "Now we have your attention. We need to have a wee word ``wi ye".

The driver pressed a button on a console, the rear passenger door opened, "Get in."

"What the hell?" He instinctively struggled, hoping it was being picked up on camera, and the security teams were watching.

"Dinnae argue with me, laddie," the Scot said, forcing him into the car. "Not here, now get in!"

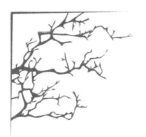

Chapter 5

"Jesus Jacko," Sir Michael blurted out as soon as he was in the car. "You are aware that it was a kidnapping, aren't you?"

"Sorry boss," was all Jacko could say. He was concentrating on the driving and getting them through the traffic. No one at Vauxhall house had responded, and it took them only a couple of minutes to get out of the building. "But we've got to talk, and this was the only way!"

"Ever heard of secure lines?" Sir Michael asked, clearly angry at the situation, "total privacy you know!"

"You mean total secrecy?" Jacko replied, "Like it was supposed to be with our locations?"

That stopped him in his tracks. He was about to give a lecture on how dumb the move was. It was still dumb, but something was coming, and he didn't like where this was going. "What do you mean?" he demanded.

They were heading across Lambeth Bridge. The traffic wasn't too busy. There were even cops on the streets, but as dumb as the move had been taking him in the car park, the intelligence officer in him wanted to know what they had.

"Like I asked," Jacko shot back, "as secure as our whereabouts was?"

"But" he replied, there was a drinks cabinet in the back of the Bentley. He reached for it. Mac blocked him, then reached out and opened the cabinet himself, satisfying himself there wasn't any nasty surprise in there. He then allowed Sir Michael to continue getting himself a drink. "I thought Joey and Sandy cleared that up. They were just in the wrong place at the right time?"

"We're not talking about how the bloody thing kicked off," Jacko replied as he took a right turn off the bridge. They were heading north, "don't worry boss," Jacko went on, "we're not going far, just far enough that we can have a quiet chat."

Sir Michael still couldn't believe it. He'd been in the most secure building in the country. He should have been safe, but he wasn't. "How the hell did you get into the building?" He blurted out, " the most secure in the bloody country, how?"

"Sorry boss," Mac cut in, "need to know, and you don't need to. Besides, that car park in Derby is more secure." He couldn't resist the jibe that a car park was regarded as the most secure building in the country.

Sir Michael couldn't believe it. *I'm the director of MI6,* he thought. 'I'm the one who decides who needs to bloody know!' but he knew it was pointless trying to get an answer.

"Look" he was getting frustrated, "just what the hell is going on? And how the hell did you know how to get in?"

Jacko brought the car to a halt. They were outside Sir Michael's club. The Marylebone club. He applied the handbrake, turned and faced Sir Michael. "you've got a leak!"

"Think I don't know that!" Sir Michael almost whispered. Whenever he was stressed, he went quieter, "and a body in the river," he went on, "I'm still wondering if they're linked!"

"News said it was male," Mac chipped in, "that right?"

"Yeah," he replied, "a young computer programmer, the name of Akbari, but part of me wonders, you know anything about it?"

Neither of them reacted, at least neither of them showed any signs giving anything away. They just sat there, a deadpan, almost bored expression on their faces.

"Boss," Jacko began, "your 'body' was found this morning, right?" He asked, "just about thirty hours before, we were knee deep in shit and drug dealers. Hell, it took us nearly twelve hours for the 'takedown', and you're asking if we've been busy here in London? Sorry boss, but Concorde went out of service, what, twenty years ago!" he wanted to add that it never flew the London to Auckland route, anyway.

They could see Sir Michael going red in the face. He wasn't used to being talked to this way. Not by anyone. The SAS were almost as well known for their 'informality' as they were for their superb training. But they were pushing the limit of what he'd tolerate. "I'll ask you again captain" he spoke slowly and deliberately, "how did you get into the building?"

"Okay," Jacko held up his hand, "sorry boss, but we've got some serious issues to deal with," he turned to Mac, "I think we'd better explain."

Mac had been listening in, a slightly amused expression on his face. He'd really enjoyed the verbal 'jousting' that had been going on. *Two Rodneys having a go at each other* he thought, *best entertainment around* but now it was time to get serious. He looked directly at Sir Michael, and said two things, "G squadron!" as if that explained everything. Both men knew exactly what, or rather, whom, he was talking about.

The man who founded the SAS, Major David Stirling 'The Phantom Major', originally formed the unit in the Sahara desert in North Africa during WWII. It originally had the sole purpose of getting behind enemy lines and wreaking havoc with his infrastructure.

Naturally, a few years afterwards, it was realised, if you've got people trained, and very good at doing it, maybe they can help prevent it happening to you? Not long after that, 'G' squadron came into being the goal, create the best counter-terrorism unit (CTU) on earth.

"Okay," Sir Michael replied, "that much even I knew," he looked exasperated, " but explain how you got in?"

"Not a chance!" Mac was smiling, "but shall we say operation Bonfire?"

That hit like a sledgehammer. He couldn't believe he'd been so dimwitted.

During the London Olympics in 2012, there was a genuine threat of terrorists doing something spectacular to get their message out. The British government had gone to great lengths to make sure that didn't happen. London became the 'most-watched' city on the planet, but two 'operations' were launched to make sure that the place stayed safe.

The first one everyone knew about. They couldn't miss it, anti-aircraft missiles were placed on every tall building in the city. All of them linked to a central command centre that was tracking every flying object within a hundred miles of the event. Anything flying that shouldn't be there wouldn't be challenged by a fighter (normal procedure). It would first be interrogated by Radar. No RFID chip and it would be blasted from the sky long before it reached London. It was called 'Operation Ring of Fire'

The second one, one no one but a few select people knew about. Then someone asked, ' what if they came another way, and took over a building?'

It concentrated on using underground networks to get from A to B, 'How can you move a strike team from point 'A' to point 'B' without being seen or heard?'

The last time London had seen a terrorist attack like this, someone tried to blow up the entire houses of Parliament using gunpowder that was back in 1604.

The perpetrators were caught and executed, but it became famous as 'the gunpowder plot' and November 5th became 'Bonfire night' celebrating their execution. 'Operation Bonfire' made sure it didn't happen again, at least, "not on my watch" Sir Michael had said when the operation started.

"I suppose that would explain it" he was resigned to the fact he would not get much more out of them. He hadn't known all the people involved in 'Op Bonfire'. It was only a select few in the planning stages. But the whole of 'G Squadron' was on 'standby' to deal with any threat within the city, and the buildings in the centre, near Parliament and Buckingham Palace, had been given extra attention. "Obviously the 'improvements' since then have made little difference?" He already knew the answer, but had to say something. "But what is this about, then?"

"Sorry that it's so 'cloak and dagger' boss," Jacko cut back in, "but there are a few things only you need to know, and too many places have eyes and ears."

"So does this car," Sir Michael replied.

"Did," Jacko replied, "We swept it, and we're jamming the transmission." He held up what looked like a small cigarette lighter. "Mildred's compliments," he added, "She doesn't want her message to get into the wrong hands."

"And what is that message?" He asked.

"You've got a leak,"

"I bloody know that!" Sir Michael's voice rose. "I've also got a body fished from the Thames. Are the two related? Is he the mole?"

"They're related," Mac cut back in, "But not the way you think!"

"And what the heck does that mean?"

"Akbari's a setup," Jacko replied, "Made to look like he was the mole, so we'd back off trying to find them. Don't accept my word for it," he held up what looked like a 'flash drive', a small piece of computer hardware, no bigger than the average Human thumbnail. "Our mutual friend Mildred sent us this recording a couple of hours ago, our mole" he waived the flash drive around, "used a different sim card, and phone, but isn't yet aware we've got most of the landline numbers, they used an un-encrypted phone, we got the details!" He gave the flash drive to the spook, "Check everything out for yourself" and with that, both he and Mac opened their doors. He was halfway out of the car when he turned back,

"There are instructions on the drive, follow them, and we can take the bastards down!" and with that he got out, closed the door and walked away as if nothing had happened.

Chapter 6

Location Auckland International Airport, New Zealand, the Departures lounge.

Time Tuesday 10am (local time)

"Got your tickets?" Peter asked them as they headed for the check-in counter. He was torn between emotions, not sure as a father what he was supposed to feel, sad to see them leave, partly worried for his 'little girl' and partly relieved that somehow they'd lived through the last week. Sad that they would not be there for Kevin's funeral, but also relieved it was all over.

"Bit bloody late if we left 'em at the farm, isn't it?" Joey shot back, a smile on his face and Sandy digging him in the ribs.

"Yeah, we've got 'em dad" she held them up for both of them to see. Turning to Joey she went on, "Didn't honestly think I'd trust you to bring 'em, did you?" She was smiling.

"No wonder I couldn't find 'em," he looked genuinely relieved, "I hoped that's where they were!"

"You'd forget your head if it was loose!" Sandy was laughing as she waved the tickets.

"Good job it's screwed on right then!" Joey picked the bags up, they both headed for the counter.

"Morning folks" the check-in attendant was cheerful in welcoming them, "you have time for refreshments upstairs if you like, boarding begins at 1 pm". She stuck the airline tags on the bags and placed them onto the conveyor belt. The bags, at least, were headed for the aircraft, or at least would be once it arrived.

"Coffee sounds like a great idea" Peter was enthusiastically heading for the escalator, the rest of the group lagging behind them, Joey and Sandy were the last. They didn't particularly want to catch up, 'just a few moments alone would be precious' was what they were both thinking.

"Right about now," Joey whispered just loud enough for her to hear, "Jacko and Mac are in London, or almost there." They were at the foot of the escalator. He stepped aside to let Sandy go first. She mouthed a 'thank you' as he followed her on. His eyes even now scanned the crowds, partly by force of habit and partly that he thought he recognised a couple of faces, but couldn't be sure.

"Don't know about you?" Sandy commented, "but I could murder a coffee!" the escalator was moving, but she took the steps two at a time.

"Sounds a great idea" Joey was right on her heels. "The coffee, that is, not the murder part!" He ducked as Sandy turned and looked as if she was going to slap him, "Just clarifying what I meant," he replied laughing.

"Two cappuccinos please" Sandy ordered from the coffee shop in the departure lounge, "and two teas, English breakfast" she added quickly, Joey and Peter had both got trays, put two plates on each, then served up sausage rolls and carrot cake for themselves. Sandy and her mum both just had just the carrot cake.

"Seems strange" Peter was the first one to speak, just after they sat down. "Doesn't feel right really, you only just got here and there's so much to talk about" everyone was in a subdued mood, and everyone knew it was true, Joey and Sandy had been in the country a couple of weeks at most, arranged so quickly that the family hadn't had time to plan a 'proper' get together. Then, what with all that had gone on, they spent more time worrying about Helen than anything else.

Helen was recovering slowly from the trauma of the accident. She'd taken Kevin's death really hard, probably exacerbated by her own injuries, but things were going to be even harder when everything settled. "Are you sure?" Peter continued on, "that you really do need to leave?"

"I wish we could stay," Joey was honest. He stopped speaking as he reached for the coffee that was his, taking the small packet of sugar and ignoring Sandy's surprised look. He gently opened the packet and poured the sugar into the coffee. There were some wooden sticks that acted as stirring spoons on the table. He took one and stirred the sugar in. Peter had done the same with his cup of tea. "But the truth is, this isn't over yet," Sandy was kicking him under the table, almost shouting with her eyes. He wasn't paying the slightest heed to her messages.

"Why do I still feel you aren't telling us things?" Peter sighed. It was a conversation he and Joey had before, and he knew the answer but had to ask anyway.

"Because it's better we don't," Joey replied, "you'll just have to trust we've got good reasons!"

Every op has three phases, the 'infill' or infiltration, where the team gets in on the ground. That part often sounds tricky, but it's the easiest part of the op. All they have to do is make sure they're not seen. Then there's the operation itself, and if that goes off well, then the next part begins. If it doesn't, then the nightmare called 'extraction' begins.

Even when an op 'runs like clockwork', the extraction can be tricky. If you got a team in without being detected, you have to get them out without detection too, and considering the mess they might leave behind, that might not be easy!

Joey and Sandy were registered with New Zealand immigration. They came into the country the legal way, therefore they had to leave the same way, otherwise, it would raise 'red flags' or warnings later. If they came in, but didn't leave, then where the hell did they go?'

"We'll call you when we get back to London," Sandy assured her parents. "Just to let you know everything's okay," They'd at least 'play that game' if it helped her parents stop worrying.

"Flight SQ286 is now boarding at gate twenty-four. Would all passengers please make their way through to the aircraft," the message came over the airport's speakers.

Joey and Sandy both reached down for their bags. Travel was a big part of their world, but it didn't make the leaving any easier. They had a job to do, and there'd been no other way to get on with it, they had to go through the left side, the other way would have been much harder for all of them, at least this way, they'd got to say some kind of goodbye.

They were just going through the final checkpoint when a hand reached out and tapped them on the shoulder, "You think you're just walking out of here?" Joey spun around not knowing what to expect, but ready for anything, Hene and Sam were both standing there, neither had uniforms on, both still had bruises, Sam had attempted to disguise hers with concealer, Hene wore his like a badge he was proud of! "Think you're getting out without even a goodbye?"

"Hene, Sam" Joey began, "What the hell are you doing here?" He grabbed Hene's hand and started pumping a vigorous handshake. It was good to see them.

"Making sure you get on the bloody plane," Hene shot back. He pulled the trooper into a Hongi, a traditional Maori greeting. Sam and Sandy were hugging each other. The rest of the family were a bit perplexed, "Er, Mum and Dad," Sandy began, "These are the two police who were investigating we mentioned, the two who"

"Please," Sam cut in, "Don't remind us,"

"Oh" was all Sandy's mum could say, still not totally understanding things. Peter understood, Joey and Sandy had pulled the two out of the 'proverbial' only to get their lives saved by them. You might say 'as clear as mud' but then again, it usually is in combat.

"No, seriously," Joey began, "what brings you here?"

"I told you," Hene was smiling, "New Zealand can't cope with the damage you do. We're making sure you're on that bloody plane!" They were laughing.

"Ignore him," Sam cut in smiling, "we just wanted to come and say a big thank you to you both."

"For what?" Joey sounded serious. "We were only." Sandy held up a finger to Joey's lips.

"Ignore this one too." She said to Sam, "He's milking it for all it's worth, can't help himself really," She laughed, "It's really good to see you, but we've gotta get going!"

"Speaking of which," Hene spoke up, "that's another reason we're here. Follow us, all of you." He turned and led them down a short path, past the Jean Batten lounge and into a quiet part of the airport, it was the 'first-class' lounge, "We had a word with the airline, and got them to upgrade you, you're in first class, compliments of the New Zealand Police, just don't tell them!"

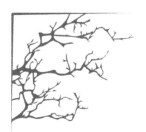

Chapter 7

Metropolitan Police Central building, Lambeth, Central London.

"So" BJ stopped for a moment, gathering her thoughts, trying to sound as if she knew where the case was going, and as if she was in charge. It felt like the case was in charge of her. Dictating everything and refusing to reveal any of its secrets, no matter how hard they pushed for a result. "At the moment, all we know is that the deceased probably didn't enter the river all that far from the place where he was found. Am I right with that at least?" It was a start.

They'd been 'hard at it' trying to track their 'John Doe' from the get-go, and gotten nowhere, or "Got sweet Fanny Adams" as they say in the UK. Nothing to show for days of work, and it niggled them, it was starting to drive them crazy.

"No identification then?" one of the officers, Frank, a middle-aged overweight cop with thinning hair. The product of long hours and late nights asked, "No licence or anything?" He had a coffee in one hand, a sandwich in the other, it was bacon, then again, they'd been at work since the early morning, it was nearly lunchtime now.

"None found" Billie was 'briefing' her team, the one that Steve Townsend had given her. She needed help, and this was beginning to get some priority. But the lack of information was almost embarrassing. 'London's the most-watched city on the flaming planet' she thought to herself, 'someone has to know who this guy is!'

"No witnesses, nothing on CCTV?" another cop, female, slightly younger than Billie and wearing the name badge 'Elizabeth' asked.

"Nothing." BJ replied, "One minute the body wasn't there, next it was, nothing caught on camera." She sounded as if she was resigned to not having any help, especially from the public.

To the team in front of her, that was strange, but she grew up in Moss Side. One of the roughest places in the country. Up there, in that area of Manchester, the gangs all knew where the cameras were, and they knew how to avoid them. *But this happened right outside the flaming parliament.'* She thought, *'the very seat of power, don't give me that crap about 'no one saw anything' I don't believe it, not for one sodding second'*

They'd studied every camera the 'Met' (as the Metropolitan Police is known) had in the area. Every square inch was covered, but nothing. Every Bank, every building that had CCTV had been issued with a search warrant. She'd even asked 'Special Branch' to ask the other security services (MI5 and MI6) for their footage. Nothing showed up. Considering where the body was, that was really odd. She just didn't dare say it too loud!

"What we do know," she cut back in, "is sometime Tuesday morning, around 2 am our friend went into the river, somewhere around here." She drew two lines across the river, about four hundred yards apart, "and he was there about three hours before he was found. That much the pathologist is certain of!"

"Cause of death?" the young female asked.

"Water in the lungs," Bille replied, "show drowning, but they're running a tox screen to see if anything else was in there. Some scuff marks on the shoes and clothes that could either be caused when he fell, or maybe defensive wounds, but we can't be sure!"

"So we might not have a murder then?" The middle-aged cop sounded deflated, "Just a bloody drunk who got too near the river!"

"What we have," Billie cut in, "is a body in suspicious circumstances, in the river whom no one can identify. And being right outside parliament, it's got everyone crapping their pants with the implications. By the way, the only thing in the pockets was a set of what could either be a rosary or prayer beads. We're not sure what. Now, I want answers as to who this boy is, and I want them ASAP. Am I making myself clear?" Her voice had risen considerably as she gave the little 'pep talk' "Now, I've got a list of all the delivery vans in the area at the time. Phil" she looked at the middle-aged cop. "You get the delivery vans, and their 'wonderful' drivers" she made the inverted comma sign as she said the last part. "Chase 'em down, get their dash-cams and any give you any crap, slap 'em with the 'prevention of terrorism' act and ask 'em how long they want in a remand centre?" She turned to the rest of the team. "Liz" the young female looked up, "you get the westside of the river, take Jimmy and cover every business within sight of the area, use a few 'uniform' if you have to, but get it done, I'll be doing the same with the other side, you two" she looked at the two youngest cops on the team "You're with me"

No one had any illusions. It was going to be like looking for the proverbial 'needle in a haystack' but with one big difference, they didn't know which needle, or haystack for that matter.

And the people who knew were staying silent!

L ondon is one of the biggest financial centres on the planet, if not THE centre. Every Bank, every financial institution has an office there. They're linked to the rest of the globe, the decisions taken there affect every human alive, and they're done by computer!

They are monitored by humans, but it's often humans who do not know how that computer does what it does, no idea whether the keys they're tapping are being monitored, and what happens when someone feeds something nasty into the system. When that happens, things can go haywire, and the hard part is that those same computers don't just monitor the financial system, they monitor everything.

Chapter 8

"Hey, you might not want to answer that, it's only the boss," the strange voice started saying. Sam stopped and gave the stupidest look imaginable. "what the hell is that?" she almost started laughing.

Hene looked sheepish as he reached in for his phone. "My ringtone for the boss," he mumbled. "Got it from an app on the phone"

"Then, for heaven's sake," Sam began. She was still chuckling, only to be cut off by her phone ringing. She went to answer hers as well, but Hene had already swiped the 'answer button' "Don't let her hear it"

"By now," a voice came on the line as soon as he answered, "They should have gone through to the departure gate, am I correct?" Hene recognised the voice straight away. It was Mildred. He took the phone down from his ear and tapped the 'speaker' icon. Sam was slightly bemused, but listened in. "Sam there too?"

"Yes," Sam replied, "on both counts."

"Good," Mildred replied. "That way, I don't have to repeat myself. Listen up, I've got some instructions for you two. Get down to the Airport Hilton, go to the front desk and ask for the keys to rooms 207 and 208. Hene you get 207, Sam, you get the other one. As soon as you've got the keys, just hit the redial last number on your phone. We'll talk then."

St Bartholomew's Hospital London.

"Hi, I'm up on the cancer ward, and I'm wondering what's happened to the medication we ordered for our patients last night. They should have been here this morning. Any ideas what's happened to them? " The nurse spoke into the phone. He was pretty frustrated, but there wasn't any use taking it out on the computer people. They were just 'small cogs in a big wheel. Even so, it was damned annoying when things fouled up, 'probably delivered them to the wrong sodding ward,' he thought, but didn't dare say it.

"Check your delivery schedule," the female voice on the other end of the line replied curtly. She'd been replying to questions from all over the hospital for the last half hour. They were trying frantically to find out what the hell was wrong with the system. But not telling anyone. Admitting a fault was serious business, and likely to get you fired in the very next breath!

"I tried that," the nurse came back. He reached for the instant coffee that he'd made before making the call. Previous experience told him talking to the computer or 'I.T.' department was a very long and frustrating process, long because they said nothing that others understood, and frustrating because by the time you got them to work, you had to persuade them that they weren't talking to people who understood 'computerese'. "But the damned thing won't even pull up the screen!"

"You are logged in, aren't you?"

"We left the machine logged on last night. No idea what the night shift did though!" He replied, "I can't even tell what's open and what's not."

"What message have you got on the screen?" she asked.

"It says," He squinted, the writing was tiny, "YOU HAVE BEEN LOCKED OUT, ACCESS WILL BE RESTORED WHEN YOU PAY A SMALL FEE OF TEN POUNDS STERLING TO MY ACCOUNT, YOU WILL BE NOTIFIED SHORTLY OF THE DETAILS!"

"Thank you for the information sir," She cut him off, "We'll get you back online as soon as we can" she cut the line, *damn, that's another department infected*' she thought as she typed out an email, one marked urgent to the headquarters of the National Health Service. It simply said, "St Barts, virus on the system, seems to be some sort of ransomware, so far unable to locate the source."

Viruses always go for the contact list in any computer system. As soon as they've got that, they've got you. And if you're connected to the internet, it doesn't matter if you send any emails out or not. It sends out an email, and a hundred others just got infected.

Within minutes, the entire system for the National Health Service (or NHS, as the British call it) was on the brink of collapsing. Every computer in every hospital, not just in London, but the entire United Kingdom, and not just the little things with screens and keyboards, but every machine that used software and was connected to other machines through the 'information highway' was shutting down. There was nothing the techies could do about it!

Everything from the mobile laptops the doctors and nurses were using to the heart monitors and even the MRI scanners were going 'offline' and no way of getting them back at the moment. They were helpless and defenceless. There wasn't even any way of knowing if they had the files backed up even when they got the system back 'up and running'. This was going to be a damn long day.

Not long after that, other computers went down as well. First, it was the Fire Brigade. Their computers in the control centres were supposed to be the 'latest and greatest', but they went down. The same message displayed on each one, "Give us ten pounds Sterling within twenty-four hours, or lose your files!"

Want to make a lot of money quickly, then hack the Banks, and lock them out. They'll pay up pretty fast. But hack their health system and you bring the country to its knees within less time than it takes to say "Help" and this one was spreading like an out-of-control wildfire, every time an email was sent from an infected computer the virus found the path and jumped. Most of them didn't have firewalls, and those that did hadn't kept them up to date. Then again, with the speed they appear, very few had the time or the money to keep up with them, but there are a few that keep 'up with the Joneses' They were the government's 'last line of defence'

When the virus got as far as the Ministry of Defence and the Civil Aviation Authority, that's when both MI5 and MI6 got a rude call.

"Find and kill this bloody thing" the Minister had screamed down the phone at them, "I don't care how!"

The young officer on the desk was stunned as the phone crashed down on the other end. *'Did he just break the thing?'* He thought as he punched the numbers. Their cyber-crime division would go into overdrive with this one. It was going to be a very long night!

Paul Johnson or PJ wasn't anything special. In fact, most people wouldn't even give him a second glance in the street, and the few that did would recognise immediately. He was a total nerd, and pretty proud of the fact.

Nearly thirty, still living at home with mum and dad, never had a girlfriend (never likely to either he'd add in sad admission). He wasn't the best with people, found them too illogical, but put him in front of a keyboard, and that was a different story.

"Shit," he spoke softly as his avatar 'bought the dust' again. It was the third time on that level. He just wasn't able to get past the gremlin that came out of nowhere, or it felt that way. Every time it came out from different places and he just wasn't quick enough reaching for 'Excalibur'. The legendary sword of King Arthur. It had magical properties, and the game gave it the power to kill gremlins, but you had to be quick to use it.

The second screen was flashing a warning. His computer had picked up an intruder, or someone wanting to get into his hard drive. The firewall was holding them off, but it still sent him a warning, kind of like an alert a sentry would send out when someone approached a unit's position. He'd called the software 'Sentinel' as it sounded a pretty cool name, and was close to what the software did.

"We'll get back to you" was the reaction he got when he tried to sell the software to NASA, and to a few other places. Right now, he had a job. Not really a job as such, but a contract to help a few places with their internet security. Especially with protection against viruses, or other bugs. Even anti-spyware that lets people know when others are watching the 'keystrokes' they're making. He still dreamed of 'hitting the big time' with the software. But that didn't pay any bills, for that he did the 'consulting' though at times it felt like 'insulting' as the pay was so low.

Computer hackers aren't always bad. Some of them called 'white hats' actually try to 'hack' the systems to show where the weak points are so that the companies can fix them. But they don't just use the virus, they've got a few other tools as well.

There's the 'bug'. Not strictly a virus, as such. The virus is like a virus in a human or animal. A virus needs software to attach to! In animals, they attach to our DNA and alter the structure of our cells. The computer virus does the same, but the 'bug' doesn't! It doesn't need any software to be running, it just gets in there, does the job and keeps on doing it until you kill the bug!

Then there's spyware, or 'bots' as they're called, they just sit in the background, watching every stroke you make, and whenever the 'master' calls, they upload all the information they have about you, including all your Bank account details, everything! Doesn't matter that you didn't store the password on your machine, if you went into the Bank account, it records your keystrokes, and sends them! With them, nothing is safe.

But the good guys, they have their own weapons, 'bots' that sit in the background and watch for any 'nasties' trying to get in, that's when places like Google send you the message 'Someone tried to access your account,' when you try to get onto your own sites from different machines, the 'bots' in the background, 'big brother watching over you' and it's not all bad.

That's what Paul had running. It came up with the message as his second screen froze. Something was trying to get into his system, but the firewall had stopped it, 'Unauthorised attempt at access, DO WE ALLOW?'

"Hell no." He whispered, frowning. Damn, he was pissed at losing to the gremlin, getting to the next level. Hell, he'd been working on getting to that stage for over an hour, and lost. He wasn't happy, "Sod off" he shouted as he hit the 'Deny' button, the message came straight back, he hit it again, it came back again, "what the?" He hit the button a third time, the screen cleared and he began the level again, the message came back, before anything happened, this was getting annoying, "Will you sod off!" He spoke again as he hit the button. Within seconds, the message was back.

This time, he stopped and looked at the message. The 'bot' had identified a piece of software that didn't belong to the programme he was running. He clicked on the icon for the 'bot'. It brought up a screen with code written on it. One line was highlighted in red, a message at the side simply said, this was updated two minutes ago, it doesn't belong in the programme!

"What the?" he whispered as he looked at the code, something just wasn't right, yeah, it was 'ransomware' that he could see from the programming, but the thing looked so simple, he reached for his phone, changed his mind and went for the Skype icon.

"Jezza," he almost shouted as soon as the other guy came on the line. "You saw this on the net?"

"Paul" the geek on the other end came back, "What you on about?" he was slightly younger than Paul, though with the amount of time they both spent in front of the screen, they both looked square-eyed and anaemic, the total opposite of the muscled, tanned avatar he used.

"On the net," Paul cut back in, "The virus,"

"What the hell would I want to look for a bloody virus for?" the other guy was laughing, "why?"

"Man, it's grinding everything to a halt!" he carried on, almost as if he hadn't been interrupted, "It's bloody awesome, but so bloody simple."

"What do you mean? I'm just turning my machine on." There was a pause. "Oh shit, look at that. What the hell?" he stopped for a moment, then came back, "Paul, you saw this? It's crippling the net. It's taken down the whole NHS! Damn, every hospital in London, nothing working, and the Civil Aviation, Shit, that means every airport in the UK, and it's still spreading!" he was looking at the screen, "You see how many aircraft are in the air and can't land?"

"Yeah" Paul couldn't help himself, he didn't see any of that. All he 'saw' was the code. He totally missed the fear. The stunned silence told it all, but Paul was missing it all. Then again, the programmer in him was seeing something else. "Jezza," he replied, "There's a kill code here!"

His screen came alive again. Someone else was trying to contact him. Another hacker. They called themselves 'White hats' because they only ever used their hacking skills for 'good' or what they deemed as 'good'. They were all coming alive to the problem.

"Are you guys following the news?" The new person, a middle-aged lady hacker, went by the 'handle' of 'Mata Hari' asked.

"Yeah, mate," Paul replied, "I'm just filling Jezza in on the situation, man this is spreading fast!"

"Yeah," she replied, "and it's got people really rattled. So far, they're only asking for ten quid off each of them!" She stopped for a moment. "It says there's two hundred aircraft can't land as their landing systems aren't working at most airports, and the ones that have manual systems can't take the bigger planes!"

"Yeah, that's for now, but next week they'll be back for fifty!" Jezza replied. He missed the panic in her voice. They knew that was the truth how these extortion rackets worked. The hacker or 'black hat' gets your info, and they never really let go of it. They'll be back for more, but Paul wasn't really listening.

"I can kill it!" he blurted out.

"What?"

"There's a kill code," he said. "How much do you think they'll pay me for it?"

"Why, what the hell are you on about?"

"I've found the code that'll stop the damn thing." He replied, "How much do you think people will pay for it?"

"They said ten pounds!" Jezza had found some information about it. "Better yet, do you want to make a name for yourself?"

"Hell yeah!" Paul screamed back. All he could think of was what it would do for his career. If it got out, he'd been the one to 'kill' the virus.

"Then just kill it!" Jezza replied, "and put it out on either Facebook or YouTube. A quick video, or a Facebook post!" he stopped for a minute, his face clouded over as if he had some form of premonition, "then again, you got to think, who's behind this?"

"Probably some idiot who wants to be a black hat" Paul was laughing, clearly unimpressed. Then again, he usually was with even the best software. This wasn't much different. "Time I taught them a lesson"

"Might not be," Jezza replied, "might be a prelude to something more sinister."

He really didn't give a damn. He'd decided, so he hit the key, and the virus faded from the screen, and disaster was averted. Or was it?

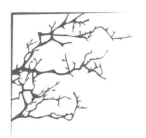

Chapter 9

"So ladies and gentlemen," the speaker looked around the room, starting from right to left. He was slowly making eye contact with every person in the room. "It appears that the virus has run its course, then?" It was a question more than a statement, but then again, very few disagreed with a prime minister. Even when they're only asking questions. "Does that mean these people were just after the money?"

Was it possible that this was just a simple heist? No one in the room really thought that, but everyone valued their jobs and positions too much to argue. Disagreeing with a Prime Minister is the fastest way to end a political career. No one wanted that, not when they were thinking of their present position as just a stepping stone, kind of like the kids' game of snakes and ladders. If the ladder was climbing, then this was an enormous snake that could get you to the bottom almost instantly.

The room didn't have any windows, but being four stories underground, under some of the most valuable real estates in central London, it wouldn't. There was air conditioning. The unit was so silent that you never noticed it. The complex, known as the Cabinet Office Briefing Room or 'COBRA' was probably one of the most secret facilities in the Western world. And the people who worked there managed every crisis the United Kingdom faces, everything from a miners' strike to nuclear war if need be.

There were a total of ten large leather chairs around a large mahogany table. The Prime Minister, or PM, sat in the middle, facing the only door in the room. On their left was the Minister for

Defence. On the PM's right, the Deputy PM and Chancellor of the Exchequer. The final ministerial post next to him was taken by the 'Home Secretary'

Nine others were in the room, other than the Prime Minister. Four were ministers of state. Two were the heads of various intelligence agencies. The Chief of General Staff, a Major General from the Army and the last two from MI6, one was with Sir Michael, head of MI6, but so far he hadn't introduced the last man. It was him that spoke up next.

"For now, Yes, but if you think you've heard the last of them, then think again!" He threw the briefing paper he'd been given down, slowly reached for the glass of water he'd poured earlier and took a sip. He looked around the table, almost challenging people to prove him wrong, or at least challenge what he'd just said.

"Sir Michael" the PM cut in, voice sharp, but not raised, "Kindly introduce us, and then let this gentleman explain himself" The PM wasn't happy at being told she was wrong, no Prime Minister ever is, and clearly that's what this man, whoever he was, was doing.

"Sorry Ma'am,", Sir Michael spoke quietly, "there hasn't been time to fill everyone in on the situation, so I thought I'd bring in the man who's been in on this from the start, this is Steve Chambers, one of our best people, he was working,"

"Yes, yes, we know where Mr Chambers worked," she cut in, "but what is he doing here? And what is he talking about?"

"If you'll let me finish, Ma'am" Sir Michael was normally a perfect gentleman, but this meeting wasn't a normal type of meeting. "I said, he's been tracking this from the start, so I'll let Steve explain!" he looked directly at Steve. The message he sent with the eyes said 'this better be good'

"First of all, Ma'am," Steve began, "This isn't the first incident we've dealt with regarding this group!"

There was some consternation in the group. Words fired off like missiles, asking questions, trying to be the one who 'got it right' and all missing the mark.

"ISIS?"

"Hezbollah?"

"North Korea?"

"All partly right," Steve replied causing total confusion, "and all totally wrong!"

It took a full two minutes for the questions to stop. A cacophony of noise, where no one could even hear themselves think. "How the hell can that be?" The Home Secretary shouted above the noise. The PM just sat there, Steve could tell. She was thinking, probably trying to guess what the connection was. "How?" was all she asked when the noise died down enough to be heard.

"First," Steve began, "the software, it was North Korean, or at least based on stuff that North Korea stole from the NSA and has used before, like when they tried to hack the Federal reserve, and the Bank of England." He let that sink in for a moment or two, then went on, "but it wasn't them!"

"So they say!" The other intelligence officer, Sir Michael's opposite number at MI5 Dame Judith, the second female in the room, "Personally, I'm not so ready to believe them." She threw the pen she'd been twiddling down. "What proof do you have?"

"The first bit" Chambers made eye contact with her, "is the coding in the program itself!" He paused, but only briefly, just enough to 'take the temperature' of the room. They would not like what he was going to say next. "We all understood that the North Koreans stole the coding they used from the NSA, right?" He looked around the room. That's what the Americans had quietly told the rest of the world's intelligence agencies, but it was only partly true. "They didn't" he went on. The intake of breath around the room was audible. Like the thunderclap of a Battleship opening fire with all her guns, and everyone on the receiving end thinking 'God have mercy on us', but Chambers went on. "They paid a third party to do the actual stealing, and that third party made copies of what they stole. That's what we're seeing here." He pointed to the file, "A copy of the original, but with a few tweaks that weren't in the stuff the North Koreans used!" he leaned back in the chair, in his right hand he had a small remote unit. He clicked it and a large screen that had so far been dormant came to life.

"So far," Dame Judith came back, "You have offered no proof, and who is this third party you're speaking of?" She clearly wasn't buying it, not yet at least.

"I'm getting to that," Chambers cut in. "Take a look at the screen. There's two samples of computer code, one taken from the North Korean hack." He showed the one on the right of the screen. "The other taken from the virus we recovered in the ransomware attack." The press already had a name for it, and they were sticking with it, just so that everyone knew what they were talking about. "Look at the third line of both, almost the same, right? But there's a couple of things there on the left, that is just aren't right, see if you can spot them."

It took a moment, but slowly each of them acknowledged they were almost, but not completely. There were two subtle differences, two small mathematical calculations that were on one, but not the other.

"Now look at the seventh and ninth lines, some changes there too," He paused for a moment, "Someone took the original, and altered it!"

"But that doesn't prove it wasn't the same people," Dame Judith butted in, "just that they made copies."

"True," Steve replied, "That is, until you see what was altered! The Korean one wasn't that sophisticated. I doubt they'd have the skills to make the changes!"

"Why?" it was the Home Secretary asking, "and for what purpose?"

"I'll answer that soon," Chambers cut him off. "But back to the original question. The first one needed you to send a message. It'd 'piggyback' onto it. Computer boffins call it a 'Trojan Horse', but it needs a message to attach to! " He reached out for the glass of water he had on the table. He was slightly nervous. You don't' get to talk like this to senior government officials every day. Taking a sip, he replaced the glass and continued on. "The first one was what the North Koreans used to infect the Banks, they relied on the Banks talking to each other"

There was a slight pause as Steve picked up the remote again, clicked a button and on his screen, the one from the right disappeared. "Now look at this baby," He began again, "the commands are different. More refined because this one's much more potent, all it needs is your email address list. It doesn't need you to send the message, it sends one for you, and to all those in your address book."

Stunned silence. It took an entire minute for the shock of what he was telling them to sink in, but Steve only waited that minute. It was important, they grasp just how bad this virus was, "your machine doesn't even have to be switched on, all it needs is to be on the address list, then when the virus arrives at the server, it'll get a 'wake up call' from the server and the message gets sent," he waited for a moment, looking around the room, even Sir Michael looked grim, and he'd heard most of what Steve was saying before, most. But not all. "Then, if your antivirus doesn't get this bitch, and it's not likely to, you go into autopilot and retransmit the virus while your machine looks to all intents and purposes as if it's turned off, they've got you!"

To all intents and purposes. Steve had just told them that the virus was, or should have been, unstoppable, but someone had stopped it. How?

"Okay" it was Dame Judith who spoke first. She was cut off by the PM.

"How was it stopped then?" the PM asked. The softness of her voice betraying nothing of the anger she felt. Knowing they were defenceless left her seething inside. Like any politician, she hated to lose a fight, even when it was against an enemy they didn't know.

"Pure dumb luck, Ma'am," Steve shot back almost flippantly, "A young kid, not much older than twenty, spotted something in the coding, a way of switching it off!"

"What?" there was an audible intake of breath, "You're telling us," the PM began again, "that potentially the most damaging attack on this country in what, twenty years," she was incredulous, "was thwarted by pure luck?"

"Actually, it was some kid with a PlayStation, Ma'am," Steve cut back in. He couldn't help smiling, knowing how uncomfortable it made all the 'power people' in the room. Normally he'd be 'hauled over hot coals' for talking this way to even a senior member of the government, let alone the Prime Minister of the country. "I said nothing of the sort, I said"

"I know what you said!" She cut him off, "but the fact remains, it was just some boy on the right page who spotted what our computer people didn't!"

"I still haven't answered the second part of the question ma'am," Steve cut her off, "and that I need to answer," he turned to Sir Michael, "You remember the group who kidnapped me a few weeks ago?"

Sir Michael simply nodded. He'd helped Chambers put this part of the jigsaw together, and he half knew where he was going, but only half knew. "Phoenix group" he offered, "Mercenaries from Russia, guns for hire working with the drug lords"

"Bit more than that Sir Michael," Chambers replied, "They've been building a global network of drug barons and the like, they were the ones who stole the virus from the NSA, we didn't have proof, that is until this showed up!"

"And it was stopped by some boy with a PlayStation?" the PM clearly wasn't impressed. "Please,"

"That 'BOY'" Steve shot back, cutting her off. "Was a computer security consultant. Yes, he got lucky and was a bit dumb putting it on Facebook, but he broke the code because he'd put a decent firewall in. Just like we told each government department to do when they shared files." He was angry. "Tell me Ma'am, when we advised each department to put firewalls in to prevent attacks like this bringing the government to its knees, was that ever done?" He knew the answer already, but they'd pushed the wrong buttons, and Sir Michael knew Steve didn't really give too much of a damn about pleasing people. He got the job done.

"We'd begun a study," the Home Secretary began.

"Oh, please!" Sir Michael replied to that. "We told you the threat was real, that there were any number of governments the other groups who'd love to see Britain on her knees, but as usual, no one listened,"

"But the costs, they were going to be tens of millions,"

"And repairing the damage now will be hundreds of millions. Not to mention the patients in the hospitals who probably died because we didn't get them the treatment they needed, the various nuclear power stations that had to do emergency shutdowns in case the virus got into their systems and reprogrammed them into meltdown,"

"Now you're being dramatic," the PM sounded almost condescending.

"Iran 2010," Sir Michael cut her off. This wasn't a time to play nice. "Israel tried to shut down Iran's nuclear programme by sending a small reactor into meltdown. Thankfully, the Iranians caught it in time, but it almost caused a nuclear exchange, read the file Ma'am," He threw a plain-looking file about a half-inch thick onto the table, "go back and check, your departments all got copies of the file. I suggest you read them!" he sounded frustrated, "and by the way," he came back, "They tried again last year, so don't tell me it's a one-off!"

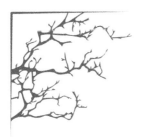

Chapter 10

"There's only one thing for it," Sir Michael spoke. He was in his office, but not the one in Vauxhall house. The one he kept somewhere else, just for situations like this. When he didn't want others knowing what he was doing. Chambers was there as well. In front of them were two screens, one had a single face on it. You couldn't see whether it was night or say where that person was, but he knew it was night there. Not that the one on the other end was looking tired. Stressed yes, but who wasn't? "We have to strike first"

"I agree" Mildred, the head of New Zealand intelligence spoke for the first time since the conference had started, they'd been there for at least half an hour, "but easier said than done, we had a plan, but this takes priority, and besides, I think we may adapt it"

"True," Sir Michael replied as he stood up and headed for the Nespresso machine, inserting one capsule into the machine, water added and seconds later a 'ristorante adrette' or long black as the rest of the world knows it. Taking the coffee he headed for his chair and sat back down. He waved to Chambers to show he could help himself, "But let's have a think of what we know"

"Akbari worked in cyber-crime," Chambers spoke up. "That tells me they needed him out of the way for the cyber attack," he headed towards the machine. "Maybe it was that he'd have spotted the kinks in the software and would have killed it,"

"If that's the case," Mildred asked the obvious, "then why didn't the people working there? I mean, it's their job to function under pressure, isn't it?"

They hadn't addressed the other screen. There wasn't any need to. They knew who was there. Scorpion One were in England, but not in London, they were outside the city somewhere, Sir Michael wasn't sure where, and it was probably better he didn't know, the less he knew about some parts of this operation the better, and the easier it would be to say "I wasn't aware of that" if the proverbial hit the fan.

"Was there anything strange about the software?" Sandy was the one who asked. She already had an idea, but wanted to hear the confirmation.

"Actually, yes," Chambers looked down. He had a piece of paper in front of him. "Sorry boss, I was going to show you this, but the meeting started before I got the chance," he turned back towards the two monitors, "It looks like there was some kind of Trojan Horse, but it was geared for one specific email address."

Troy was an ancient city in what is modern-day Turkey. Legend has it that the walls were impregnable. No one could break into the city.

War had raged in the region for ten years, and the besieging Army was still no closer to defeating the Trojans, as they couldn't get through the walls. Then someone came up with a plan that was as simple as it was audacious.

Build a model of a horse, a huge model capable of fitting fifty trained warriors inside. Then, when it's finished, leave the 'horse' on the beach with the warriors inside while the rest of the army moves away as if leaving. They even made it look like a 'peace offering' to the Trojans.

The Trojans fell for it. Thinking that the horse was a 'peace offering' they took it inside the city and partied all night. Only to wake up the next morning with their city in ruins as the warriors stormed the gates from the inside and let the main force in, the city fell within hours, could this have been a 'Trojan horse' designed to take down the security services defences from the inside?

There was a stunned silence. It lasted a full minute before anyone spoke. Yes; they had firewalls, but if the enemy had gone to the trouble of removing one of the people who'd be looking after those firewalls, then did they have someone on the inside? They all knew the answer to that.

"Actually Sandy," Chambers broke the silence, "I'm inclined to agree with you, it was a Trojan horse. I think that when we sent the command code to disable it, there was meant to be a second part that would allow it behind the firewall. Once behind it, they'd have access to every bank account the government uses. There'd be no way of knowing how much they would steal!"

"We have to get this Pig" Sir Michael almost threw the coffee cup across the room, "and I don't mean behind bars!"

"We're expecting them to hit again then," it was more a statement than a question, "But where?"

"Why wait? Let's give 'em something, or someone to go after!" Jacko spoke up, "we've been playing this game on their rules. Let's change things around, give them something to think about!"

"What do you mean?" both Mildred and Sir Michael asked pretty much at the same time. It was Sir Michael that went on, "explain yourself, Captain"

"Look boss," Jacko knew Sir Michael didn't really like being referred to that way, but they both knew it was part of the Regiment. So he just went on, "so far everything we've done has been reacting to whatever they did right? Sure we've had some good takedowns, but all we've done is put a slight delay in the supply at best, right?" He stopped momentarily before going on. "Let's give 'em a target they can't refuse and be ready to grab 'em by the short and curlies when they do,"

"Are you suggesting?" Chambers began. "What would we use?" he wasn't sure he liked the idea of where this was going.

"The kid that stopped the virus," Jacko jumped in. "His address is in the public domain, right? They'd have no trouble tracking him down, especially if we gave them an incentive, like letting it be known MI5 wants him as he might have tracked the source!"

"You mean you'd put a defenceless civilian in harm's way?" Mildred wanted to make sure she was hearing this right, "am I understanding you right?"

"Sorry Ma'am," Joey chipped in, "but so far they haven't exactly shown much allowance for civvies from their side, I mean the farmhouse and what happened to Hene and Sam."

"But they were coppers," Chambers cut in. Everyone wanted to be totally sure that this was the way they were going. The idea had potential, but could also go spectacularly wrong.

"My family weren't," Sandy spoke up again. She'd been searching for something on her laptop. "The stories in the press hint at the possibility of the Russian Mafia involved. What if we told the intelligence people that we needed to talk with him because he knew who was behind it? Might just shake 'em loose enough to try something,"

"But we'll need a head start," Smithy spoke up for the first time. "I want a good camera. I'm assuming I may not be able to shoot the sods yet, so I'll get photos so we can hunt 'em down instead."

"It seems you've got this all worked out," Sir Michael huffed. Somehow, he had the idea that the team had planned for something like this all along. They just waited for the right time.

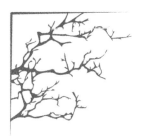

Chapter 11

"Bravo two, where the hell are you?" He spoke louder than he intended to. The adrenaline from the gameplay kicking in. "I've got bandits on my tail!"

"At your five o'clock high," a voice came back, "you've got two right up your arse, when I say, do a barrel roll and break right."

"Are you nuts? " he shouted back, "I'm in a mark three Spitfire remember!" He grabbed the computer joystick, ready for the manoeuvre. In real life, it would be nearly impossible and only a superb pilot would even try it, but this was a game and he might just pull it off.

"Yeah, I remember. It was your choice, remember. They're dead level with you. Break either way and you'll go across their gun sights. You need to lose a bit of height as you go. Throw 'em off balance, the roll is the best way!"

That was true. The original Spitfire had one weakness. A gravity-fed carburettor sat on top of the engine. Roll the plane and the huge Rolls Royce Merlin engine would be starved of fuel, resulting in her almost cutting out, and losing height. The original pilots found out the hard way and turned it to an advantage when they attacked formations by flying above. Then pulling a half-barrel roll and a dive. That way they got an extra ten miles an hour, vital when you're taking a Messerschmitt Bf109 on, and the game simulated it all.

The screen almost blanked out as he started the turn. In real life, the pilots would pull four 'g' turns causing them to black out, or at least nearly so, that's what the computer was simulating.

"Shit, engine failure," he called out as a buzzer sounded, "I might be hit" he spoke into the mike. There wasn't any way of knowing until his avatar recovered.

"Looks okay to me," the voice came back, "no trails,"

The 'trails' were vapour. If he'd been hit, then either oil or fuel would stream out of the engine. There weren't any. The plane wasn't 'vibrating' either, so the computer wasn't simulating a stall.

The buzzer sounded again, just as the screen was coming back to life. Next thing was to check power connections. It took an entire minute before he realised it wasn't the machine. Someone was at the door.

"Sorry bud, gotta go, someone's at the bloody door." He was annoyed. It was bloody frustrating, especially as he thought he'd disconnected the buzzer. He reached over, flicked the switch, and was just getting up.

"Don't bother" the voice was female, silky, and almost seductive, "we let ourselves in".

"Whoa, what the?" he looked up, startled at the voice. "Where did you come from?" He was half surprised, and the other half, well, probably not printable. 'She's gorgeous' was all he could think, 'and she's smiling' hopeful delusions setting in and not taking the scruffy tee-shirt, paunch and two-day-old facial growth into account.

"It's okay bud" another voice, a male one, shattered any hope he had, "She has that effect on all the boys" the voice sounded slightly amused, which was annoying. No one enjoys being 'read like a book'

The intruders, there were two of them, didn't seem to be causing trouble, apart from the fact they'd broken into the house. No threats of violence, no 'smash and grab'. The girl was just sat there, in his one armchair. Shapely legs crossed, smiling. He felt weak at the knees, seduced by a simple smile.

Sandy was loving it. She couldn't help herself, it was something that just came 'natural' to her. The ability to get what she wanted with just a smile, 'something you just have to love,' she thought to herself.

Paul couldn't believe his own eyes, a gorgeous redhead just walking into his place. Wild dreams were being unlocked in his mind, a mind that somehow managed to not even realise she was escorted by a scary dude carrying a concealed gun. *'I mean she's gorgeous'* he thought to himself, hoping that the words didn't actually come out of his mouth, "Whoa, who are you?" sounded as if it came out instead, but he couldn't take his eyes off the redhead sat in the armchair.

Sandy was loving it, not the attention so much as the effect it was having. Holding the guy 'riveted' to the spot while Joey did what he needed to, the navy blue polo neck along with the tailored tight black jeans gave her skin an almost 'alabaster' look, coupled with her shoulder-length flame-red hair. It kind of lit a bonfire for the guy. She always enjoyed having that effect on men, but that's as far as things went for her. She was Joey's girl through and through, though seeing Joey squirm a little at the attention was 'kinda fun'

"Relax," she spoke softly, "we're here to help."

"What?" Paul was confused. "Where'd you come from? What do you want?"

"Not a lot," Joey replied. So far he'd stayed in the background. Just watching, checking the room, and anything that moved outside. He had seen nothing out of the ordinary, but that meant little. He noticed that the street was quiet, a little too quiet for the time of day. "Let's just say we're here for your health, not ours"

"Excuse me?" Paul was really confused, and more than a little spooked. "Who put you up to this? I can take you" he jumped up and started moving towards the door, only to be met with a wicked backhander that knocked him halfway across the room. "That's assault," he screamed as he launched himself for his phone. The headset he'd been wearing was busted with the blow. Joey got there first.

"Relax knucklehead," Joey was almost laughing, "If I'd wanted to hurt you I'd have done so, and not given you a gentle tap like I just did. You don't know it, but you need our help!"

"Why? What the hell have I done?"

Sandy spoke again, "Couple of days ago you came across this on the net" she was holding a small black bag. She unzipped it and lay the contents out on the table. A flash drive fell out. She took it and plugged it into his computer.

"Hey, that's mine. What are you doing?" He launched himself at the computer screen trying to push her out of the way. The big guy behind grabbed him by the shoulder and wrenched him back into his seat.

"Sit" was all Joey said.

"Just want to show you something" Sandy tapped the keyboard a few times. The screen changed and was filled with a series of numbers. It looked like lines of computer code, "This got onto the servers of most government departments"

"Oh, shit," was all he could say. Slowly, he began turning white, the blood draining from just about every muscle in his face. He looked at the screen, then saw a piece of paper he reached for that as well. It was the same code, and he knew exactly what it was. It was as if the paper suddenly ignited in his hand and burned his fingers. He snatched his hand back violently. "It wasn't me!!" he blurted out.

"We know that, you moron," Joey shot back. "We know where it came from." He'd been watching the window. Now he turned and looked directly at Paul. "You're a hacker, but not that kind of one, isn't that right?"

"Yeah, yeah, that's right, yeah," Paul's colour slowly returned, "I stopped the damn thing,' the verbal 'swagger' coming back.

"And in doing so," Sandy cut in, "Pissed off some pretty serious and nasty people,"

Paul stopped mid-sentence and slumped back into his chair, all hope of 'fighting' lost. He was in deep shit, and he knew it. "Oh shit," was all he said.

"Relax" Joey's voice was calm, almost soothing. Which was strange considering a few minutes before he'd been pretty violent, "we're not here to hurt you, we're here to stop you getting hurt!"

"I'm calling the police" he reached for his phone. Blinding pain bit in as Joey knocked the phone out of hand. It went flying across the room. "What the hell? How'd I know you aren't the ones wanting to do me harm?"

"If we were" Joey began, his voice an emotionless monotone. "You'd already been in a body bag!" He sauntered over and picked the phone up, a quick wrist action and he had the sim card out. Next, within seconds, the battery, which wasn't supposed to come out was just that, out, Joey wasn't taking any chances. "As of now" he paused for a moment, "You're going off-grid, and I mean literally!"

Somehow, Paul knew the 'body bag' thing wasn't an idle threat. *This guy has ice in his veins,*. He thought, but didn't dare say. "Just who are you people?" was all that came out as he slowly massaged life back into the hand. He was convinced there'd be permanent nerve damage.

"We've already told you," Sandy spoke softly, "we're here to protect you." She shifted slightly, "look, you're in a lot of trouble, and need our help,"

"Why?" He whimpered, "what have I done?" the hand still hurt, life was coming back into it, but slowly, "besides" he began again.

"a couple of days ago," Joey cut him off, "remember the ransomware?"

"I've already damn well told you!" he screamed. "I didn't bloody do it! I stopped the sodding thing!"

"We know that" Sandy's voice was silky smooth, almost seductive. The contrast between the two was throwing him off balance. One he wanted to jump into bed with, the other seemed to want to throw him off the nearest roof, and while Joey suspected that's what he was thinking, if he'd confirmed it, he would have been tempted to. Except he knew Sandy wasn't interested in the guy. It was all a ploy to throw him off guard. They needed Paul scared and compliant. He'd fear Joey and comply with whatever Sandy told him. "It's the people who created the virus that want you dead! We're here to make sure that doesn't happen"

"What?" he was almost crying, "Why, all I did was stop a virus from destroying a heap of stuff! Why?"

"Because you stopped them stealing about twenty million pounds, Quid, Nicker, Smackers, anything else you want to call it, a whole heap of dough," Joey wasn't playing all that hard, he was genuinely surprised at how naïve this guy was.

Paul was almost in tears. His life was being ripped apart, and all because of one stupid move. A click on a keyboard that he just hadn't been able to resist. He never even thought for a moment how these guys might actually have found him, never thought that it was his own social media that had given him away.

"I can't believe this," he was almost crying, "How the hell?"

"Did this happen?" Joey couldn't resist trying to guess what he was going to say. He didn't know whether to feel sorry for him or tell him to get a life he'd been watching out of the window, the street looked clear, Joey knew otherwise, but that's what he was counting on, they just couldn't say anything, Paul was the bait, but Joey's job was keeping them alive. "Listen bro," Joey began again, "Long as we're here, nothing's going to happen to you," he lied.

"Really?" Paul stopped crying. "How?"

"Believe me," Sandy was the one spoke up, "If you can avoid finding that out, then do so. You really don't want to know," she stood up, "anyway, it's time to get you out of here," she began moving towards the door.

Joey was still at the window, scanning the street, there were a couple of cars there, but one, in particular, had caught his attention, it was parked, and had been for over ten minutes, the exhaust fumes said the engine was running, the two men inside the car were waiting for something, and he was pretty sure what they were waiting for, before heading towards the door a quick text put the last piece in place.

The text simply said, "Black Ford Mondeo, engine running, end of street" Smithy would know what to do.

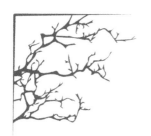

Chapter 12

The two men were smoking. Not that either was too bothered. Both were concentrating on the job at hand. Both getting ready and using the cigarette to calm the nerves. "Where the hell are they?" The driver, a big gruff bear of a man growled, he didn't like to be kept waiting for anything. Normally, it wasn't a good idea. Lives had been significantly shortened by keeping him waiting.

"How the hell should I bleeding well know!" The one in the back, the 'trigger man' had a distinct Irish lilt. The guy in the front knew his comrade had been with the provisional IRA or 'Provos'. He'd done time in prison for that, and thought that when peace came. He'd tried to settle down, but well, too much money was made running drugs and guns!

"Yer man on the inside said they should be in that house there, about five doors down." The Irish accent came on strong. "You sure about them?"

"Boss says they good" bear-man replied, "They make good money from deal" he really didn't give a damn whether they were, they got paid for the job, so that's what they'd do, fact was, if the money was right, bear man would kill anyone, even his own mother, and the money for this job was good, it was very good, but doing it in broad daylight? In a place where there were cameras everywhere. That made him nervous.

"But they're English, and selling their country out, you know! Trust but verify, maybe?" He paused before continuing, "I don't trust the bastards, never have."

"If they set us up" bear-man turned and faced his companion in the back, a huge sickening grin on his face, "I take great delight in killing them slowly"

Somehow, the Irishman knew it wasn't an idle boast. He didn't push things anymore.

"We're good to go, boss," Joey whispered into his lapel mike. Neither Paul nor Sandy saw or heard him. Not that it would have made any difference, Sandy knew the situation, and Paul was too scared to know what to think.

"Roger that," a voice came back through their earpieces. Both Sandy and Joey were wearing them, along with the mikes. They knew Jacko and the rest of the team were monitoring them. "Three, check-in"

"All good here boss," another voice, with a Geordie accent, came back, "Street's quiet, but we've got a bead on the gremlins,"

A 'bogey' in any operation is a 'callsign' you can't identify. They might be your side (known as Angels) or your enemy (known as 'Bandits'), a 'Bogey' could be either. And a 'Gremlin' is one you think probably is the enemy. Either way, you 'lock and load'

Except for this time they wanted them alive, preferably not realising they'd been 'rumbled'. Making them think they did their job, but somehow keeping their 'target' alive, "Should be a walk in the park" Jacko had said, Joey's reply had been something like, "I'd hate to be your dog if that's how you walk them!"

"We're coming out," Joey spoke into the mike as he reached for the door. Sandy was the first one through, eyes scanning the entire street before moving off.

"Bogeys are on your three o'clock," Smithy's voice came over the mike. "Got 'em on my camera, just waiting for the move, then we roll,"

"Roger that," Sandy replied. Anyone watching wouldn't have known she was speaking into a mike. "Joey?"

Paul was the next out, though he didn't actually know it, just as he got to the door. Joey had shoved a black bag over his head. It had no eyeholes and the bloody thing felt heavy. "It'll keep you alive." He'd said as he forced the thing down. He did not know where he was going. "Trust her," Joey had nodded in Sandy's direction. It didn't occur to him that Paul couldn't see Sandy.

But he was literally tied to her. She was pulling a leash that went around his waist, 'Like a sack of sodding spuds', he thought, though he daren't say anything.

"Black Mondeo closing faster than it should," Smithy gave instructions. Joey spotted it immediately in his peripheral vision, though he didn't show it. Joey had just come through the door, looking as if he hadn't seen a thing. He reached inside his jacket. He was already reaching for his Browning 9mm.

The Browning was in a shoulder holster. Joey checked that the keeping clip was undone. He wanted nothing to get in the way.

The car was at the south end of the street. It was about seventy yards away. It slowly pulled out from the place where it had been parked and began coming towards them. The window at the back on the left-hand side was halfway down. Smithy saw something poking out.

"Joey, it's a pistol shot, repeat a pistol shot," Smithy spoke calmly into the mike. There's no way even a professional could make sure of a kill from a moving car with a pistol. They all knew that but evidently these guys were either super confident or did not know, "Correction, an Ingrams" he screamed the last part.

The Ingrams submachine gun, better known as the MAC 10, is a favourite for the criminal world. A thirty-round magazine can be emptied in less than two seconds. The suppressor on the barrel makes it so quiet the only thing you hear is the cocking action of the bolt as it slams back into place. Mind you, it is doing it a thousand times a minute (if you can change magazines that fast). Not very accurate, but with a hose down rate like that, you don't need to be.

Joey didn't wait. He launched himself at Paul catching him right in the middle of the back; They began falling just as the first hiss was heard. Glass shattering as windscreens gave way to the hail of bullets. Sandy dropped like a stone as soon as Smithy's given the warning. She was down behind a car, out of the way, Makarov in hand, ready for any attempt if they got out of the car.

As soon as the hiss stopped, Joey was up on one knee. The Browning was out and barking. Two shots into the back of the car before it took off down the street, two more through the rear windscreen. His orders had been clear, not to kill them, but he couldn't resist giving them a real scare.

"Trackers are in," Joey called into the mike, "how're they reading?"

"We're all good here," a voice they recognised from halfway around the world, "Signals coming in clear as a bell, shit. I thought they were in the next room!" it was Mildred on the radio.

"Good to hear from you, er boss?" Sandy didn't really know what to call Mildred. Technically, she was running the show, but only because they made it plain. No one inside '6' was to be trusted until they said so, and considering the huge amount of cash they'd just delivered, she was happy to spend some of it helping them out, besides, in the spying game, it's always good to have your 'allies' owing you favour!

"What's the news on the other two?" it was Joey asked. "Back on the beat yet?"

"Officially?" Mildred replied, "They're on stress leave, really, they're on their way to Manchester. They're there as your backup. Like we agreed, I'm sending you contact details so you can contact directly."

"That figures," Mac broke in, "anyone who spends a day with Joey needs at least a month off to recover!" A few laughs were heard on the net.

"Okay folks," Jacko cut in. "Sorry to be a sourpuss, but what's the situation with the trackers?"

"They're reading good. The car's doing about fifty miles an hour down the street. We're following using the CCTV cameras, should have a location for you within minutes of them parking up,"

"Don't forget about the car switch," Smithy came back on the line, "They'll probably switch at least once if not three or four times."

"Did I tell you how to do your job?" Mildred shot back, not angry, but clearly wanting to put him in his place. She knew what she was doing. Switching cars is one of the first things that criminals think of. At least the smart ones do, and until the CCTV camera was invented, it was a sure way of getting away. If you had enough space between you and the pursuing cops, today was a different story.

But this time, they wanted them to get away. These were the 'small fry' of the operation, and the team were after a much bigger prize. Hopefully, the 'small fry' would lead them to the 'bigger fish' in the pond. But that was going to take some handling.

London has the dubious title of being the 'most watched city in the world. Literally every street corner is covered by a blanket of CCTV cameras that stretch from one side of the city to the other. But what no one tells anyone is that the blanket extends out much further than the security forces let on. Right from one coast to the other, every junction, traffic light and intersection, and it's all 'off the books'

"They're heading out of town," Mildred came back on the radio. "Looks like they're heading for the big smoke just like we thought!" She used the Londoner's favourite expression for London.

"What about the phones?"

"A couple of calls from the numbers we knew about," one of the other operators came on the line this time. "Seems like they're pretty rattled!"

"**I** damn well hate this," Sir Michael spoke for the first time since the operation began. He'd listened in on everything, "Flaming foreign agents working on British soil, doing a job we SHOULD be doing!" He almost threw the headset across the room, instead he tore it off and threw it into a pile on the desk where his laptop was. It was still connected, and on a secure frequency, but the anger was getting the better of him.

"Boss" it was Chambers who spoke, they were in the same place, near to the action, but far enough away that they couldn't see any of the players. "We have a mole! If we try anything, they'll know, we have to let it play out this way"

"I know, I know," he sighed, "but it doesn't mean I like it!"

"Boss, we gave them a hell of a mess to clean up, and ours won't be clean until we finish this. Let the Kiwis do their thing!"

"Doesn't mean I have to bloody well like it," he huffed as he sat down again.

Even Chambers would not correct him, and point out that the team was all British. It was just that control of the op wasn't his, and it ate away at him. He paused. They both had coffee, and something to eat where they were, their computers linked to Skype, along with the radios. They had everything they needed to listen in.

"Everything's in place boss" Chamber tried to smooth things out. It only had a limited effect. We're ready to go with the deception.

"We're under fire" Sandy's voice broke over the radio channels. They all knew GCHQ at Cheltenham was listening in on that radio frequency. Hopefully, they weren't listening in to the secure chat over the system they'd been using. It was a gamble, but they were using encryption techniques that even if they were on the right frequency, they'd have to have the right settings to break the code, otherwise it'd be gibberish.

Jacko had laughed when he first saw the radios they'd be using for the security line, an old-style mobile phone, "is that a phone?" He'd asked, "or a bloody brick?" The thing was so big it looked like an enormous bulge in his pocket.

"Old she may be boss," Joey replied as he cracked open the back of the phone. He took a few small packets out of his pocket, passing them round he carried on, "There are three papers I've colour coded for you uninitiated in the fine art of communication." He chuckled as he tore the end off the one he'd kept for himself. "Green first, then amber, then red, just like the traffic lights! Put them in the wrong order, and all you'll get is static." He looked around at each of them. "By the way, I colour coded these before we left New Zealand, so there ain't no copies here!"

"So?" Jacko asked

"So, get the wrong order, and all you get is gibberish, get the wrong cards, and all you get is static. They're unbreakable encryption. Even Cheltenham can't break the codes, unless they know which cards to use!"

"He's right," Sir Michael cut in, "back in the day we used them to fool the enemy, you had a one in three chance of getting the first card right, a one in nine chance of getting two of the cards right and a bloody astronomically small chance of getting all three right, and that's without knowing the frequency!"

To put all three cards in the right order was a one in two hundred and forty-seven chance of getting it right, and that's on a good day.

Sandy was talking on the 'open' system, the one that Cheltenham thought was their 'secure' system, they didn't want the cops to pick up on anything until after MI6 had seemingly 'cleaned the area', that was all part of the ruse. "We're taking fire, the package is down, repeat package is down, require immediate evac!"

"Roger that," Jacko came on the line, "evac on the way, help on the way" Mac and he were in a car at the end of the street, Jacko turned the key, gunned it and went screeching down the street.

All this was being picked up by the street cameras. By now Cheltenham would have heard the call, hacked the feed to the street cameras, put a few minutes' time delay into the feed so that the cops got the details minutes later. Enough time for either '5' or '6' to sort out a response, and hopefully get someone down here to 'contain' any damage to national security, all part of what they needed. The 'mole' had to think it'd been successful. Hopefully, a few calls on phones would report it, and they'd have the location.

Paul was hurt, but he wasn't shot. Joey'd hit him hard enough to knock 'the stuffing' out of him. He'd gone down hard and damn near 'popped' his kneecap, He howled with pain, but Joey'd thrown something damned heavy over his head, and was lying on it, holding him down, he was beginning to have trouble breathing, and was beginning to panic.

"Let me up, Let me humph,"

"Shut up and lie down" Joey punched him in the back and screamed in his ear.

"Get this bloody thing off me!" He shouted. His ears were ringing with the noise. The voice sounded kind of muffled. He'd no idea a weapon could be so loud, he wasn't even sure the firing had stopped.

"It's a Kevlar vest," Joey shouted back, "Bulletproof, now lie still until we tell you to move," He pushed down harder.

"You're clear" Smithy's voice cut over the secure channel, he was their 'ace in the hole' but this time 'over-watch' had been different, his job had been to just 'spot' the enemy, and keep track of them. They needed their enemies to get away this time!

Less than half a second later, he was being physically lifted. Whatever it was still over his head, bundled into the back of a vehicle, "Keep it on" Sandy was right beside him and pushing him down, "we've gotta make 'em think you're dead"

"What?" He was terrified.

"They want you dead. The only way to keep you alive is to make them think you are. Now shut up and lie down!"

"Control, this is Scorpion Team," Sandy began a 'sitrep' report over the official channel, "Two gunmen, dark Ford car registration Yankee, Charlie, Pappa, four two five Xray, heading north on Victoria Crescent. Am evacuating the package, damaged, but not destroyed, heading for the 'Prince of Thieves' over"

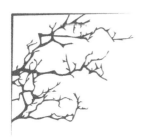

Chapter 13

"We got 'im guv" the young detective shouted down the phone.

"Whoa, hold on Jimmy," she reached over to turn the volume down. Billie was driving, so she was using the car's Bluetooth tech on her phone. Jimmy was coming over the car speakers. "Now, whatcha got?" the Manchester slang slipping out.

"I've got him guv, found yer man!"

"Where?" she shot back. Suddenly, the traffic wasn't as important as before. "We've been looking for days. Where was he?"

"I know boss" Jimmy might be the youngest one on the team, barely in his twenties, but he was probably the brightest. "That's why I did some lateral thinking." He stopped for the slightest moment. Billie was genuinely curious where he was going with this, but let him carry on. "You told us to search the river banks, right?"

"Yeah," she began. By now, she'd found a parking spot. She pulled over. "Carry on"

"Well," He began again, "I remembered something from my school geography class,"

"Not so long ago for you," she quipped. She just couldn't help having a dig at his age, or lack of it, "but go on"

"You had us checking all the cameras upriver, cos rivers normally flow downhill, right?" The comment about his lack of age either went totally over his head, or he ignored it.

"Yeah" she was genuinely curious. "carry on". She really wanted to see where this lead.

"Well guv, the Thames isn't a normal river, it's what they call a tidal river. It ebbs and flows with the tide. Sure, mostly it flows downhill, or downstream, but what if the fella went in the river when the tide was coming in? He could have drifted from the east, possibly the east end."

"Please don't tell her he's a sodding mobster!" She exhaled, speaking softly, yet the voice was full of fear, "That's the last thing we need, a gang war in the middle of tourist season!" Then again, she thought to herself, 'it's London when aren't the tourists around?' She switched the car ignition back on, "Listen, Jimmy, I'm heading right back to the station, have the whole team get together, you can brief us all when I get there!"

"Tower Bridge,"
"What?"
"Tower bridge, that's where he went into the river,"

"But now, it's a river right, and they run downhill, don't they?" One of the others asked. It was Frank, he was number two on the team now that the 'brass' had decided the case wasn't such a priority, Though how you can go from 'top priority' to almost a 'cold case' in the space of a couple of days mystified BJ.

"Not the Thames," Jimmy replied, "at least not all the time. It's what's known as a tidal river. The tides can affect the way it flows." He stopped and took a sip of the water he was holding in the plastic beaker, he was nervous, very conscious he was the 'junior,' here and it's the older more experienced cops meant to be showing him how to do stuff, "the Thames has tides, and they go all the way up as far as Teddington lock, you know, right past here." He pointed to the place on the map where the body was found, "and all the way to Hampton Court, so flowing upriver isn't a problem!"

"But how did you work out it was Tower Bridge? That place is closed to traffic, and the public!" Frank came back, "Been closed for months, working on the drawbridge aren't they?"

"Yeah, they are," Jimmy replied, "but I asked the database for people who went into the river for that night. There were three altogether, one in Dulwich, he got rescued about five minutes after he went in, the second was down by Dartford, pulled herself out, and then there's this guy, the only one I couldn't account for getting out!"

"But if he fell in," Billie started, "How come no one noticed?"

"Like Frank said, boss," Jimmy replied taking a sip of the water he was holding, "It's a construction site, the weekend, no one really around to see it,"

"But what about the security company?" the young female on the team, her name was Joanne, "aren't there CCTV cameras? Wasn't someone watching?"

"There were," Jimmy replied, "they've got cameras, and they're working, but because it's a construction site. They're only really interested in when people nick stuff from the site. They only look when stuff's gone missing!"

"Just great," Frank spat the words out. He'd got a coffee in his hand, standard practice for a cop with ten years 'on the job',. "A deserted building site, no cameras worth a shit, and no one taking responsibility"

"Oh, and that's not all," Jimmy butted in, "we also got the time he went into the river wrong. He went in at eleven the night before. The high tide was at three, so the body drifted downriver, got stuck and was found where he was," Jimmy was a little more precise than me meant to be. He was getting carried away with the excitement of the moment, no one stopped him though.

"What did he get stuck on?" Frank asked. No one really noticed that Jimmy had switched from the personal of talking about the man to the impersonal of talking about the body.

"Not sure boss," Jimmy addressed his comments to Billie. He wasn't ignoring Frank, just following the protocol that everything goes through the boss in these situations. "But there are a few ships moored nearby. The Pathologist says there's paint. *Navy grey*' he called it." He made the two-fingered sign for inverted commas, "apparently it used to be known as Mountbatten pink, and only the Navy ever used it, and only during the middle of WW2. There's only one ship that's ever been painted that colour on the Thames. That's HMS Belfast, but there are other boats that the body may have washed up alongside"

"This gets bleeding worse!" BJ was beginning to regret being given the case, not that she'd had much of a choice in the matter. You never do. She knew from the start it was a 'make or break' case. It would either make or break her career, and right now it was looking like the latter. "What you're saying, or at least seem to say" she went on. "Is that the Royal Navy's floating museum and two of London's most iconic tourist attractions are our crime scenes! Sodding wonderful!!"

"Boss," Jimmy cut her off, he was about to deliver the biggest blow, "I'm not even sure there was a crime. Here' take a look at this" he'd had his laptop with him. He reached down, opened the laptop, turned it on and flipped it around so that everyone could see. Three clicks on the inbuilt mouse pad and he was onto the camera footage from the time of the incident. They all watched with interest. "I downloaded what footage the construction company had, here look." He clicked the mouse a few times, brought up the footage and swivelled the machine around so they could all see.

Everyone could see the victim. There was something or someone glancing off him, but it happened so fast, and at such an angle, they couldn't see clearly. Then they only saw about two steps before he fell from the bridge, but he was staggering as if he was drunk.

"So" BJ was annoyed, really annoyed. She was trying to hold in the anger, but not succeeding very well. "What you're saying is we've been sent on a flaming wild goose chase through the bleeding streets and cesspits of this sodding city just to come up with this bullshit?" Jimmy looked sheepish. They'd all done their jobs to the best of their ability. But all they'd come up with was that the man seemed as 'drunk as a skunk' fell over and drowned in an accident!

"Wait a minute boss," it was Joanne who stopped the flow. "We've got the pathologist's report. I put it on your desk an hour ago. Figured you'd look it over when you got back. That should tell us if it was alcohol or drugs." She started for Billie's office. Fifteen seconds later, she had the report and presented it to her boss. She already knew what Billie would find, but there was no way she was going to 'steal her thunder. She gave it over, "Here you are, guv."

BJ snatched the report. She'd normally have the manners to say "thank you", but she was too frustrated at the wild goose chase. She studied it for a moment. "Wait a minute," she blurted out. She leaned back against a desk and read out loud, "Blood alcohol level was nil, no drugs found in his system," she went through the rest of the report. "Nothing" she looked up, holding the rest of the team in her stare, she blurted out, "anyone care to explain how we can have a man 'drunk as a skunk' on video, yet no alcohol or drugs found in his system? Do we even know who he was yet?"

Everyone looked sheepish. It was clear the answer was 'no' on both counts. Billie's eyes were boring into each one. They'd done their jobs, yet it felt like they were naughty school kids being told off by the school principal. Nervous fidgeting was going on around the room.

Something clicked in her brain. She figured the same thing had either clicked in their brains too, or was about to, and that was someone out there who didn't want the cops finding out who this guy was. That someone was either in the government, or had connections very high up. That made her very uncomfortable.

"We still need to find out who he was," BJ ignored the stony silence. She knew she'd be pushing the limits. "A family had a husband and possibly a father who didn't come home a few nights ago. They're probably frantic with worry. We owe it to them to find out and let them know what happened. We'll use that angle to cover our arses with this," she pointed to the board where all the details were. "meanwhile, I'll get hold of the pathologist, and see if they can explain what we saw, that sound like a plan?"

Chapter 14

"**999** Emergency. Which service do you require?" The voice, that of a young female, seemed so ridiculously out of place, yet so very English, yet totally wrong for the situation.

"Er, not sure," the young man on the phone spat back, "There's been a shooting down Hucknall street."

"Thank you, putting you through to the police." The voice came back, "please stay on the line" like he was going anywhere? He'd just entered the street and a hail of bullets seemed to come his way. He'd dived for cover and prayed like he hadn't since he was five years old. At least that's what he was about to tell them, and it was all a lie. A few moments later, another voice, that of a male, came on the line.

"Police emergency, how can I help?" the voice asked.

"There's been a shooting. A shooting, down in Hucknall street" he played it as if he didn't realise the nerves causing him to repeat himself.

"Thank you. Can I clarify where you are, where exactly was the shooting?"

"I'm on the corner of Hucknall and Bracegirdle streets,"

"Is that in Bath?" the voice cut him off, "or?"

"Bristol you bloody idiot," the young man screamed. He was beginning to lose the plot, "There are bullets everywhere, a couple of people have just bundled a guy into a car, I think they're taking him to the hospital!"

"Has an ambulance been called?"

"I just damn well told you, someone took the guy to the hospital! Besides, you're the flaming emergency services, you should know that!"

"Stay with me sir," the voice was calm, bringing order to the chaos, "I need to ask you, are the shooters still at the scene?"

"No,"

"Are they injured?"

"How the hell should I know? They left in a car!"

"The shooters? Or the victim?"

"Both!" he knew it probably wasn't making sense. That was good, a panicking civvie wouldn't, and that's what Smithy was trying to be. But he was telling things as they happened, "Look, all I heard was a hail of gunfire, and a car speeding off followed by the other two bundling a guy into the back of a car."

"How do you know it was gunfire?"

"There are holes and broken glass in at least half a dozen cars in the street. The car alarms are going nuts,"

"Okay sir," the voice was still calm, "Armed police are on their way, as well as ambulances. Please stay where you are and don't touch anything,"

"**G**et in and stay down," Joey screamed as he pushed Paul hard to the floor in the vehicle. "Move your legs" he reached down and violently pulled them up into the back of the estate car. Slamming the back down, he ran round to the rear passenger door. Jacko was waiting in the driving seat. Sandy was already buckled into the front passenger seat. The second the door slammed shut Jacko floored the accelerator, wheels spun and tyres screeched as they hurtled down the road, so far everything was going to plan, though to the rest of the world it looked as if everything had fallen apart, just what they needed people to think.

"I thought it was Mac coming for us?" Joey sort of asked the question.

"You just wanted to see my awesome driving skills again" Jacko was laughing. His driving was legendary in the unit for being totally reckless.

"Yeah right," Joey replied as he climbed into the backseat. Sandy was already in the passenger seat at the front and buckled in. "Sorry to disappoint you boss, but even I'd prefer to take a pass on that one!"

"And I thought you had a sense of adventure" Sandy was almost laughing, a nervous laugh.

"We've just been bloody well shot at," Paul blurted out, "and all you people can do is make a joke about it! Who the hell are you folks?" he was trying to raise himself up. Joey had thrown a heavy blanket over him. It was hard work, but he was moving it, and his wits were slowly coming back.

"Your guardian angels," Joey quipped as he slapped him hard on the back of the head forcing him down again, "It's Kevlar, keep the sodding thing over you, we're not out of the woods yet!" He turned to Jacko, "let's get the hell out of here, boss!"

Jacko floored the accelerator. The front wheels spun as the car jumped forward, forcing Sandy and Jacko back into their seats. Joey was already hanging on and watching the back of the vehicle, pistol still drawn 'just in case.

"Sorry to disturb you sir" the voice on the phone sounded apologetic, Sir Michael knew it was the duty officer at Vauxhall House, and he was performing the task everyone at MI6

dreaded, giving the director of intelligence bad news, "but we've got a bit of a situation, sir, a code yellow,"

"Casualties?" Sir Michael cut him off. He knew the codes. 'red' was an ambush with fatalities, yellow was injuries, green was 'bloody lucky'. He thought he already knew all the information, but it was vital he played the part. They couldn't let the 'mole' know it was a setup, and that mole was a part of '6's infrastructure!

"We have at least one injury, sir," the junior agent replied. "the one they were protecting took a hit. We're not sure how bad yet."

"Why not?" Sir Michael asked, doing a good job of sounding alarmed, "aren't you in contact with the team?"

"Sorry sir," the agent sounded flustered, "I've only got the information my superior gave me. The team is mobile to one of our safe houses, one with medical facilities,"

"Which one?" Sir Michael already knew the reply, and he knew the team wasn't on its way there, at least not with the 'target', but MI6 wasn't to know that.

"The one they were sent to protect, sir," he replied.

"What the?" Sir Michael cut him off. "Weren't they SUPPOSED to be damn well protecting that one?" He acted angry. It was pretty convincing. He carried on, "what about cleanup? Has a cleanup team been dispatched?"

The desk officer was taken a bit by surprise. "Negative sir, a call was made to the police before we could respond. Armed police are sealing the area off as we speak!"

'Cleanup teams' have one job, and that's removing any trace of agency involvement. They're often the best forensic people around. The challenge of 'hoodwinking' the police is just too much to resist, but there just wasn't time. The 'plods', as the cops were often known, were on their way.

"In that case," Sir Michael began again, "we better get a liaison officer down there. I want to know everything they know, and preferably first, I want a lid screwed down tight on this, and I mean NOW!"

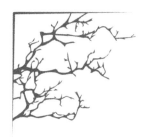

Chapter 15

"Just what the hell is going on?" Paul tried to raise himself up. He was being held down by someone. "This is kidnapping, let me up"

"In case you haven't realised yet," Joey pushed him back down, "those bullets were meant for you, now sodding well stay down until we tell you otherwise."

"But what, why?"

"You're forgetting the first one," Sandy chipped in. "the who?"

"Whatever!" He shouted. "One minute I'm playing a game on my laptop. The next I'm being bundled into the street, and people are shooting. Just who were they, and why me? And where's my laptop?"

"You're on a 'tech-free' diet as of now!" Sandy spoke loud enough to be heard over the engine. The big Ford wasn't noisy, but Jacko was 'pushing her' a bit. Sandy saw the speedometer touch eighty miles an hour just as they merged onto the M5 motorway. He backed off as soon as they were in the flow of traffic.

Ten miles further up was a motorway service, petrol, restaurants, accommodation, truck stop, the works, almost perfect for the car swap. If the CCTV didn't catch them, that is.

Back in the 1950s, a rather well-known author wrote a book about the Britain of the future. A book that painted a bleak picture of CCTV cameras and microphones everywhere. Watching every move, listening to every word, checking every person to make sure they're 'towing the line'. The book became a classic, and everyone thought that what he predicted would never happen in a democracy, how wrong they were!

But, even with the best cameras, the most potent mikes, there are always 'blackspots' parts where the camera doesn't see, the mike doesn't pick up the noise. There are two kinds of people know where they all are. The criminal, and the spy. Big brother might watch the masses, but he misses the ones he needs to watch!

"You and Joey take the Ford," Jacko yanked the handbrake on. They only had seconds before someone suspected something. Even in the black spots, there's a security guard watching who goes into and out of them all the time. Anything out of the ordinary and someone will be 'sent to investigate', especially here on the motorway, where a truck's entire load can go missing in seconds. "Head for the RV with Smithy. By then he should have info on where those arseholes are, but wait for Mac and me OKAY." He turned and faced Joey. He knew Sandy would wait. Joey was a bit of a different story.

"Gotcha boss," Joey replied as he climbed out of the vehicle. They were leaving the explorer here, the 'Ford' was a Grenada Sedan, 2.8 litres of pure mean under the bonnet.

"You drive or me?" Joey asked as they stepped around the vehicles.

"Me," Sandy replied, as she took the keys out of his hand. Slotting the remote into her handbag, she reached down, turned on the ignition, put the car into gear as Joey clambered in. "We need to be in one piece when we get there!"

"Are you insinuating?" he began.

"That you're a maniac?" she shot back with a cheeky grin, "absolutely" and they took off, wheels spinning.

"And just how do you come to that conclusion?" Joey was starting to relax. There's nothing like humour for relaxing tension.

"Let's see," Sandy cut him off, they were both laughing slightly, "Jumping out of a bloody aircraft with just a skimpy parachute. Jumping off a cliff with nothing but a darned wingsuit. That was after rigging a bomb to blow half the mountain up. That explains why I've come to that conclusion?"

"And I'll add" he cut her off, "You were right behind me in all those." He turned and looked at her. She was gorgeous. She glanced his way. "Takes one to know one as they say where I come from!" She gave him a playful, dirty look.

Joey reached for the car speaker controls. He'd already enabled the 'Bluetooth' on his phone. It meant the phone would make the calls he needed but would play over the car's speakers and mike system. As soon as he set the controls, he spoke, "Call Smithy" within seconds the Geordie accent could be heard over the speakers.

"About bloody time man" it sounded like he'd said "mon" but that was just the accent. "Where are yer?"

"Motorway services on the M5," Joey replied, "heading back in as fast as we can."

"Stay away from the area, it'll be swarming with bloody cops in a couple of minutes," Smithy warned them. "I gave yer a five-minute start before I called her in, told 'em I was just walking by, they'll be looking for us all soon." He paused for a moment. From the sounds of it, he was on the move. "Tracker's still active. They're about four miles away. I had a look on Google and it looks like a warehouse of some kind. The car has been inside for about five minutes. Meet me there!"

"Shit," Joey didn't mean to say it on the phone, but it came out anyway, "Jacko said to hold off anything until he and Mac get there, Smithy hold off, we'll be there as fast as we can!"

"Where are we with communication?" Mildred didn't sound polite. They were monitoring everything remotely, and things didn't sound too promising, yes the mole had taken the bait, but the car switch wasn't something they needed. Needed 'like a hole in the head' as Joey would say. Just about every thief who knew what they were doing would have something like that planned, but most of them didn't know where the cameras were, and that was often their downfall. These people seemed to know where everyone was, and that meant only one possibility, it had to be an 'inside job'. It had to be the 'mole' telling them where they were.

"Sooner we catch this Bastard the better!" She swore under her breath, not really caring who heard her. There wasn't much that angered spies. They were trained to stay calm under pressure, but when one of 'your own' goes over to the other side, that hurts.

"We're monitoring the phone numbers we have," the young girl with the studs spoke up, "but so far nothing,"

"What about the tracker?"

"As Smithy said," Cody cut in, "Went into the warehouse seven minutes ago, nothing since it's still there!"

"Have we got camera footage from around there yet?"

"Working on it," Mark, her second in command chipped in, "Not easy, each area's compartmentalized, preventing hackers from getting in and taking over the system, should,"

"Don't give me excuses," she cut him off, "hack the bloody system!"

"Was going to say, should be any second, and I've gone back fifteen minutes so we can see what vehicles left around that time!" He let his frustration for a little, Mildred could be short and rude, but she believed in 'do unto others as you'd like them to do to you,' and that meant she didn't mind them getting 'stroppy,' back when she got 'stroppy,' with them, as long as they got the job done. "Here we are boss, coming through now."

"My terminal" was all she said.

Chapter 16

"Here we are" Jacko wrenched on the handbrake as they came into the yard. The car skidded to a halt outside what looked like a farm shed.

A small stone cottage sat to their left. The two buildings were separate, but connected by a small dry stone wall that formed a rectangle shape encompassing the cobbled courtyard.

"Stay inside the vehicle, and out of sight until I tell you otherwise." Jacko addressed the heap that Paul was under. He'd been too scared to move since he'd been bundled into the vehicle 'like a sack of spuds'. Jacko exited the car and headed for the door to the farm shed.

The door was closed but had a few unusual features, one of which was a keypad and screen. He quickly punched in a ten-digit code. The door moved as he headed back to the car; it was fully open by the time he got in.

"Glad you made it," a female voice spoke from behind as they were getting out of the car. They recognised it as being the cop 'Sam I think,' Jacko thought.

"We've been keeping up to date with things over the radio," Sam continued. They noticed both she and Hene were wearing shoulder holsters. They both had Glocks in them. "Is he injured?" she motioned to the 'sack of spuds' that was shaking. Paul was trying hard not to even move, but the sheer terror of what had happened had taken hold. Shock can be delayed, but never stopped altogether.

"Nothing' that a cuppa Cannae cure" they couldn't miss the Scottish brogue.

"No physical injuries then Mac?" it was Hene asked.

"Nah," the big Scot replied, "psychological' a different story though!" He frowned, then resignedly went on, "still, cannae be helped, c'mon laddie" he prodded Paul, "yer quite safe now"

Paul moved, though it took a few seconds for the words to register. "Safe?" he mumbled. "I've been kidnapped, shot at, damn near killed, beaten to a bloody pulp by my SUPPOSED protectors, and HE says it's safe?"

"Safer than staying where you were," Mac retorted. None of them had the time or the patience for whining. "Lead tablets are bad for the health," Mac went on, "and they were Tungsten tipped, that's even worse, one will kill ya, and there were about sixty, all headed for ya!" He reached in and virtually yanked Paul out of the car, "now get a move on!"

Paul stumbled as he was wrenched from the car. His left foot caught the back of his right leg, just above the ankle. He went down, only to be caught by Hene, who held him up.

"Do you have to be that rough?" Sam quietly asked Jacko as they made their way towards a small trapdoor in the floor. She was a cop and used to being rough with the criminal she arrested, but Paul wasn't under arrest. He was just an average bloke.

"When your armed offenders squad clears a building in a hostage situation, do they stop each hostage to give 'em tea and biscuits on the way out?" Jacko shot back, "bloody hope not," he replied to himself before she had the chance, "they're still in danger, get 'em out of the danger first, then be nice to 'em,"

"But we're at the safe house!"

"He's never going to be safe," Mac cut her off, he'd been listening in, "until we nail these pricks, and dinna forget," he went on, "one of 'em is MI6, they bloody well know the safe-houses!"

"That's why we're not using one of theirs" Jacko cut in, "this one's '5's, but Mac's right, he's gonna have a target on his back until we get these guys!"

Chapter 17

"This is bloody unreal" BJ put the file she'd been reading down, rubbed her eyes and stared down at the desk. They'd been on the case for days. It felt like months, but they were getting nowhere, and fast! "Nothing, we've got sodding nothing, five days and zilch!" the frustration getting the better of her, she stopped and looked up at the wall. The clock said eleven pm. That didn't make her feel any better. It just reminded her she'd been working sixteen hours straight.

"I suppose he'll still be dead tomorrow." She said to no one in particular. Even that late in the evening, there were still a few in the office. The detectives on the night shift, and a couple of other workaholics. No one paid her much attention. They all had their own cases to deal with.

Pushing back her chair, she was just rising to grab her coat when her mobile rang, 'strange' she thought, the only people who had her number worked in that room. It sure as hell wouldn't be her boss. *'That prick's strictly nine to five. Who the hell is it?'*

"Who's this?" She demanded as she answered the phone.

"Detective Sergeant," a voice on the other end replied, "Is that a good way of greeting someone with information?" there was a gentle rebuke in the voice.

"This isn't the hotline number," she replied. "it's known only to a couple of people, and you're not one of them! So, who are you?"

"You've got a stiff in your mortuary, right? No idea who he is, and no one's saying anything. Am I needing to be a rocket scientist to figure that out!" There was a pause. "Let's cut to the chase, shall we?"

the voice came back, "Now to the important stuff, you do not know who he is, right?"

"I suppose that was in the news, so nothing new there." She was tired, and this, while the banter might be enjoyable when she wasn't tired, right now she really couldn't give a damn. "You better do better than that if you want this conversation to continue" by now a couple of the others in the room were looking over. She indicated for one of them to get into the cyber division and trace the call. One of them jumped towards his phone and got things moving. He gave a thumbs up indicating the trace was in progress.

"Check out a name, you'll find nothing on file after 2005, but the name is Mohammad Akbari, Egyptian born in 1978 in Cairo, came to Britain to study in 1995, studied Oriental languages and computer sciences, became a naturalised British citizen in 2004, then disappears off the radar." The line went dead as the phone was hung up. A very confused BJ was just looking at it, wondering whether it could be legit, when the phone pinged again. This time an email, from a 'Hotmail' account, which meant it was practically impossible to trace. All it said was "in case you're unsure." She opened the email, there was a crystal clear photo of the deceased, and it wasn't the one they released to the press, this one was recent, but he was alive in it, and it had been 'clipped', all it said was "He worked in computers, for someone important!"

This was getting stranger by the minute. First, the body appears 'within shouting distance' of parliament, no ID or anything. The Police throw all their resources at solving the case, but someone starts pulling strings. And they're re-assigned pretty quickly, then phone calls in the middle of the night?

She stopped, swung the bag she was holding back down by her desk, and sat down again. Picking up the phone she pressed a number on the speed dial. A grumpy voice came on the line, "Guv, you know it's eleven pm, right?"

"Yeah, sorry Jimmy, but I need you to look into the customs and immigration files for me,"

"Ya got any paperwork we might need?" Jimmy didn't like to poke around in government files without the correct signatures. "Doing it without the right signatures can bite us in the arse you know?" He knew BJ knew that, but sometimes it's good to remind them, 'just in case'

"Not really," she was honest with the reply, "but I might have the ID of our victim. You're looking around 1995, probably from Egypt, and the name's Akbari, while you're there check the DVLC records,"

The 'DVLC' stands for the Driver and Vehicle Licencing Centre. All the driving licences and vehicle registrations are registered there. If Akbari's name was on the lists, it would tell them what kind of vehicle he owned, and more importantly, where he lived.

"Guv, we ran the photo through the DVLA before. Got sweet Fanny Adams from it, remember." He began.

"Run it again" she cut him off, "and this time with the name!" the fact was the info she'd been given showed that someone didn't want her to find out whom it was, this would flaming well show them she was better than they were, and she'd get the ID eventually, she was sending them a message, "Stop screwing with me or get ready to pay a steep price!"

"Okay boss," he replied meekly, "It'll probably take me a couple of hours to get the info Guv. Want me to come in?" He wondered if this was going to be 'official.'

"Nah, better do it from your end," BJ replied, "Your coffee's much better, send the results to my mobile." and clicked the phone off, as soon as it clicked a message came up.

"While you're waiting for the reply, grab a coffee at Starbucks on the corner, table nearest the door." This was damn strange, but she had to follow through. She had to find out who was sending the cryptic messages.

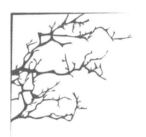

Chapter 18

"Just what the hell do you think you're doing?" The acid in the comment was so caustic he could feel the phone melting. Just who the hell was this punk on the other end? "You screwed the whole thing up."

"We did what we were told!" He spat back down the phone. "We dumped the car, found another, cleared out, no one followed." He was getting impatient. He wasn't even sure if it was a man or woman, as they were using software to disguise their voice. It sounded more like a computer he was talking to. The only thing that gave it away was the anger in the voice.

"And you screwed up the hit, you moron!" the voice came back, "you were meant to take him down, as in killing him!"

"No one says he got protection. We were supposed to get there first, REMEMBER!"

"You take nothing for granted in this game" it was almost a shout, as if the person saying it couldn't believe these people. The supposedly trained assassins needed reminding of the 'golden rule' of their profession. "He's still alive, and thanks to you morons, they've got him stashed in a 'safe house' somewhere" the phone went dead as the caller clicked off. The call had taken less than thirty seconds, not enough time to trace it if anyone was trying, which they doubted very much.

They'd done everything they were told. The brief had been 'make it look like a gang thing', so that's what they'd done. A gang drive-by, but no one had warned them of the *protection* the target had. That made little sense as they'd been told he was just some geeky computer nerd, and they don't get armed protectors.

"I think we should have demanded more," the driver, a big bearded guy with an East European accent, said. He was Russian, not that he'd told the Irishman. Neither of them knew each other that well, and neither asked questions. They just did the job they were paid for and went their own way. That was much safer. Too many questions can get you killed.

"Nah," the passenger's Irish lilt came through, "better stay alive than ask too much"

That was true. These people didn't take kindly to greed. They paid well, but don't try asking for too much. The only addition you'd get from them was about nine-millimetre diameter and travelling at about four hundred feet a second.

"We better get outta here," the big Russian said, "before someone turns up." He was out of the vehicle and moving, he didn't even turn around, "come on, get moving!"

"We got 'em" Smithy's Geordie accent came through pretty strong as ever. "We got the bloody sods,"

"Have we tracked 'em then?" Joey fired the question. They were still mobile, driving to the rendezvous point. Sandy was at the wheel. Joey was 'prepping' for whatever came next, and that meant anything could happen.

"Nah, not tracked," he replied over the phone. They were using the 'Bluetooth' technology in the car. It was coming over the car's speaker system. "I've got an idea where they are on that though." The phone went silent for a few seconds. Just as Joey was about to ask Smithy to go on, he came back on. "Got a mugshot of the shooter."

He sounded excited, that was unusual, Smithy was only ever excited when he'd made a kill shot from over a mile, then again, taking a 'usable' mugshot of a shooter with an Ingrams took a special kind of skill, one that most professional photographers don't have. Even Police sharpshooters struggle with it, Smithy had it in spades.

"I got the shot," Smithy went on, "put it into the Interpol database like the way Sandy showed me, and we got a hit, bloody Russian, sending you the details!"

"Thanks," Sandy was still driving. "Where do we need to go?"

"Sending you the details now, the car pulled in there ten minutes ago, so it's likely they did a swap, and might not be there."

"Roger that," Joey came back on, "We'll check it out."

"Wait until we confirm," a third voice, one instantly recognizable, came on the line. Mildred had been following everything they said. The last thing they needed was the team going in half prepared and being in a firefight of any kind, at least not until they were ready to initiate it!.

Mildred may have been twelve thousand miles away, but the clarity on the phone made it sound like she was in the next room, even the delay was so small that it was hardly noticed that the signals had travelled at least 24,000 miles, if not further. "We lost the signal as soon as they went into the building, but we're working on finding out, as fast as we can."

"Any chance they'll torch the vehicle?" Joey asked, knowing the answer beforehand, but still needing to hear confirmation.

"Only amateurs and desperate people do that," Sandy cut in. "These people have the resources to make the vehicle totally disappear. My guess is it's going to a 'chop shop' in a few days."

Movies often portray the villains as getting rid of evidence in a fire, but fire doesn't always destroy all the evidence. Sometimes it gets preserved, and the fire draws the wrong kind of attention. The fire service puts the blaze out, then the police or fire brigade go through it with a 'fine-tooth comb' and any evidence you tried to destroy is going to send you for a long stretch in prison! Those with the resources make sure they get left in a place the cops will not look for them, then in a few days pick 'em up and take them to be dismantled. Simple, easy, and you make money off it as well!

Twelve thousand miles away, things were frantic. "Where the hell did they go?" Mildred was shouting at her operators, none of them was paying too much attention, they'd been half-expecting something like this, just hoping that the criminals weren't as smart as they seemed to be, and that was bloody annoying, the thought of 'criminal masterminds' is a product of the fictional detectives, or so the wisdom of the world said, these guys were showing different.

"It's a bloody car park!" Joey let out a frustrated shout as they came into the street where signal disappeared, "multi-storey, paid and monitored by the looks, security cameras on the outside,"

"Shit" was all Sandy replied. They could barge in, demand camera footage, and if the perps were still there, it would be like arriving with the sirens blaring, "any chance they're still there?" she demanded.

"Still working on that," the terse reply came back, "meanwhile stand down, repeat, stand down, do not approach!"

"What?" Joey wasn't sure he was hearing right. "What about a recipe?"

"You go in there and they're still inside, you could blow the whole thing," Mildred cut him off, "We're trying to confirm either way, but you stand down, even if they've left we'll pass the info on to the cops. They can take this side from here! GOT IT?" the last part was more a command than anything.

"What do you want us to do?" Sandy cut back in. They'd parked the car a couple of hundred yards from the entrance, they were both watching the entrance.

"Head for the RV point like we agreed" Sir Michael's voice came through clearly. He'd been following everything, but not interfering. The agreement was that Mildred and her people would take them so far, but after that, he'd take over. This was that time. "You have the mugshots, use them to identify the perpetrators, after that clear the mess your way" the less he knew about what the team did the better it would be, but he was positive it wouldn't be pleasant.

"And the trackers?" Joey was concerned they were leaving evidence behind.

"Are standard MI5 equipment," Sir Michael replied. He knew Mildred was still listening, but it was important that he take over now if there were any issues from this. He had to be the one to take the crap. As the politicians would be annoyed, MI6 was running an op on British soil, but they'd be 'baying for blood," if they found foreign involvement, even if it was an ally! "We'll try to retrieve them later, but for now, leave them there. When, or rather if the cops see those they'll get really nervous, and that's going to benefit us, also if our friends find them, they'll realise it's a multi-horse race, they're going to be looking over their shoulder all the time now, watch your backs".

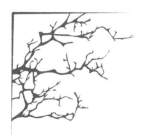

Chapter 19

"So," BJ spoke into the phone as soon as the voice answered. "You've got my attention. How come you know so much?" She was looking round to see anyone watching. Trying to spot whoever had the phone. There were a couple of people there talking on their phones, but they'd been on them since she arrived three minutes before. There was another guy in a corner using his like a writing tablet. No one stood out.

"All in good time, detective." The voice said, "all in good time, there's a package taped to the underside of the table, when we finish this call take it home, use your own desktop to access what's in the files, but DON'T connect to the web. You'll see why when you open it," the voice preempted her next question.

This was weird! No other way to describe it fits. Yeah, as a copper she was used to informants not wanting to be seen talking to the cops, but going this far? Weird was the only word she could think of.

Someone didn't want the cops to know who the victim was. You didn't have to be a rocket scientist to work that much out. But who? It would make sense if it was the killer, but they would have hidden the body better. *The killer doesn't give a crap* she thought. In fact, it was almost as if the killer had sent a message with the body being by the river, so close to Parliament. No, someone else didn't want the identity known to the Police, and that really made little sense.

One thing was obvious. She was being watched, and they knew more about her than she was comfortable with. Hell, they'd got her private mobile number. Only three people had that, two were family, and the other, well, the boss never called. He texted, and my boss, not the idiot who'd given her the case. He was just a link in the chain. She meant the man who'd recruited her for the 'Met' , Townsend's boss.

Slowly moving forward, left elbow on the table. She made it look as if she was fighting a losing battle with the dreaded sleep. Meanwhile, the right hand went under, searching for the package that was meant to be there. She found it, actually; it felt like two. The first one felt to be just as thick as her finger, and about as long as going to her middle knuckle, but it was stuck on top of something larger, but a lot thinner, and flatter.

It was about the length of her hand. As wide as the width of her hand, but about as wide as a woman's nail file, she had an idea what they were, but this was no place to stop and look.

As soon as the items were free, she guessed it was stuck there with Bluetack. She dropped them into her pocket. She had a handbag, but never trusted the really important stuff to it. Too easy for a thief to make off with the thing while she wasn't looking, or worse, while she was bowled over in the street as they came hurtling past on a skateboard or something. The packages went into a pocket.

The hand came back up as she reached for the drink. Hot chocolate downed the drink and got up to leave.

The couple were totally engrossed in talking to each other. They weren't watching her. She was sure of that, but the guy in the corner, she wasn't sure about him. He was still texting, and laughing when replies came, 'could be a girlfriend' Billie thought to herself. "Oh, for a normal life." She said quietly to herself, sort of envious of the mediocrity that was around her. Going about their daily lives without the stress of tracking down the worst scum London offered, just accepting safety and security with a few inconveniences. Very little thought of those who worked night and day to make sure it stayed that way.

As soon as she left the coffee shop, the guy in the corner stood up. He ambled to the door, opened it and seemed to go the opposite way. As he left, he hit the send button on the phone. His message read, "She's on her way, taking an Uber"

The reply was a few seconds in coming. It simply said, "follow to make sure".

She was being watched, that was true, but so was the watcher.

Chambers wasn't in the coffee shop. He'd been in a car nearby, and saw the copper get into the cab. He also watched the guy leave the shop. Saw him go the opposite way, but something told him things weren't right. Seconds later he saw the guy ride past him on a Vespa. Not the fastest thing on the block, but there's no way a taxi can dodge a scooter. They're perfect for following through the streets.

And he was in a bloody car, only one thing for it, forget tailing the scooter, go straight to her apartment and pray they don't make a move before then.

Chambers hit the speed dial on his phone. A voice came on asking, "Number to call?" He spoke one word and the phone dialled the number.

"How are we with tracking these arseholes?" Joey almost shouted as they entered Smithy's lair.

"Nice to see you too!" Smithy shot back, "Got sweet nothing from Mildred, they reckon the car went into some carpark and the clowns went to ground,"

The 'lair' wasn't much, just a small room, a table, a couple of chairs, a couch for sleeping on and a laptop with a power lead. Sandy headed straight for the laptop. "Want me to run the facials?" she asked Smithy.

"Yer can," he replied, "If you want to, I already did Interpol. Not much there. Got a name, though. Pietr Igor Gromatski." He went on, "Russian Mob turns out, not much on him though, just a couple of bloody arrest warrants out in Kyiv, of all places. Evidently the Ukrainians would love a friendly chat with him for some bodies they found floating in the Dnieper river a couple of years ago. And I bet they won't be too gentle either!"

"That might be summat we can use" Joey's northern accent came out, as it did when he was getting frustrated. He was starting to, "If we ever catch up with him, that is"

Sandy stepped forward and sat down. The laptop was open and running, "Photos are where?" she asked.

"Here" Smithy leaned over and clicked the mouse. The screen changed and the photos on the hard drive came up. She selected the one she wanted and minimized the screen. Next, she took out a flash drive and plugged it in. The screen changed. Fifteen seconds later, they saw the screen change as the insignia of Her Majesty's government came up. The lion on the left and the unicorn on the right, holding up the shield with the four emblems of the United Kingdom, came up. "We're in." She said as the screen changed. "Might take me some time to get the information through"

Just at that moment, their phones pinged a message. It simply read, "Code blue, London. Tower Bridge, ASAP"

"Shit," Smithy looked at Joey, "we're supposed to wait for Jacko and Mac. What ya reckon?"

"Code blue's a code for a kidnapping," Sandy replied. "Who?" they sent the reply.

"Don't piss me around" the reply came back, "How soon can you get here?". They recognised the number. It was Chamber's number. Did that mean?

"Sir Michael safe," the next message came back easing their fears, "will explain when you arrive. Assistance required urgent. How soon?"

Confused was an understatement. Then a message came from another number. It was Jacko, it simply said: "Haul ass, GO!!"

"How far is London?" Joey asked as they were in Reading, a large town outside the M25 motorway ring road, about two junctions along the M4 motorway heading towards Wales and the West Country. "About an hour," Sandy was the one that replied. "At this time of night, you can do it in forty-five minutes, maybe less, get moving, you two. I'll stay here and sort through the information we've got!"

Joey and Smithy ran for the car like two kids let loose in their favourite playground as Sandy texted, "Scorpion three and four on the route, ETA 45"

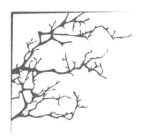

Chapter 20

BJ still felt uncomfortable. She'd taken the Uber knowing they'd be next to impossible to follow. But something just wasn't right! She wasn't sure if it was the stuff she'd been given or the fact that she just felt like she was being watched.

Investigations follow the evidence. A copper follows the evidence wherever it leads, but sometimes there's none, and the cops have a choice. Either wait and see what 'breaks' or take a chance and see if they can force their enemy's hand, knowing when to do that took what every copper called 'going with their gut', but something just wasn't right. Ask her and she wouldn't be able to tell you anything, 'just doesn't feel right'.

She checked the street. Nothing out of the ordinary. Everything seemed quiet, almost too quiet. Just a scooter in the street. She opened the car door and headed for the front door of her apartment building, what Brits affectionately call 'flats'

The lights were out in the passageway. Nothing new, or major really, as they were out when she went to work that morning. *Wish he'd get a damn move on and fix the bloody things* she thought, about the local caretaker' it's only a sodding fluorescent light after all!

Reaching for her keys, she let herself in. She stepped through the door relieved to be home, but something wasn't right. The wrong light was on. Before she could back away, a hand reached out and yanked her inside.

"Come here bitch," a harsh voice rasped as she hit the wall. Another shove sent her flying into the lounge. 'Gang?' Her brain tried to guess what was going on. She still had hold of her bag.

Swinging it she caught one of them square in the face. He didn't even flinch. "got some fight, have we bitch?" the voice had a cockney accent, "gonna be fun this".

She landed on the coffee table; it was teak, a hardwood. Hitting bone on a hardwood usually means broken bones. The pain was almost unbearable, but she wasn't going down without a fight, another swing, but the assailants easily dodged even in the confined space.

She had a pepper spray canister on her belt, on her left-hand side. She went for it. The pepper spray would blind them if she could just get to it. She was quick, but the assailant was quicker. As soon as she reached it, he reached for her arm.

"No you don't!" He shouted as he slammed her arm down into the table. The pain was unreal, but she wasn't letting go of her only chance. She tried again. The canister bounced across the floor, frantically reaching for the face she tried clawing at the eyes. Both men were wearing some kind of mask. One of them kicked her hand hard.

"Where's the hard drive?" He shouted at her as he punched her in the mouth.

"Piss off" she screamed back, struggling to kick him between the legs. It was a feeble attempt. She was fast losing the fight, but that didn't mean she was giving up. She'd go down fighting.

Still trying to reach the canister, she reached out, but another fist caught her square in the temple, almost knocking her unconscious. But that's when her world did strange things.

Later, when the police took her statement. She described it as "the bloody door just flew open, some guy in a ski mask stepped in and beat the crap out of the first two!"

"Did you get a good look at the assailant?" It was a dumb question, but they knew it had to be asked. The cop interviewing her looked pretty sheepish asking the questions. He was a 'plain clothes copper, from the local nick as police stations in the UK are known. BJ vaguely knew the guy. She was pretty sure they'd been on the same courses a couple of times, but couldn't for the life of her remember his name.

"Which one?" She replied holding the ice pack she'd been given against one side of her face. She knew it was going to be an absolute 'shiner' of a black eye on that side. "They all wore ski masks!"

"Were they carrying weapons?"

"The first two, those that attacked me were." She screwed her face up as if trying hard to remember, "they had knuckle dusters, and I think they might have had other stuff, but they only used the dusters,"

"What about the other one?" from the question, it sounded as if he wasn't totally buying the idea that some dude in a ski mask had come to her help.

"Didn't see any," she replied truthfully. "He was so fast, then again." She paused, reached over, wincing with pain, but finally reached the glass of water that was on the small hospital table that fitted on the bed. She took a sip before continuing, "I was pretty out of it by then, you know Frank" she wasn't sure what his damned name was, but at least trying to remember might change things a bit.

"Actually, it's Peter," the cop began, sounding almost apologetic. He'd really fancied her on the course, and it kind of deflated the ego to think she'd forgotten him. "It's just that there are a few things that don't make much sense. We didn't find any evidence of anyone else in the flat!"

"You think I clocked 'em one?" She chuckled. It sounded ridiculous. The words were hard to piece together, and she wasn't shouting, but the whole idea sounded too much. "How the hell am I going to do that with what? A broken wrist, dislocated shoulder, and God knows what else?"

"We found three of 'em in your flat," the copper replied, cutting her off. "And you were the only other one there. We figured maybe you used the coffee table or something," He shrugged, he clearly had no answers, "do you have any idea what they were after?"

"No" she lied. She'd known something was amiss as soon as she got to the flats. The hard drive was hidden. There was no sodding way they were getting their hands on it, not even the cops. Not until she'd seen what was on the damn thing.

Joey and Smithy had tossed a coin to decide who went in. Smithy had won, "You deal with the prick on lookout." He nudged Joey as he got out of their car. They were a couple of streets away, but knew exactly what was going down. Sandy had activated Billie's phone remotely. They heard the sound of the beating she was getting, and the protector in them wanted to jump in and kill the swine slowly. They needed some things to happen for the plan to work, granted the cop getting beaten hadn't been part of that plan, but they needed to cut all lines of communication before taking them out, and that meant Joey was 'up first'.

The scooter was a 'nifty fifty' on the street under a streetlight. Its rider thought he was safe. The street wasn't busy, but only an idiot would try to approach when he had three hundred and sixty degrees of vision. But he didn't count on the shadows, and Joey knew all about them.

It took Joey about two minutes along the street using shadows. He was about ten feet behind the guy when he saw the phone he'd been using. He was texting. The rider did not know what was coming next.

Crash helmets are great for protecting you against accidents on a bike, but they're useless when the assailant is coming for you from behind, and even worse than that, they give your attacker a dangerous advantage; they hinder your sight and hearing.

There was an empty beer bottle in the gutter. It was perfect. The visor on the helmet was up. Slowly, Joey reached down and took hold of the bottle. He was in the crouch nine feet away. Fingers wrapping around the bottle, he sprung forward launching himself at the lookout. Swinging the bottle for the back of the neck as the other hand reached out for the base of the helmet and ripped it up over the guy's head, the bottle came crashing down on the collarbone, splintering it in one fell swoop.

The guy went down fast, dropping the phone and screaming in agony. One fist to the mouth soon shut him up. It also removed a couple of teeth. "Wanna live?" Joey hissed, "Then shut the hell up and I'll think about it!" Taking something out of his pocket, he simply spoke into the device, "One down, the rest are all yours, buddy"

As soon as he'd spoken into the device, Joey turned to the guy on the ground. He wasn't struggling and looked terrified. "Who paid you?"

"What are you on about, bro?" The guy replied, trying to pretend like he was innocent, "I'm just dealin' a little, you know, the good stuff!"

"Cut the crap," Joey punched him hard in the mouth. Blood was oozing out. "We both know what you're doing, so who sodding well paid you?"

"Dunno what,"

Thwack, Joey hit him again. This time, the nose gave way. "I can do this all night," Joey said. "Can you take it? And by the way, don't count on your friends coming to help. They're in even worse shit than you are. My buddy's a hell of a sight meaner than I am." he let that sink in. "Now, who paid you?"

"Dunno, no, stop." The guy tried to hold up his good arm. "I'm serious, I don't. I got a text to be a lookout, no reason was given, just be here!"

"And you thought it would be a picnic" Joey got ready to hit the guy again, more out of disgust this time.

"I don't ask questions," the guy offered hastily, "you ask them and you die with these people."

"Well, take my word for it," Joey hissed back. "You ever do something like this again, and you can book your place in the cemetery. GET MY MEANING!" He threw the guy onto his stomach and began one of the roughest searches he could manage. The guy did his best not to scream, but from the broken collarbone, a busted nose and crushed nuts. He was in agony.

Finally, after the search, Joey flipped him back onto his back. He'd found the mobile, and few other things he'd expected to find. Namely, how they'd been able to find BJ's flat, along with a weapon he'd not had time to get to it. It was a BB pistol. "Listen, shithead," he began again. "You and your mates just tried to kill a copper. They have eyes and ears all over the hospitals here. How do you think you'll fare when we let them know they're treating one who tried to kill their own? Go near a hospital and you're a marked man. Go near a doctor and we'll know about it. You're a marked man. Try to call your bosses, and we have every number you've ever called. We'll hunt you down. Your only hope is to get out of London, and never ever come back. AM I MAKING MYSELF CLEAR? Now piss off." Then he had second thoughts of letting the prick go and king-hit him straight in the face knocking him out like a light. He crumpled to the ground. Joey had a plan. He'd debated with Smithy whether they let the guy go, so he could spread the fear of who was coming for them, or, well, let's just say, Smithy lost the argument. He had a set of zip ties in his pocket. He thought about using them as well, but stuck with the plan.

The guy began coming round. As soon as he was semi-conscious, he got up and made for the scooter. "Not so fast" Joey waited until he was about to put the scooter into gear before yanking him off it. He landed in a heap at Joey's feet, "that stays with us, Now piss off." He'd already ripped the crash helmet off, next he king-hit the guy straight in the face knocking him out like a light. Next, he pulled the zip cords he was carrying out of his pockets. They were gardening ones, one for the arms, the other for the legs. Fifteen seconds later, he was trussed up and Joey waited for Smithy's 'all clear'. He'd never intended that the guy would go free, but wanted to put the fear of the Good Lord into the creep at the same time as playing a psychological game with him. That way, when the cops asked him, he'd be more than ready to talk, and do so freely.

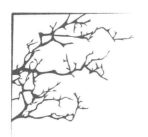

Chapter 21

"Just what the hell were you two doing?" Sandy didn't sound impressed. "I couldn't get hold of you." She went on, "I turn the radio on," she pointed to the police scanner she'd been using to track what the cops were up to, "and get this crap about masked vigilantes beating the crap out of two guys doing a copper over. Know anything about it?" She asked pointedly. It had Joey's 'trademark' all over it.

"Three," Smithy replied.

"What?" Jacko was also in the room. He was enjoying seeing her 'chew them out'

"Three," Smithy said again, "there were three of them, one lookout, and two bozos in the flat. Joey did the lookout. I had fun with the others!" He almost looked like a kid caught with his hand in the cookie jar. He'd enjoyed it so much.

"Leave me out of it!" Joey held up his hands. He'd crossed Sandy before, "apparently the word came from the top."

"Why?" Jacko asked. The place they were in was a small one-bedroom flat, a small kitchen at the back leading out to the main lounge. The bedroom was on the right, as the kitchen was on the left. Sandy had everything set up in the bedroom. The front room or lounge was where Mac positioned himself. To all who looked in, it was just someone watching sky sports. The nine millimetres were concealed, but within easy reach.

"Why what?" Sandy asked.

"Didn't MI6 want this thing kept 'under wraps', you know, secret?" He made an inverted comma sign. "She was investigating the body in the river, the one he thought we put there," he reminded her. "So why protect her?"

"Six wanted it under wraps, as you put it, but not Sir Mike!" Sandy replied. She stopped and looked at each of them, looks of confusion on their faces. "Six has a mole, remember, standard procedure for them is to keep things under wraps, anything else and the mole would know we're onto them."

"Yeah, that makes sense," the confusion in the voices said the opposite. Joey voiced it though, "but why leak the information."

"What got leaked?" Sandy asked.

"No idea," Joey replied, "but whatever it was, caused some serious injury to the copper!"

"Yet we don't know what it was, and it's got someone spooked!" Mac finished the thought off, "bloody Bugger did it to put pressure on the mole, force a mistake maybe?"

"And we got the fruits," Sandy looked at Joey and Smithy, "did you get 'em?"

"No," Joey replied to her obvious disappointment, "but we cloned them instead," there was an audible sigh of relief as he went on, "if we took the phones they'd know something was up, so we took these and cloned the hard drives, two replicas, we can listen to any call they get. We've got the details of every message sent or received, and with a little magic." He handed the two cloned phones over. "We can get every location they've ever been in."

"Then let's get to work," Jacko took over. "Sandy, how long before you'll have intel we can work with?"

"We've already got some stuff from Smithy's photos." She replied, "you're gonna love this" the sarcasm coming through strongly, "recognise this one?" She threw the first photo, a slightly fuzzy image, but there was no mistaking the features, a long scar down the right side of the face, running from the temple to the mouth. "Or what about this guy?" the second picture, someone more stocky, yet not an ounce of fat, short black hair.

"The first rings a bell" Jacko picked the first photo up, brow furrowed. "is that?" he began.

"Patrick O'Flanagan," Sandy finished, "one time IRA trigger man, and just about everything else." She turned towards the laptop. "Finished a ten-year stretch in France two years ago, for drugs and extortion, and a few kneecaps removed from people."

"A nice guy then," Joey chipped in.

"Keep him off your guest lists, that's for sure," Mac piped up. "Then again, maybe we need to send him a calling card?" He was hitting his left fist into the palm of the right hand.

"But first," Sandy spoke again, "we've got a bit of a doozy for you. This you're gonna love" she placed the next photo down so that they could all see it, obviously enjoying the suspense she went on. "O'Flanagan will be next to impossible to find, at least with our resources and time." She handed a piece of paper to each of them. It was a fact sheet for the other guy. "This boy took the trouble to let us know where his boss works, not just that, you won't have to kill the swine, just hand him over to the Ukrainians, they'll do with a smile in their faces" she was actually smiling, it wasn't often you got carte blanche to send a scumbag down a deep and very dark hole.

"This 'Pietr' Gromatski clown,' Joey said. "It says he's also known as 'Igor', he looks like a real nasty piece of work, what is this?" He was looking at the Interpol 'rap sheet' with the photo, "suspected of three gang-related killings in Kyiv, one where an innocent kid was gunned down." He threw the sheet of paper back down onto the table, raising his head. He looked Jacko right in the eye as if asking the boss what he thought.

"You're right," Jacko spoke softly, every syllable deliberately chosen to drive home the emphasis, "killing this piece of crap would be too quick. A few years in a Ukrainian gulag first would be more fitting." He stopped for the slightest moment, then went on, "and the Ukrainians just love sticking it to their old masters, the Russians!"

There are some places where prison is a really harsh punishment. Then there are places where it's a fate worse than death. Ukraine, while not the worst, is enough to strike terror into the heart of the hardest criminal, and Gromatski would have reason to fear. In their eyes, he was a child killer. The worst punishment was reserved for them.

One by one, they replaced the photos. Sandy gathered them up. She would shred and incinerate them later, but for now, she had a briefing to run.

"Gromatski works for Alexei Serkhov, the 'businessman' in the East end" she passed a piece of paper round. Nothing in this briefing was going via electronic channels. There was no way of knowing how much was being passed to the other side, especially when they couldn't be sure exactly how much information the mole had access to.

"I take it you've got an address then?" Jacko was all business.

"On the paper, I just gave you," Sandy replied, "along with the details about his boss, might be good to pay the boss a visit too. I can't see him letting his employees go freelance." She turned to Jacko, "so how do you want to run this?"

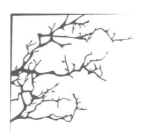

Chapter 22

"Am I a prisoner or what?" Paul still didn't know what to make of the situation. One minute he'd been playing a computer game. The next he was being shot at, bundled into a car like a sack of spuds and sent careering across the country. At least he thought it was across the country. The driving had been fast and furious and he'd spent the time sweltering under a huge heavy blanket. That the 'blanket' had kevlar plates in it had escaped him. It was one of the things that had kept him alive.

"No, you're not" Sam replied. He began to say something, but she cut him off. Holding up one hand, she went on, "you're under our protection".

He looked uncomfortable, unsure what to say. "Still feels like a prison to me," he mumbled. "Can't go anywhere. Where are we, by the way?"

"Couple of hours from your house." Sam replied she had 'this shift' looking after 'the pax' as Mac had called Paul when they handed him over. Impersonal but practical.

"I gathered that!" He shot back, slightly frustrated, "but where the hell is that?"

"Well, you're still in England." She sounded almost apologetic, "that's all I can tell you, the less you know about your location, the safer you'll be."

"I don't even know what I've done. I mean one minute I'm minding my own business." He was mumbling, half talking to whoever would listen, but half talking to himself, expecting no sympathy from anyone, "next minute I'm"

"Bundled into a car," Sam cut in, "after being shot at by some pretty serious firepower," she went on, "let us not forget someone wanting to kill you." She'd been making coffee. One mug went down with a little more force that she originally intended in front of him. The 'nursemaid routine was beginning to grate on all of them, especially Sam.

The two of them were sitting around what looked like a kitchen table. The place looked old. Not the 'tired' or worn down old, more like a house from previous centuries, yet kept as if to preserve the history, but there was a distinctly utilitarian feeling about the place.

The walls didn't have the smooth plaster of the modern house, just whitewash over the stone. It reminded Paul of the prison movies from the 1930s.

"Place even looks like a prison!" He grunted as he reached for the mug. He slowly lifted it and took a sip. At least the coffee was okay. "How old is this place, anyway?"

"Dunno really," Sam replied, "but I was told at least a couple of hundred years old, kinda impressive, don't you think?"

" Depends on if you're impressed with prisons," Paul shot back. "looks strong enough to be one!"

"Fortress would be a better word," a voice from the left spoke up. They both turned. Hene had just walked through the door. "Think about it," he went on, "thick walls, no musket ball would get through them. Hell, most modern weapons wouldn't penetrate them!" He pointed to the walls. "Small windows, heavy wooden shutters, probably oak." He showed a place on the wall where evidence of stonework could still be seen if you looked hard enough.

"What ARE you saying?" Paul asked. "so far I've been,"

"Yeah, I know," Hene cut him off, "spare us the speech." He sat down at the table, "the fact is when you took down that ransomware, you pissed off some pretty seriously bad people,"

"I've heard all that," Paul cut back in, "but all I did was stop the thing! It's not like it was going to make 'em lots of money. The damn thing was simple."

"It was meant to be," Sam replied, "but not for you. They wanted someone else to do it!"

"But that makes no sense" Paul pushed his chair back, frustration coming through. "Why?"

"Do you have any idea who they were?"

"Men with guns?" He shrugged.

"Try the Russian Mafia" Hene went to pour himself an instant coffee. There was no water in the jug. He got up and sauntered across the kitchen. "Oh and the Triads, ever heard of them? Yeah, and the Yakuza"

"Who the hell are they?" Paul did not know who they were talking about.

"Japanese Mafia," Sam added, "Kinda like the criminal Samurai, only worse, and they don't usually take prisoners. You're lucky they let the Russians do the job!"

"Shit" was all he could say.

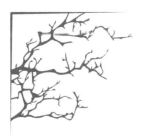

Chapter 23

"Thanks for picking me up Jimmie, I owe you one." Billie struggled to stand. She wasn't entirely sure discharging herself was her brightest idea. The doc had made it plain. Even though she didn't think it was a good one, *'but doctors are like that'*, she thought.

"Don't talk soft, boss." Jimmie reached out to help her. She brushed him off. If she was going to do this, she had to do it herself. "You'd do the same for us."

"Nah" she replied. "I'd tell you not to be such a bloody idiot!" She turned to him, "but don't you even think about saying it!" her face looked stern, but there was a mischievous twinkle in her eye.

Jimmy might be the youngest on her squad and the keenest. But he was reliable and could keep his mouth shut when he needed to. Right now, she didn't know who to trust, but Jimmie had been trustworthy in the past.

"We've got some digs arranged for you. Wanna go there first?"

"Maybe second, take me to my place first," she replied, "there are a few things,"

"Are you sure about that?" he said. "it's pretty rough,"

"I can handle it" she wasn't offended that he'd asked that she would ask the same thing if it was anyone else, actually she'd probably be forbidding them from even going near. Using the excuse of 'not wanting to tamper with the crime scene' even though everyone knew that the Crime Scene forensics unit had finished with the scene. "Besides, what I need isn't actually in the flat!"

They got to the car and made their way back towards the flat. Traffic was pretty light for a major city, thanks to the extension of the traffic monitoring system that London uses. A very simple and effective way to cut down on traffic within a certain area.

Back in the late 1990s, London was grinding to a halt with the sheer volume of traffic on its streets. Around the centre of the city, a journey of just a mile could take up to two hours. So the local authority came up with a very simple system.

Every vehicle within that area would have a 'tag' that they could purchase, which would allow them to drive within the area. Every vehicle needing to drive within that area could also purchase them. They would be displayed on the front left-hand side of the windscreen. You could purchase a tag for a day (24 hours) a week, a month or a year.

The system was monitored by CCTV cameras set up in a 'ring' around the perimeter. Each camera was linked to a computer that would ensure that every vehicle in the area would be photographed both entering and leaving the area. If you were a permanent resident in the area, you could pay by direct debit from your bank. In that case, you'd only pay for what you'd already used (on a monthly basis) and would only get the bill for the hours you spent within the area.

The real 'kicker' or punishment was any vehicle caught within the area without the 'tag' would be identified by the computer, which would then interrogate the Driver Licencing Centre (D.V.L.C) where all the vehicle records were kept. And the owner of the vehicle would be sent the bill for an entire year. Some thousand pounds (the fee for a day's use was about three pounds) and anyone who didn't pay within the month got their vehicle impounded and crushed. It paid to either pay up or stay away.

Portobello Road, where Billie's 'flat' had been, was well within the boundaries. It was also ideally located for working in central London. Just north of the world-famous tourist mecca of Hyde Park. It was in an area known as Notting Hill. A working-class enclave within what had become middle-class inner London. A vibrant and colourful community from just about every nation on earth. It wasn't uncommon to go about your day speaking Swahili with the Africans, Hindi, Punjabi, Tamil or Gujarati with the Indians, or any one of the hundreds of languages from the subcontinent. Not to mention Arabic, Farsi or even Aramaic, to name a few of the languages, sometimes using two or three of the languages mixed with English in the same sentence. Billie loved it, it made her feel at home, 'Just like Moss Side' she thought.

"I need to pick something up from the old place first," Bille spoke up as she gently eased herself into the car, "then I need to go get a cheap laptop, then you can take me wherever the new place is."

"Guv" (a slang expression cops in London use for their boss, any senior ranking officer in an investigation is 'the Guv' short for Governor) Jimmy began. "We took everything we could from the flat," he tried to reassure her, thinking she wanted to confront the demon of fear. "It's all at the new"

"It wasn't at the flat," she cut him off. "I knew something was off, so I hid it before I got there. It's what those bastards were looking for,"

"Scuse me?" He formed a question.

"When I got dropped off, the lights were out in the entry, broken." She began, "Five years I've lived here, and they've never once been broken at night. The folks in the flats value their safety too much to leave them that way. Someone had just busted them. I knew something was coming down, so I hid what I'd just picked up."

"Then why the hell didn't you call and?"

"And sound like a little girl crying because of the dark?" She shot back, Jimmy was taken aback, "not to you maybe," she went on, "but to the likes of that prick Townsend, that's exactly what it would sound like, and get me busted out of the position for wasting police resources. I didn't have any proof, just a gut feeling." Her face was a picture of determination. "Nah, I would not give him the pleasure. Now take me there so I can get it."

"But what's so important about this, whatever it is?"

"That," she replied, "we'll only know when I get it, and a cheap laptop, one that doesn't have an internet connection built-in, so I can open the file without them being able to stop me,"

"So it's a computer file then?"

"Dunno. I was just told to make sure it didn't have an internet connection when I opened the file," she shrugged.

"Guv" they'd stopped at the car park barrier arms, they were rising, but he took the opportunity to give her an enquiring look, "how can you not know?"

"Bloody easy," she replied sarcastically, "someone with enough clout to find my number, not the one you guys have, but my personal phone. Hell, only my mum and sister have that number! It's not even in the phone book, but they got it and wanted me to have some pretty serious information about our body in the river." She shifted in the seat as Jimmy sped up away. She was still nervous, trying to see if they were followed. "somebody else doesn't want that information getting out," she stopped for a moment.

"And?" Jimmy asked.

"And they're prepared to kill to stop it getting out!" She stopped for a moment, then went on, "But someone else wants us to have that information, and I want to know why!"

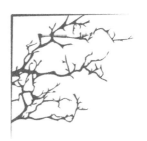

Chapter 24

"Serkov doesn't go anywhere without at least one bodyguard," Sandy was conducting the briefing. They were still outside London, holed up in the *safe house*. Preparing for the next part of the operation. They'd found a 'tentacle' of the organisation. Now it was time to cut the thing off, and see who squeals. "Gromatski is one of his lieutenants, usually gets the job of 'disciplining' the others" she made the inverted comma sign, making it clear she was quoting someone, "kinda valuable to him, but he's not usually the bodyguard"

"If he's a valuable asset," Smithy asked, "Then why take such a big risk?"

"Yeah," Mac added, "they had to know it would be picked up by cameras?"

"Unless they already knew they had the cameras covered," Jacko replied, "our mole would have done that!"

Notting Hill is northwest of the famous Hyde Park, it's a multicultural area with a large Jamaican and Caribbean community, but there are also Indians, Africans and dozens of other nationalities living in that area and it's all working class, just Paddington that sits just to the east of it. The North and South of the park are just like the famous horror novel "Dr Jekyll and Mr Hyde", with the North being whichever you think the working classes should be.

If Dr Jekyll's opposite was a 'Mr Hyde,' then the opposite of Notting Hill and Paddington would be Knightsbridge and Chelsea.

Knightsbridge looks just as multicultural until you look beneath the veneer. That is the Middle Eastern oil money being spent in places like Harrods. Chelsea is just rich. Even the smallest place fetched five or six million pounds sterling, and that's the starting prices. They're like two different planets, yet only a couple of miles apart.

"Will ya look at the bloody money around here" Joey was constantly flabbergasted at the incredible wealth in some places. The wealth and poverty that seemed to exist 'side by side', It didn't help that almost every car in the street they were in was either a high-end Rolls Royce, Ferrari or a Bentley, "Makes yer wanna weep"

"Welcome to the financial capital of the world," Sandy replied almost wistfully. She loved London, but the sheer opulence at times was too much. Especially in Knightsbridge, where most of the wealth wasn't even English, it was Arab oil money. Very few English people could afford to live here.

"Gromatski is in there at the moment," Jacko pointed to the front door of the enormous department store that was Harrods. "He's looking after one of Serkhov's mistresses. She's in there buying whatever she wants"

"Sugar daddy?" Jacko asked.

"He's nearly sixty, she's nineteen," Sandy replied.

"Talk about cradle snatching," Joey replied.

"Only one he smuggled here that it turned out well for," Sandy came back, "but even she's on a very short leash, gilded prison, if you know what I mean?" it came out more like a question. "And besides, as soon as he tires of her, guess where she'll be going. It won't be pleasant!"

"Hence Gromatski," Joey replied as they saw the man leaving. He was looking around, as if trying to spot any unwelcome visitors, like journalists, or cops, no one was looking at a black taxi cab with two tourists arguing over a fare, Jacko was decked out as the driver, Joey and Sandy as the tourists, Mac and Smithy were close by, they would be needed for the next part, "I take it, no one ever found any evidence then?"

"Always a whiff," Sandy replied. "Never any proof. Too many friends in the right place to make sure no one asked questions,"

"And here we are," Jacko came back into the discussion, "One of his men driving the vehicle that takes potshots at one being guarded by MI6! Makes you wonder,"

"No one ever said criminals were the smart boss," Joey chipped in cheekily, "But it must be hellishly important to them, whatever they were hoping for,"

"About a billion reasons and I'm talking pounds sterling, not US dollars," Sandy replied. They both turned and stared at her, their jaws on the floor. "What?" She went on, "where did you think the new toys you got to play within Iran came from? You don't honestly think Her Majesty's government would put up the money for the Op, did you?"

"Sandy," Joey said slowly, "we knew that it's just that amount, it's bloody huge."

"And it put a serious hole in the drug trade worldwide," Sandy replied. "We were getting nowhere with the old methods. So we turned things around. We knew we could get some of the money, but rather than just locking it up in bank accounts, and getting them to freeze the accounts, you freeze an account, all you do is to reward the Bankers for being corrupt. Take the money and everyone is at each other's throats. No one trusts the others. That's what we did,"

"And what did they hope to achieve?"

"Simple, really," Sandy replied. "They've got someone on the inside. Once the ransomware got as far as MI6, with Farid out of the way, their person on the inside could send the deactivation code, but with a difference. It would have MI6's Banks listed, and they'd be able to clean us out. Not just of the money we took, but everything, secrets as well, and that means every agent in the field, the motherlode!"

"Here they come," Jacko cut across the conversation. He reached for his phone, tapped in a few letters and numbers, then pressed send.

Joey and Sandy both broke off and walked hand in hand towards the entrance. To the rest of the world, they looked like lovers who only had eyes for each other. That was only partly true. Both of them were scanning their 'peripherals' making sure everything went to plan.

"They're not bothering to watch," Joey whispered to Sandy as they got level, "get ready"

Sandy tripped 'right on cue' flailing slightly as she went down. Joey reached out and caught her just as she 'fell' against the big 'bear' of a guy escorting a young blonde towards the Mercedes. What people didn't see was Sandy slip a small metal device inside the wheel well at the back. "trackers in place," she whispered into the small lapel mike.

On the other end, about two hundred yards down Brompton Road, the main road through Knightsbridge, Smithy and Mac were waiting, Mac's phone went off, the message came up. "It's a white Mercedes 280 SLK rego"

"There she is," Smithy started the car. A Nissan Pulsar, he pulled into the traffic three cars behind. He'd been following the GPS screen.

Anywhere else in London a white Mercedes convertible would stand out like boils on a baby's bottom, but in Knightsbridge it was the Pulsar that stuck out. No one is poor enough to want to own one!

"We just turned left" Mac spoke, they were using earpieces, everyone was on the same frequency, "Old Brompton road"

"Roger that," Sandy replied. "Her place is near Earl's court. We're heading there now. Should be about ten minutes."

"I'm south of there," Jacko cut in, "got a visual, any minute now he's gonna try to lose any tail."

Gromatski would be careful. It was almost second nature to him in some ways. A lifetime of crime kind of built the skills he had. They were good, but not good enough. He was looking around, using the car's mirrors. That made little difference, though. He was still cautious. The light ahead had been on green for a while. He got ready for the light change.

The light changed to amber. He floored the accelerator. The car sprang forward like a thoroughbred racehorse unleashed and gave her full 'head' to sprint to the finishing line. The Mercedes shot forward, tyres squealing. As soon as she was halfway through the junction, he yanked the wheel hard right narrowly squeezing between two oncoming cars, both of whom 'stood' on their horns, not that he was worried, he shot down the street, tyres squealing and speeding up away, at the next junction they went right, again without indicating, this time narrowly missing a cyclist.

"Ya bloody maniac" the cyclist screamed as he fell off his bike, "I've got yer sodding number on camera, ya moron" he was cursing, and Jacko was watching it all from a safe distance.

"Gromatski just came round the corner" Jacko spoke into the Bluetooth device he was using, "Just as we thought, he's on Bolton Gardens, just missed a car at the intersection of the A3218." The fact was, his training was such that he was actually predictable, and that's what they'd done. The tracker had helped, but they knew every journey he made. At the third junction, he always made the same move.

"Roger that," Joey replied, "we're ready to roll, everything in place."

About three hundred yards down on the left was a four-story building that looked like a house from the Regency period, early nineteenth century. The distinct red brick build on top of the first storey of granite with carvings that looked as if they came from the Roman period, the window frames all painted white, giving off a stark contrast to the red brick.

The car pulled up outside the red-brick building. Double yellow lines showing 'no parking' were totally ignored, not that there were any parking wardens around. The building had secure car parks, but he was taking the car somewhere after if Sasha needed transport she'd call him.

He jumped out and moved around to open Sasha's door. She may be a teenager, but she was the boss's mistress. Piss her off and Alexei was likely to hear about it. That wouldn't be pleasant.

"Where's my purse?" Sasha was mumbling and fumbling as Gromatski moved round to open her door. She found it and climbed out as the door opened, "Ouch, YOU BIG, what the hell?" she knocked her head, her foot was stuck, trapped in the half-opened door with an unconscious Russian bear-like man falling against it.

"I think he's had a heart attack," someone shouted from the other side of the door. They were trying to pull the big guy away. She got her foot free, got into the car, and locked the door. "Did you hear me?" the guy shouted, "Call a bloody ambulance!"

"But I have no phone" Sasha replied through the closed door, her strong accent giving her away, "Not here in the car"

"Then bloody haul ass and go get your phone," another one, this time a female, shouted. She'd seen what was going on and came to help. "Look, I know first aid, and can help here, but you need to go get a sodding ambulance! RUN!"

She wasn't sure why she obeyed the voice; it sounded more like a school headmistress than anything else, a voice that in her native Russia must be obeyed at all times. She was out of the car and off at a sprint up the steps to her apartment.

It took Sasha fifteen seconds to reach the apartment, twenty seconds to unlock the door, and dive into the apartment. She heard a car start, but nothing much out of the ordinary.

"Emergency services, state the service you require," the voice demanded. She wasn't totally sure. She'd only been in England six months.

"My friend, he has a heart attack," she began, "he is dying,"

"Where are you, madam?"

"Earls Court, Bolton Gard,"

"Bolton Gardens Madam," the voice was male and speaking gently, "is your friend breathing?"

"I not know, I ran inside, make a phone call," she moved back outside, the phone was cordless, "I check for you,"

"Thank you, meanwhile an ambulance is on its way,"

"No," she cried, "NOOO" outside there was no Pietr, no car and no people helping a man who'd had some kind of attack and been rendered unconscious.

Chapter 25

"You sit tight," Billie said as she opened the car door. "I'll only be here for a couple of minutes." She was obviously still stiff and struggling from the beating. Even Jimmy could see that, but she was too proud, or stubborn, (pick your own words for it,) to ask for help. She struggled out of the car, left hand on the top of the door, right gripping the doorframe. She stood after a few seconds. Billie had been given a crutch to walk with, but was refusing to even contemplate using the thing. Jimmy had a pretty robust umbrella in the car. He was from the North, just like her, where it rained at least once a day, even on the hot summer days. You never left home without either a raincoat or a 'brolly'. He offered her the umbrella. She took it grudgingly.

"Boss," Jimmy said as she got out of the car, "you know we took everything from the flat, don't you?"

"And I told you, what I'm looking for isn't in the flat," she replied leaning back in. She closed the door before he could say any more and headed for the entry.

The flats were in the shape of a rectangle, sixteen apartments side by side, all emptying into a central walkway. Lifts at either end went up the four floors to the other dwellings, sixty-four dwellings.

"Good," Billie whispered to herself, "nothing's been touched." She could see from the large pot plants there that nothing had been disturbed. She made her way towards one of the enormous pots. It had a medium-sized bush that needed serious watering in it.

At the base, just visible through the nearly dead leaves and thorns, was a bit of earth that looked as if it had been disturbed. She didn't go for that patch. At about ninety degrees, there was a flat patch with a few leaves covering the area. She began digging with her fingers.

Halfway through uncovering whatever it was, she stopped. Trying not to make it look obvious she looked around, no one seemed to be there, she whipped the device out with one hand while still making look as if she was digging, slipping it into her pocket she stood up and headed back to the car without a second look.

"Took yer time boss," Jimmy said as she gently lowered herself into the car, "I was beginning to get a bit worried"

"Nah, only been gone a couple of minutes," Billie replied, "anyway, let's get the hell of Dodge." She slipped the seatbelt on, "did you get me a laptop?"

"Yeah, it's at your new place, a separate modem too," Jimmy replied, "though the sales assistant thought it strange. Normal people want internal modems and Wi-Fi you know!"

"Who said I was normal?" BJ smiled, "besides, all normal is," she went on almost laughing, it was a nervous laugh, "is what the majority do, doesn't mean it is the 'sane' thing to do."

"Speaking of 'sane' and insane," Jimmy butted in, "you're aware what DCI Townsend has done?"

"That jerk," she spat out, "gave us a nearly impossible case, then just to make sure he damn well stitched us up, yeah, I'm aware he's been dismantling the bloody team before we did much!"

"We're the only two left," Jimmy added. " apparently someone with real clout wants this investigation to go away,"

"Not surprised," BJ replied, "someone doesn't want us finding things out," she held up the package, "and whatever this tells us, they were prepared to kill to stop us finding out, and even kill a copper!"

There's a code the Police live by. It's unwritten, but the criminal who knows it tries very hard to never break the code. It's known as 'appropriate response'

It works like this: commit a crime and they'll send whatever's appropriate. Burglary and you'll get a couple of 'uniforms' taking statements and fingerprints. A bit of violence would get the local C.I.D (Criminal Investigation Division) involved. Murder gets an entire team, and they track you down, eventually. Kill a copper, and the whole of the Metropolitan Police comes after you, and there's nowhere to hide. They'll take London apart if they have to.

But someone had called the 'rottweilers' off!

The rest of the trip, all fifteen minutes of it, was done in silence. Jimmy wondered just how much trouble he'd be in if he kept working the case. He hated to let things go, and he knew there was no way BJ would drop it. Hell would freeze over first.

She was trying to think which side wanted the investigation quashed, and why?

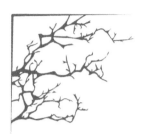

Chapter 26

"Can I help you mate" someone offered as Joey eased the big man down to the pavement.

"Need an ambulance?"

"Got one on the way, mate," Joey replied, pretending to speak into his phone. He was speaking into the device, but not to the Ambulance people. Mac was on the other end. Seconds later, Smithy pulled up in the car. Mac, who was in the passenger seat, sprang out. He began running towards Joey pretending to be slightly unfit and out of breath.

"Let me through." Mac bellowed, "I'm a doctor," which was partly true. Mac was a 'doctor'. He didn't have the fancy title or degree, but he had years as an Army combat medic, and a few years working as a junior doc at Hereford General's Accident and Emergency department. Mac crouched down and began examining Gromatski. It was all part of the charade. He knew exactly what Joey had administered, and how much he'd prepped the syringe with the Chlordiazepoxide.

Chlordiazepoxide or 'Librium' is pretty easy for Doctors to prescribe. It's a sleep serum you mix into a liquid and inject directly into a vein. In this case, they'd gone straight for the Jugular, and Gromatski had gone out like a light, similar to what they were going to blame it on.

"Sudden heart attack" Mac looked at Joey. He had a stethoscope out and was doing a check of the heart rate. Partly to make sure everything was going correctly, but mostly for show. They knew exactly how much they needed to give the guy, and not one milligram more. *'This prick isn't getting away so easily'* was the thought. *Death is not an option.* He looked at Joey, "we need to get him to a hospital, and the Ambulance will be too slow, gimme a hand, we'll take him in our car" he motioned to Smithy to come and give a hand, "how far is the nearest Emergency department?"

"That'd be the Chelsea and Westminster," one of the people looking on said, "Five minutes away, that way" he pointed down the street, the way they were intending to go, anyway.

"Right then," Mac replied, indicating for Joey and a few of the others to grab an arm or a leg and lift the big Russian into the back of the vehicle. "No time to lose. The bloody ambulance will be at least five minutes. He hasn't got that long. Come on, every second counts"

If anyone had stopped and thought about things, they'd have realised that everything they were doing was probably the wrong thing to do in the situation. But that's what the team were counting on. No one would have a clue! No one would challenge *a doctor* who seemed to know what he was doing, yes there was a chance that there'd be another health professional on hand who would challenge things. But the risk of that was so small, they ran with the plan. Besides, all they'd really challenge would be the choice of vehicle. Then Mac would get them to listen to the rapid heart rate. A precursor to a major cardiac arrest. They had everything covered, except that none of that was happening.

As soon as everyone was busy loading the big Russian into the car. Sandy scanned the area for anything they'd left behind. She already had Gromatski's phone and wallet. Enough to ID the guy and figure out his contacts. She slipped them into her bag and 'aided' them by seeming to support the body in the middle. She checked each pocket to make sure nothing was missed. Ten seconds later, Mac was in the passenger seat. "You two," he pointed at Joey and Sandy, "the docs are gonna want to talk to ye," the Scottish brogue coming through, "Get in the back with him, come on MOVE" he shouted, no one questioned.

As soon as they were in the car, Smithy took off. Tyres squealing to make it look good. They shot through the traffic lights at the end of the street as they turned red. Two cars had to do emergency stops and narrowly missed them, their horns blaring as Smithy sped down the street.

Round the next corner, he eased off the gas. No need to race. Gromatski was just asleep. There was no risk to life, at least not yet, and he wasn't likely to wake up for at least five or six hours.

"No wonder this prick could get through immigration here" Sandy had looked through some of the things she'd retrieved, she had a passport, it was Russian, and had Gromatski's photo, but a totally different name on it, "He used a false identity"

"Probably a genuine article," Smithy chipped in, "the passport that is bought and paid for on the black market. These pricks have so much money and power, that kind of stuff isn't a problem for them,"

"Problem?" Sandy half asked. "We've suspected Serkov of controlling that kind of stuff, along with some of the seedier sides of London's underworld. Never been able to prove it though!"

"And to think" Joey began. He was looking at her with his cheeky grin that she both loved and hated. Often both reactions at the same time, "all you had to do was kidnap his chief enforcer." He was lucky the big Russian was in the way' she would have silenced him in a painful way otherwise. She had to settle for giving him a filthy look instead.

The one place they were not heading for was the Hospital. The Hospital was on the A3220 and they wanted that road. But as soon as they were on it, they hung right and headed south. The Hospital was on the left, but they kept going.

"As soon as we're over the Thames, take a left," Sandy advised, "onto the A3205. It'll take us around the back of Battersea Park,"

"Better if we carry on down a bit further, and get onto the A3," Mac suggested. "That way, we can go directly to the destination."

"Where are you folks now?" A voice came over the car's speakers. It was Sir Michael. He'd followed everything over their secure comms network, but couldn't track the vehicles by GPS. If he did that, then MI6 would know what was going on, and so would the mole.

"Just coming over the Thames now," Sandy replied, "should come past your location in a few minutes." She didn't say the name of the location. There was no need.

"Negative," Sir Michael was emphatic, "stay away from here. Go further south and take the A3. We're having a few issues with the cameras there. Technically, we're 'blind' on the A3 inside the city, and will be for the next half hour,

The last thing they needed was a 'trail' from the scene where Gromatski went missing leading them to where the car actually took him. Sir Michael had just arranged a corridor where the cameras would not work, and whoever tried to find them would be at a tremendous disadvantage.

Most international cities have two, or maybe three, airports, and a port. London has five airports and literally a dozen wharves where big ships can come in. Heathrow has five terminals

and deals with forty million passengers alone. Then Gatwick deals with thirty million. Luton and Stansted. both dealing with a couple of million, but sitting in the city's heart, dealing almost only with small charter flights or the odd private plane from a very rich person who wants 'no questions asked' is Docklands airport. Right next to the financial capital of the world, the City of London.

Sitting on the tarmac was a solitary plane. No markings to reveal what airline it might belong to, it didn't; It belonged to a government, but not one that wanted it known that the plane was there. Beside it, three men stood. One they recognised straight away. It was Jacko, the other two, both of whom were military or ex-military. The short hair, bulky frame and ill-fitting suits made them stand out a mile.

"Took yer time, didn't yer?" Jacko joked with them as they climbed out of the vehicle. "How's the 'pax'?" His only concern was that Gromatski was alive. That was the deal with the Ukrainians.

"Sleeping like a wee one," Mac replied cheerfully, "I think I got the dose slightly wrong, not that it's gonna harm him any, it's not lethal, just means he'll sleep a little longer, should be out for most of your flight," he turned to the two stood with Jacko.

"We could just get 'em to kill him here!" Joey suggested. "None of us would say anything." letting him go just didn't feel right, even if it was to a very black hole.

"Nah, Killing's too good for this one," Jacko replied, "besides, this way families in the Ukraine get real closure for what was done to them, and besides, we need this creep gone. What better way than to make sure he's never found," he turned to the two men, "Right?"

The one nearest Jacko smiled, a sickening, almost glazed-eyed smile. It said volumes, "Da, and we have a special room in the 'Hotel' Litvanska in Kyiv specially prepared for him. Please, don't disappoint us!"

"Oh no," Jacko replied, "that will not happen." He motioned Mac to open the door so they could get the sleeping giant out of the car. "All we ask is if you decide he should learn to fly without a parachute, please wait until you're outside British airspace,"

"Da," the Ukrainian replied, almost laughing, "you don't want the mess, da?"

"Nah," Joey butted in, "personally I'd waste this arsehole with a smile on my face, but we've got bigger fish to fry, and if he shows up, it'll screw everything up,"

"Though cleaning the blood off the concrete will be a hell of a job," Mac added, "better to do it over the water, if you're going to do it that is!"

By now, they had Gromatski out of the car. The other Ukrainian picked the Russian up in a fireman's lift and headed up the stairs towards the door of the plane. He wasn't being gentle. The loud crack as he smacked Gromatski's head against the doorpost made everyone cringe.

"Careful," a voice from inside the plane shouted, "you'll damage the plane"

"Shut up and let's get going," the first Ukrainian shouted back as he released Jacko's hand from the handshake they'd given each other. As soon as they were on the plane, Jacko descended the steps and pulled them away.

As soon as the steps were clear, the pilot opened the throttle, the engine noise began to rise.

"Let's get outta here," Sandy headed for the vehicle, "we've got work to do."

Chapter 27

"This place is so boring." Paul was at it again. He was driving Hene crazy. "Are you sure I've got to stay here?"

"Yep" was the simple answer, and Hene was the one said it. They were around the kitchen table. Sam had gone for groceries down to the local village. She'd been gone about half an hour.

"Where are we anyway?" Paul asked for the tenth time that morning, "you can tell me, it's not like I can tell anyone!"

That part was true, the place didn't have a phone, and the only access to the internet was through their devices that 'Mildred' had supplied at the start of the mission. Even with those restrictions, both phones had 'fingerprint' identification. So Paul wouldn't be able to use them unless he hacked his way past the security procedures. Anything was possible. Later on, they were counting on him doing it, not that he knew that.

Hene had his phone on the table. He was cleaning the Glock he'd been given. Joey and the team had literally hammered it home how important keeping weapons in good working order was. Yeah, he'd learned how to clean them with the Police, but working with the team, even the couple of days he'd spent getting to know them had really 'rubbed off' on him. It also gave him the excuse to have the phone where Paul could see it without making it obvious what he was doing. Laying the bait for part of the plan.

Paul noticed the phone was a mid-range Chinese brand, Huawei, pretty good, but not 'top of the range' and it had fingerprint ID. *'That wouldn't be too hard'* he thought to himself *'If I can just get the phone for a couple of minutes, I can let people know I'm alive'* was all he could think of.

"You aren't English are you?" he asked Hene. "Where are you from?"

"True bro" Hene replied, dropping into Kiwi slang, "I'm a long way from home." He was cleaning the barrel of the 9 millimetre with a piece of linen threaded through a small rod, called a pull through. He worked it through the barrel half a dozen times before he was satisfied it was clean enough. Then he got another piece of the linen, dipped it in a little gun oil and threaded that through the slot where the first one had been. This time, he only sent the linen through once. He only wanted the barrel lightly oiled. "Too much creates smoke" he heard Joey saying in his mind, "and smoke blinds you"

"Where is home, then? And why are you in England? Are you some kind of 'Hitman'?"

Hene started laughing. He was laughing so hard he was nearly crying, "Nah bro," He replied, "Just the opposite, I'm actually a copper back in my home country, or at least I was,"

"And what's with the Tattoos?" Paul asked, pointing to the Maori art on Hene's forearms, "what are they about?"

"Full of questions aren't you," Hene replied, "The Tattoos are Maori art, and that should tell you a bit about me and where I'm from." he tried to close the subject.

"Australia?" Paul asked, genuinely not knowing what Hene was talking about.

"Aotearoa," Hene said with pride. He also knew Paul would have no idea where he was talking about, leaving him even more confused, "Land of the long white cloud".

"Where?" Paul probably looked as confused as he sounded. "Where's that?"

"A long way from here," Hene chuckled.

"How come you're over here then?"

"Truth?" Hene asked. Paul nodded. "We owe your friends big time," he replied.

"Oh?" Paul didn't realize it came out as a question. "How's that?" The whole time, he was trying not to look at the phone. He was thinking of a way he could get hold of it, bypass the fingerprint ID and just send a text to a couple of mates, *just to let them know I'm okay'* or at least that's how he reasoned with himself. Hiding the fact he was addicted to social media.

Hene finished cleaning the weapon and began reassembling it. It took him about fifteen seconds. All the time he was trying not to seem as if he'd noticed the attention that Paul had been giving the phone. The last thing they needed was to 'rattle' the man. They were 'playing him' but really needed it to seem like he was coming up with the ideas. They just had to control 'when' he got the chance to send the message.

"Everything will be monitored," Sandy had told them. "Every phone call in England is picked up by GCHQ in Cheltenham. We'll be off the grid, and 'six' will look for us. You can guarantee they'll be looking for us. So it's important he gets the access when we want to, not when he wants!"

"What's with the questions?" Hene asked, trying not to sound too intimidating, but wanting to guide the conversation away from where it had been.

"Can't help it" Paul was truthful, "I'm curious, I'm a hacker. We always want to know things. It's why we do what we do!" He smiled as he replied, it was true, but not totally the truth. He had to get his hands on the phone.

Chapter 28

"Alexei, Alexei, it's me, Sasha. Alexei, please, pick up the phone," the voice sounded hysterical, not that he cared that much, "please Alexei, if you can't pick it up, then call when you get the message, Something terrible has happened." he heard the click as she hung up.

'What's she done now, the stupid cow?' He thought to himself, 'what kind of trouble is she in?' Sasha seemed to have a habit of getting into trouble, speeding tickets, abusing shop staff. He just hoped she had done nothing stupid.

"Da" was all he said. She knew straight away who it was, and what he wanted. 'Da' is Russian for 'yes' but when barked like a command, it's more like "WHAT DO YOU WANT?" except more unpleasant.

"Alexei," she whimpered, "I'm so sorry, I didn't know what to do," she was crying.

"What is problem woman?" He didn't have the time or the patience to deal with Sasha's little problems. That's why Pietr was there. "Can't Pietr deal with it?"

"Alexei," she replied, still sniffling, "it's Pietr, he's been taken!"

"WHAT?" he'd been slouching in the huge leather office chair that had pride of place in his office. He jumped up so fast that the Oak desk went flying back six inches. The vase that had sat at the end of the desk went crashing onto the floor. His criminal brain immediately kicked into overdrive trying to work out who might do something like this. Was it the first blow in trying to take him down? And if so, then who was behind it? "What do you mean, taken?" he asked in a slightly softer voice, trying hard to both calm Sasha down and working through the issues.

"He had some kind of fit," she started saying, "right on the street outside my apartment. Luckily, there was a doctor near. He said it was a heart attack, they took him."

"Where?" he didn't bother asking if she was okay, Pietr Gromatski was one of the fittest men Alexei had ever come across, he was virtually a fanatic on fitness and health, with the one tiny exception that he liked to smoke, but there was no way he would have a heart attack, it just didn't sound right.

"Outside my apartment, like I just said," she replied.

"Not that, you idiot," he shot back. "Where did they take him?"

"Hospital,"

"Which one?" he was getting angry. He began pacing up and down his office, "Which Hospital you stupid woman" he shouted down the phone. "Did they take him in an ambulance?"

"No," she replied. "They said an ambulance would be too slow. They put him into a car and took him, one called Chelsea and Westminster Hospital, I think."

"Where are you now?" He barked as he made his way to the office door. Two rather confused and apprehensive henchmen were just outside. He signalled for them to give him a piece of paper and a pen. They did so promptly, he wrote 'trace this call' in Cyrillic. Pointing to the one on the left, he clarified that's what he wanted to happen. And he wanted it now! The guard took off. There was no need to get the number. Every call that came into the building was intercepted and monitored downstairs where Alexei's bodyguards were stationed. Within seconds, he was in the small office and kicking the operator into action. Sasha wouldn't need to tell them. They would find her within seconds, but it would go better for her if she was honest.

"I panicked," she began. "As soon as they said the Hospital, I thought the Police might arrive. I took off, I'm North of London,"

The other guard came back with a beaming smile. They'd found her location. He had the information on a piece of stationery. He passed it to Alexei.

"You're at the Services on the M1 motorway, at Watford Gap." He replied, "stay there, I'm sending people to meet up with you." He waved to the two guards, the meaning clear, "Move your arses, what are you waiting for, GO" they ran out of the building, not wanting to anger the boss.

As soon as he pressed the speed dial for another number on his phone. Two seconds later it was answered, but before the other person could say anything he barked an order, "I want you round to Chelsea and Westminster Hospital now. Find out if Pietr is in there, NOW!"

It just didn't sound right, that right outside Sasha's apartment, the man he sent to 'protect' the woman had a heart attack? Something wasn't right, but he couldn't be sure.

He felt groggy and had a thumping headache. The constant noise didn't help. It wasn't loud, but the whine was constant, and when you've got a sore head anyway, even the smallest whine is magnified a hundred times.

"He's coming round" the voice didn't sound concerned, and it spoke a language he hadn't heard for a very long time. He started to move, except he couldn't. His arms had some kind of restraint on them. He slowly opened his eyes. Man, they hurt like he'd been on the Vodka all night. The eyelids felt like sandpaper being dragged across the soft eyeballs.

He began to recognise things, he was in restraints, at least his arms were, he couldn't feel his legs yet, 'some kind of drug' he thought to himself, he didn't ask why, there were at least a hundred reasons, and most of them very unpleasant to think about, the real question was who?

The whine he worked out was engine noise, a jet engine.

He opened his eyes. At least he tried to open them. Something prevented him. He tried to take whatever it was off, except his arms couldn't move.

'Restraints' he thought, "Wass ist Dass?" He shouted as he tried ripping them off, "What, get them off!!" he screamed.

"Shut up" a voice replied in a long-disused language, one that instilled fear as a fist ploughed into his face, slowly he realized what was happening, the language, blindfold, restraints and the noise of the engine meant something that would pump fear into the heart of even the hardest criminal, it was an 'Extraordinary rendition' of the worst kind. He was being taken to a place you don't come back from, Pietr Gromatski no longer existed.

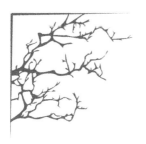

Chapter 29

"

Holy Shit!" She couldn't finish the phrase as she was too dumbstruck. "How many of us are still on this case?" Billie turned and asked Jimmy, being in hospital meant she was out of touch with where things are at.

"Townsend reassigned everyone," Jimmy replied, "except me. He wanted me to finish the paper trail, then put everything into storage, you know, the cold case," he shrugged. "Why?"

"Because I need to let you and anyone else on the team know what we've got here!" She tapped the laptop's screen, "now I know it's only us two we can go grab a coffee" she stood up and headed for the door, grabbing her coat she came back, switched the laptop off and put it in the holdall they'd bought for it.

"Okay boss," Jimmy said, "spill the beans,"

"Not here," BJ replied. "Walls have ears!"

"Eh?" Jimmy didn't know what to make of what she just said, "what you mean, boss?"

"All will be revealed, in good time that is!" She replied as she reached for her phone. Flicking through to the number pad she punched in a number, two seconds later it was ringing, five rings and a female voice answered, "Jo, Jimmy and I are heading out to the Duke, I'd love for you to join us if you've got the time" she hung up the phone and headed for the door, "leave the car Jimmy." She headed for the door, she stopped at the door, turned and said, "By the way, you're buying, and mine's a Carlsberg"

'The Duke' is on the corner of Portobello Road and Elgin Crescent, a traditional English pub that doesn't bother to cater to the almighty tourist dollar. The pub would only have locals in, and most of them knew her, not that she was a regular. She was a copper, and seeing a copper having a 'liquid lunch' wasn't all that unusual, though with BJ it usually ended with her still being sober. Today would be no different. The beer was just to not look out of place as they put things together.

The pub was half full. Two locals gave Billie a wave as she walked in. No one really paid much notice. Then again, in a London pub, it pays to not take too much notice of what's going on. Not that it matters, it's the kind of place that's got its own code for things, and even its own language that was specially invented in the 19th century to keep the local 'Bobbies' (as the police were known back then) guessing what the hell was going on. Jimmy went up to the bar to order the drinks while Bille found a table and waited for Joanne to show up. She'd sent a text saying she was on the way.

"Okay boss," Jimmy started as soon as Joanne got there. He'd already ordered drinks for the three of them, Carlsberg for both him and BJ and a Heineken for Joanne, "what's the big secret? Whatcha got?"

Billie put the laptop on the table in front of them. She began opening the machine up, but not turning it on yet. "How long have we been trying to find out the name of the guy in the river?" she asked, "Ten days?"

"Yeah," Joanne replied, "Body went in the water last Tuesday, actually probably Monday night, but we found out about it Tuesday. That was ten days ago" Joanne had been part of the team as well, and she was someone BJ had known from previous investigations. She was good at what she did. Damn good.

"Ten days," BJ began, "and we got nowhere, not even a name, in the financial capital of the world, and right next to the seat of power. Does that seem strange to you?" she stopped for a moment, observing the two. Their looks said a big fat YES.

"It was a bit strange," Jimmy acknowledged, "But I've seen stranger things!" He shrugged, "But yeah, I'd say someone didn't want us finding out,"

"And I think I know why," Billie replied. She leaned forward and activated the screen on the laptop. "Say nothing," she warned them. "Just read the file"

The file had the initials MI6 stamped right across the top, and a red seal saying 'Top Secret' right in the next line. Next came a picture, and a name, followed by the personal details of the person in the picture.

MI6 Top Secret

N *ame Farid Akbari*
      Country of origin Egypt
Age 30
Nationality British (Naturalised)
Languages spoken Arabic (Mother tongue) Coptic, Hebrew, English and German (fluent in all these) French, Italian and Spanish (conversational)
   Skills Phd in Computer science (Oxford University), degrees in Political science and sociology.

   Further information. Farid's parents came to Britain in the late 1980s to escape persecution in their home country. His father was a Muslim and his mother was a Christian. This wasn't a problem in Egypt, as the child would be raised in the father's faith, but his father was a secret Christian who didn't want this. So they came to Britain to escape the persecution and death threats.

   During the Arab spring, the father believed he could help Egypt because of the changes and went back to try to work with the democratically elected government. But the new government was an Islamic extremist group who had him arrested and executed as an 'Apostate'.

   Farid was studying computer science at Oxford. He was recruited and given the chance to work with MI6 against the Islamic extremists. He works in the cyber division tracking the links between extreme Islam and organised crime, particularly the drug world.

   "Is this for real?" Jimmy's face was ashen, "I mean this guy,"

"Was a spook?" Billie asked, "I believe so. This is what those swines were after. They wanted to stop this from getting to us!"

"But why?" Jo was confused. "Who were they?"

"That's what I'd like to sodding well know!" Billie said ruefully, "Then I'd know who to slap the flamin' cuffs on after I've got my revenge, that is!" She took a sip of the beer. Jimmy had ordered a plate of sausage rolls as well. They arrived just then. She reached out and took one. The flaky pastry was delicious. She stopped for a moment, savouring the pastry before carrying on, "but here's what we have. An employee of MI6 is murdered on our turf, and someone's hiding stuff from the cops. You can guarantee that 'someone' was MI6, but then someone else wants us to find out what the hell is going on! That's the strange bit. You can bet your bottom dollar it wasn't the killers or MI6!"

"Let me get this straight" Jimmy looked totally confused. He reached for his pint, took a swig of the beer and put the schooner back down on the table. He was careful not to spill any of the precious amber liquid, "We've got a body in the river"

"Had a body," Joanne interrupted. "It was cremated yesterday on someone's orders. The ashes are being put in a pauper's urn,"

"What?" both Billie and Jimmy were stunned, "No one contacted the family?" Bille got the next part of the question out, but both were thinking, "Why? And How?"

"It's what you sign on for with MI6,!" Joanne replied, "It kind of makes sense they could, they tell you you might be killed in service, and there's no way they could recover the body, so you sign all rights like that away. Hell, you don't even get any memorial. At least the CIA has a star on the wall at Langley. MI6 doesn't even get that!" She drained the last of her drink, Billie offered to buy another round of drinks. It was obvious they were going to need them. She gave the money to Jimmy to 'do the honours,'

As soon as Jimmy was back Joanne continued, "it's what they agree to at the start." She shifted a little. "The pathologist was overridden and told to find a 'death by misadventure' in the report, though even he said it was bloody strange,"

"I thought it was strange," Bille cut her off, "I've been trying to get hold of their office for a few days, well I was before the attack, no one answered, there was some weird stuff in that report,"

"You mean like being pumped up on adrenaline?" Joanne asked, "I got hold of him before he went on 'holiday'" She made the inverted comma sign, "by the way, he said to say hi, and don't call," she almost giggled, the beer was having an effect, not that it was anything serious. She was finished work for the day, "he told me to tell you, and make sure it was no one else," she stopped for a moment, then went on, "oh well, I suppose if you trust Jimmy, then I can,"

"Thanks for the vote of confidence" Jimmy wasn't sure if it was a compliment or an insult, but he took it anyway. He was still very much the junior member of the team.

"He said there was a hypodermic needle mark in the back, right where the shoulder blades meet the backbone. Left-hand side, it went straight into the heart, Adrenaline injected there would cause a sudden and massive heart attack, he said it could look like someone 'drunk as a skunk' staggering along, they wouldn't feel the needle, but the effects would be deadly within minutes,"

"So," BJ looked at the two, "what did Townsend say to that? I presume you told him,"

"Didn't want to know," Joanne replied, "I tried to say something, but he just wasn't interested, and told me to drop it like a hot potato."

"Someone yanking his chain, you think?" Billie asked. She already knew what she thought. She just wanted to see if what she was thinking stood up to scrutiny.

"I'd say much further up the food chain than him," Jimmy was the one to reply.

"CTC," Joanne replied, "we had a visit from them just before they shut us down."

"Put the fear of God into everyone, right?" Billie asked. She didn't wait for a reply. "Those bastards shut us down, probably saying they're gonna deal with it, yeah right," she was angry. She'd dealt with them before.

'CTC' are the initials for 'Counter Terrorism Command' or what was the old Special Branch and the Metropolitan Police's own Anti Terror unit called SO13 (Special Operations section 13) they were rolled together to do everything 'in house' including investigating and taking down the 'bad guys' with the power of arrest (something that MI5 doesn't have, but 'five' calls on the SAS when they need things done, something that causes huge rivalry between the two.

"We know this guy was MI6," Billie began again, "Killed by someone. CTC doesn't want it investigated, nor do some parts of MI6. He worked in computers, linking it all back to terrorism. What are they hiding?"

"You said some parts of MI6 boss," Jimmy cut in, "care to explain?"

"Take a look at the file itself," she replied, taking a swig of the beer. Replacing the glass she leaned back in the seat, the pub was still only half full, and no one seemed to pay too much attention, she went on, "it's an internal file, a personnel file, someone on the inside got that file and sent it to us. That's why I say some parts, someone else wants the truth to come out, then there's my guardian Angel from the other night. How the hell did he know I was going to need help?"

"Let me have a look at that file again" Joanne leaned in closer. She took the laptop and studied the contents of the file, her face changed, "Oh Jesus" she let out a quiet shriek, "I think I know what it's about," she reached for her phone, flicked through to Google and started tapping away at the screen.

"What?" both of the other two asked at the same time. They stopped with their glasses in mid-air, "what is it?"

"Look." Joanne swung the phone around. "We found the body ten days ago, right? He worked in computers, the cyber division, then seven days ago the ransomware hit," She showed the screen, it had the first news reports of the damage the ransomware did listed, "If I'm right, he would have been our last line of defence, taking down the ransomware.`` She was getting excited. She began tapping the screen of the laptop.

"Except that it was stopped," Billie replied. Not sure where things were going.

"By pure fluke!" Joanne replied, "some geeky hacker still living at home with Mum and Dad just happened to find the kill switch, what if he wasn't meant to find it, but someone else was, and they were meant to do something else with it!"

"But what? And why?" Jimmy asked.

"I don't know, but here's where things get really strange," Joanne replied. "Five days ago, MI6 sent a team to pick this guy up, take him into protective custody,"

"And?"

"They were ambushed. They tried to shoot the team down in the streets. The MI6 team has gone to ground, and no one knows where the hell they are! Not only that, but they've got the hacker with them, and he might be injured!"

Chapter 30

Stunned would put things mildly. Both of them stopped mid-air with the drinks on the way to their mouths, "What the F?" Bille almost slammed her drink down on the table. "When did this happen, and how come we haven't heard about it? And flaming well where?"

Joanne stopped. She suddenly realised she'd probably said too much, "My flatmate." She said quickly, almost too quickly. "Works in the call centre," she went on. "She was on shift when the 999 call came in. Took the details, and got things moving, then she got a 'visitor' said he was from the home office, wanted all the recordings and stuff, kinda strange really," she reached for her drink, "it was in the West Country, just outside Bristol, I can find out for you,"

"Do that!" Billie replied, almost shouting, a few heads turned their way, she quickly quietened down, "then let's see what this is about, any chance you can ask her now?"

"That would be suspicious," Joanne replied, "though we can search the Police database and see if anything pops up like that, I know they got the files for the calls, but surely they can't delete everything straight away, there was an armed response unit sent, you can't make that disappear off the files overnight, can you?"

"Even if the police files vanish," BJ began.

"There's got to be press coverage. And that's a different story" Jimmy replied. He flicked to Google on his phone. A few strokes of the keys later, he had what he was looking for. "Here we are" he turned his phone so the other two could see it. He had a news article showing, 'Police respond to an armed incident just outside

Bristol' with the name of a reporter on it. The details were sketchy, but enough to give them some idea which station would have been dealing with the incident.

"What's the betting they're getting shut down as fast as we are?" Jimmy asked as they got up to leave the pub, "bloody good odds they've already been shut down,"

"Nah," BJ replied, "this was gunplay on the streets. Most likely, the best way to deal with this is to shift the blame. Fit someone up for it. Preferably one of your more unsavoury criminals. One you know has done some pretty serious shit, but you can't prove it. So you get 'em to plead guilty to this and tell 'em you'll ask for a lighter sentence, makes everyone feel good, feel safer, but the real dickheads get away with murder,"

"Not in this case, boss," Jimmy quipped, "just attempted,"

"You know what I mean," she shot back, "Let's give this guy a visit, Jo, you head back to the office, see what else you can dig up, Jimmy and I'll get down there and pay a visit to the cop lumbered with this,"

"**Y**ou sure these are even linked Guv," Jimmy asked as they climbed into the car. He'd had two pints of Lager, He was right on the legal limit for driving, but he'd also had food with the drinks would absorb some of the alcohol, it wasn't the best idea they had, and both would love to leave it for another day, but there just wasn't time, things were slipping away, and fast.

Bristol is directly west of London. The easiest way to get there is to pick up the M4 motorway in London and simply drive west for about eighty miles. Then, just as you come to the junction of the

M4 and M32, take the M32 straight into the heart of the city. They headed that way.

"Hi there," Billie started the conversation over the phone, "this is DS Jones. I'm wanting to talk to Sergeant Harris of your ARU, is he in?"

"Hang on sergeant the voice came back, I'll just try his line" the phone went to music. She was on hold. About fifteen seconds later, she heard someone pick up. "Sergeant Harris, how can I help?" A male voice came on the line.

"This is DS Jones from the Metropolitan Police," she began. "I'm calling about a case you're investigating at the moment, the shooting in Little Stoke," she stopped, waiting for a reaction.

"Yes," he replied, "what about it?"

"We've got something that might tie in with it up in London. Can we get together and have a talk?"

"We already handed the case over" he began, "Special Branch, or whatever they call themselves today, some kind of international link yadda, yadda, ya." She knew he didn't believe a word of what he'd been told, but had gone along with it, because that's what you do if you value your career and pension, Not to mention wanting to stay out of jail.

"Oh, sorry to hear that," she clipped the phone off, *'shit'* was all she could think, *'all this effing way, and for what, diddly squat!'* She was about to tell Jimmy to find a place to get off the motorway and head back, wasted journey and all when her phone started ringing, she glanced at the number, didn't recognise it, but it couldn't be a coincidence could it? I mean, she'd only just got off the phone with the guy. Swiping the screen she spoke, "Yeah"

"Listen up" she recognised the voice, one she'd just been talking to, but calling from another phone, one that wasn't being monitored, "I'll be at the Blackbeard on the wharf in fifteen minutes. We can talk then. I'll be at the bar, on the far right." the phone clicked off.

"How far's the wharf?" she asked Jimmy.

"No idea boss, look it up on Google,"

Before she could, the car's Bluetooth had already connected and began the search, 'twenty minutes' was already displaying on the screen with the directions on how to get there, "The Blackbeard pub?" she added to the query, the computer went blank for a couple of seconds, then came back with the information they needed.

Bristol's most famous son isn't known by his real name, but by a name the put fear into the heart of every man who took to the seas in years gone by, one that still lives on in legend and movies, and was the inspiration for one of Johnny Depp's best-known characters, Blackbeard.

Second only to their exploits on the seas, pirates were also famous for their drinking and the general trouble they caused on land. So it was only fitting that Bristol, once the second most important port in Britain, would celebrate her most infamous son by naming a pub after him, and that it should be down on the wharf, where he probably first went to sea.

The pub was a typical 'Olde Worlde' kind of place. It looked old, but the old that's well maintained. Fresh whitewash on the stone walls, fairly new black paint enhancing the Oak beams that formed the frame of the Tudor style building, the low door was a dead giveaway that the pub actually was old, and probably dated from Blackbeard's time, not that they were there for the sights.

Gone are the days when walking into a bar your senses are immediately assaulted by the cigarette smoke, and battling the haze was the first challenge. Instead the pub looked clean and fresh, Bille could actually see around the room, not that it was large, just four or five tables. Two of which had people at them. Three more patrons were propping the bar up, two junior staff were behind it, making sure that drinks were kept full, and anyone wanting to order something to eat could do so with a minimum of fuss.

There was a board with a menu up behind the bar. The fish and chips was 'fresh cod' if you count two weeks in the freezer on the trawler as being 'fresh' but beggars can't be choosers as the saying goes, she indicated to Jimmy to order them some 'grub' and a couple of drinks while she headed to the table Harris had said he would be at.

"Sergeant Harris?" She asked. The guy sat at the table. He was tall and thin, but with an athletic frame, short black hair gave the game away that he was ex-military. He indicated to her to take the seat opposite. There were two more seats at the table. He flicked one of them around so that it was pointing towards the next table.

"You must be DS Jones." He didn't wait for her to reply, "What can I do for you?" He was polite but direct. She liked that.

"As I said on the phone earlier," Billie replied, "I'm interested in the events of the other day!" She tried not to mention the actual incident. It wouldn't do to give too much away,

"Not a lot I can tell really," Harris replied truthfully, "The whole street got bloody well shot up, but when we got there no one to be seen, just a bunch of cars with bullet holes all through them, broken glass all over the place, but that's what you get when someone's spraying and praying if you know what I mean,"

"Haven't heard that term for a while" Billie was surprised. She'd only ever heard ex-squaddies use that term, and it wasn't complimentary to the shooter! "Where'd you serve?"

"What?" he was a bit surprised. "Iraq, Operation Enduring Freedom, and Afghanistan in '04, why?"

"Only people I heard use that term were men and women who knew what they were talking about with weapons, that's why?" Billie replied truthfully, "anyway roughly how many shots were fired?"

Jimmy was back with drinks. He had a Carlsberg for Billie, but he was on Coke. He took the other chair; they waited for him to sit before continuing.

"We counted fifty holes in the vehicles," Harris replied, "all nine millimetres. In other words, it was a submachine gun, or possibly two."

"What makes you say that?"

"Where the shell casings were found," he answered.

"Really! What was so special?"

"There were two shooters, or at least two people using weapons, possibly one of them was the guys taking the kid into protective custody, but they're missing, so no one could confirm that!" He shrugged.

"I'm guessing it's where the shell casings were found that gave that away?" Jimmy was actually asking a question but trying to sound observant.

"No," the reply came back, "we only found two casings, and that's why I'm saying two shooters."

"Why?"

"If you're firing from a moving vehicle," Harris explained, "chances are you'll have only the end of the barrel outside the vehicle, you'll probably have a casing catcher fitted. Otherwise, you stand the chance of hot casings hitting the driver causing them to swerve and crash,"

Both Jimmy and Billie looked a little confused. Harris tried to explain a little more. "Look, we drive on the left-hand side of the road, right?" they both nodded, "that means our steering wheel is on the right, and the shooter, unless he's in the back is on the left, almost all weapons are designed for right-handed people, that means the cases eject flying to the right, straight at the driver, so the best way to stop that is a sock or something over the ejector to stop the casing flying off and hitting the driver, pretty much all military people use them as brass isn't cheap!"

"Hence, no casings for the bullets fired inside the vehicle, but two were found," Jimmy replied.

"Meaning two were firing, one inside and one outside. My guess is the one outside was returning fire, but until we get to talk with them, I can't confirm that!"

"Who was the guy they were picking up?" Billie asked.

"Don't know," Harris replied truthfully, "we were told it was some government operation, some kid who helped stop the Ransomware, but otherwise they've clammed up tighter than a duck's arsehole," just a hint of frustration came out.

"What are the locals saying?" Billie asked. She'd seen that 'Little Stoke' was a run-down place, so it wasn't likely that they were saying much to the cops. Especially if they thought it was gangs or drugs. You just don't cross those people, and you certainly don't 'snitch' that could seriously cut your life short.

"Not much." He replied, "it was the middle of the day, so all the decent people were at work. The CCTV cameras were on the blink, had been for a couple of days. They weren't due for repair until later in the day."

"Sounds to me," Billie said, "Like someone knew there would be a blind spot, and set the hit up, but why?"

"That's what I thought" Harris replied, "but it's been taken out of my hands." He shrugged and sat back in the seat, clearly frustrated at the turn of events. Looking up he asked, "how does this tie in with you?"

"A case we're looking into," Jimmy jumped in, Billie aimed a blow right at his shins with her right foot. He looked at Billie, a little confused.

"Just something of interest," she cut in, "in a case the Met thinks is gang-related, any idea what kind of weapon was used?"

" I just said they were nine millimetre," He replied, "both weapons that is, I'd say the one we got the casings from was probably a handgun, a Glock or something like that, the other I'd guess was an Uzi or MAC 10, they're the only ones with big enough magazines," He reached for the plate of sausage rolls the waiter had just brought over. Taking one he took a bite, the flaky pastry falling onto the table as he chewed, "and before you ask, there was only one mag used, there's never enough time to reload in a drive-by, it's a blast away and get the hell away kind of deal, anyway, you didn't answer my question, why the interest, especially if it's gang-related? You'd have all that information on your own, wouldn't you?"

"Truth is," Billie said, "it's a murder and the guy who was killed worked in computers, cyber-crime." She waited for a reaction. She got none, at least not that she could see, so she went on, "If he'd been alive at the time, he'd have been the man the government turned to when the Ransomware hit, as it was" she shrugged, "He was killed two days before the attack" she stopped, watching Harris closely to see if there was any reaction, there wasn't 'I wouldn't like to play poker with this guy' she thought to herself.

"And my one," Harris said, "was the snotty-nosed kid who lived with mum and dad, yet foiled the whole thing, right?"

"And I'd say someone was extremely pissed off that he did," Jimmy cut in. They both gave him filthy looks. "What?"

"Yeah, that about sums it up," Billie replied, "that and the fact that someone is trying to shut both investigations down," She reached for a sausage roll, they were a decent size so she took a bite and held the rest of the roll in her hand, "someone wants both investigations to go nowhere,"

"Not quite," Harris replied, "I was told unofficially the reason the home office took over the investigation is they think the team doing the guarding of the kid has gone rogue, and they've got no idea where they are, they're literally shitting big bricks over this. That's why they took over. They don't want a panic, at least that's what the word is". It was plain as the nose on his face. He didn't believe a word of what he just said, but it was the 'official line'

"What can you tell me about them?" Billie asked.

"Nothing" he replied, "apart from they were obviously the government, and one was packing some serious firepower, and whatever went down, they didn't have the time to clean up!" He reached for another roll at the same time as taking a swill of his drink, he'd had a drink in front of him when they first arrived, it was three-quarters full at the time, and this was the first swig he'd taken since they started talking.

The more they talked, the more both of them became convinced the two things were linked. There were just too many coincidences for it to be a chance. Billie didn't feel the need to talk about the 'Guardian Angel' who'd shown up at her place or the fact that they had three people in custody over the incident, the police put that down to a simple 'home invasion' that she knew was pure Bullshit, but as long as it kept those bozos off the street, she wasn't too concerned what they called it. Mind you, two of them were still in the hospital, albeit a prison one.

"So," BJ said, "we've both got a situation where things just don't add up!" She shifted slightly in her seat. It didn't matter what was being said, proper procedure wasn't being followed, and that worried her, "is there anything you can tell me about the shooting?"

"Only other thing is the car involved. The report said it was a dark coloured Mondeo, a couple of years old, but in good condition, didn't get a registration number though,"

"Cameras?" Jimmy asked.

"As I said before," Harris replied, lifting his glass to drain the last of his drink, "the cameras were offline bloody convenient if you ask me, and,"

"Bloody unusual," Jimmy interrupted, 'aren't yours in this neck of the woods supposed to be state-of-the art?'

"The cameras are monitored, aren't they? How come a team wasn't dispatched to get them back online?" Billie asked.

"It's not London here," Harris shot back, "we don't have those kinds of resources, they'd only gone down that morning, here they give themselves twenty-four hours to get them back online, as long as the team gets to them and gets 'em working again within that time it's not a problem normally."

"Until something goes wrong," Jimmy added.

"Hindsight's a wonderful thing?" Harris was getting a bit frustrated with the young copper. The tone gave it away.

"We're not meaning to criticise,' Billie was glaring at Jimmy, 'back off' her eyes were saying, "But it's damn strange that the cameras were down when the hit took place, it can't be a coincidence, can it?"

"Tell the truth" Harris' tone softened slightly, but only slightly. "I'm convinced it wasn't, and that's what worries me. Whether it was one of the spook agencies or someone with a man on the inside, the whole thing stinks to high heaven, and it has me worried!"

"Okay, what about the witness, you know, the one that made the phone call?"

"Disappeared into thin air," Harris replied, "Oh and one last thing, that really throws a spanner in the works"

"Go on" they waited, eagerly expecting what he was going to say.

"All the damage done, four cars riddled with bullet holes, windows smashed and all that," he went on, "the government were there later that afternoon, fixed everything up immediately and literally took the people whose cars got shot up down to a dealer to get a new one, all on one condition,"

"Let me guess," Billie butted in, "that they say nothing about what went on, maybe even deny it took place, am I right?"

"Give the girl a prize" Harris smiled, it was a sarcastic one, not that either was offended, "You got it in one"

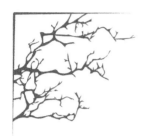

Chapter 31

Serkov's office was at the back of one of his nightclubs. He had three of them in London. They were all set up the same way, identical 'offices' in each one.

They had the latest gadgets in them, but all hidden away behind facades that looked like they came straight out of the Hermitage in his hometown, St Petersburg.

The clubs were the 'in place' in London. Anyone wanting to be 'seen' went there, especially Alex's place, as it was called in Knightsbridge, but that one was for 'A' listers only.

But they were only a front for where his real money was made, a way of 'greasing the wheels' to get things done, and moving 'product' without too many questions. After all, the 'A' list wasn't just movie stars.

He accessed the security feed from Sasha's building, saw the footage, and cussed.

"Show me the face," he screamed at the monitor as it showed the abduction for the fifth time. He was going through it almost frame by frame and getting nothing. Not even the 'doctor' was turning to the camera. It was as if they knew they were being filmed. The movements seemed natural, but if they were, he should have had a picture from at least one he could check against his facial recognition software. But nothing. He threw the pencil he'd been holding at the monitor screen, shoved his chair back forcibly, and stood up. Ten paces and he wrenched open the ornate Oak door, it flew back hitting the stopper with a thud.

"SERGEI" he bellowed into the next room. The unfortunate man he was shouting at was nearly deafened as he was only five steps away, "Have you found anything yet?" It was more a command than a question.

"Niet," the unfortunate replied in Russian, "I was in contact with all our people going to hospitals, none found anything" he was nervous. Alexei Serkhov wasn't a boss you wanted to annoy, even if it wasn't your fault.

"Agh" Serkov wheeled around, grabbing the door handle. He slammed it shut so hard that the doorframe shook. He went back to the desk and slumped back down into the chair.

There was a half-full bottle of Russian Vodka on the desk. As the owner, he didn't need to hide it; he was tempted, but today he needed a clear head. Something was going down, he just didn't know what?

'Rule nothing out' he remembered that from his days with the SVR or the 'renamed' KGB from the old days of the Soviet Union. it's the first thing they teach, 'when the crap happens, rule nothing out, and eliminate the possibilities starting with the easiest'

He'd sent men to every hospital in London. The hospitals had security guards there, but they 'don't get paid enough' to tangle with Serkov's thugs. As long as his men weren't causing trouble, they were left alone, but his men had found nothing, none had found Gromatski, and that was worrying.

"Who gains from this?" was the next question.

Gromatski had been kidnapped, that he was sure of. The question was, why? And who gained by it. Every name he thought up just made little sense. They all had too much to lose. It just made little sense.

"If I find the bastard," he said to himself, "I will kill them" he sat back in his office chair. He stopped to think things through. Too many things had gone wrong. First, the money going missing from accounts, bosses wanting answers and getting nowhere. Then an old 'friend' as he liked to think of them, caught years ago by the SVR in a 'honey trap', finally earned his keep and came through with information, but this time "for a price".

The 'honey trap' is one of the oldest and most effective ways spies and criminals use, but for Serkov, it wasn't about money. Sure, they'd made billions, but for him, it was about control! Controlling the supply often meant you needed to control those trying to hinder the supply, paying off those you needed to, and using 'other means' was the way to go about it. The 'honey trap' is one very effective way. All you need is someone willing to sell their soul and a camera, and often they don't have to be a willing partner. One trapped in poverty lured by the promise of bright lights and freedom in the West is enough.

That was the promise. The reality was little more than slavery, and he was good at that business.

The girls were attractive. That meant men would pay for a night with them. Some. Those not rich or powerful got an hour, but those with influence. They got what they wanted. He got photos or recordings 'for future use' and it was amazing how compliant people became when it became known you had these things. Those who didn't, well, that's where Gromatski came in, and he was good.

That was the issue, Gromatski knew too much! He knew who was on the 'payroll' and who knew to turn a blind eye. Whoever took him could cripple Serkov's operation overnight. He had to be found, and fast!

He'd even put 'feelers out' through his contacts. Quietly, a manhunt was going on, but nothing turned up.

It was a comment on a Facebook post. It just didn't look right. Something about it, something about 'Blueberry picking' at the 'old firm' just didn't look right. He nearly threw the machine out, but the more he looked at it the more he realised what it really was, he threw his chair back, reached into the top right-hand drawer of the desk, took out his SIG Sauer, it was in a shoulder holster. He slipped the holster on before putting his jacket on, then headed for the door, bellowing for Sergei and whoever else was around.

Guns are strictly controlled in Britain. Every owner has to have a firearms licence, they have to be kept in a registered armoury, and are never allowed to be carried in public, they are all registered by serial number so that the police, at least in theory, know where every weapon in the country is at anyone time. Serkov broke those three laws daily, and he didn't give a damn about them. After all, with so many Judges and Lawyers as 'partakers' of the delights he provided, he never had a problem with petty things like the law.

Chapter 32

"Package delivered," Jacko's voice came over the phone, "we're on our way back."

"Cheers for that," Sandy responded, trying to make things sound more conversational, more like what friends would sound like than what they really were. "When you get back, I should have some updates for you" she clicked the phone off.

Joey was in the other room making a cup of tea. "Mum's cure for all ills" he'd told Sandy a couple of times already, and that was just that day, she could tell he was stressed, but trying not to show it, they all were, but they weren't the kind to buckle under pressure, "When the going gets tough" she'd heard him say, "the tough get going" it was a creed they all lived by.

"Here you are." He brought a steaming mug of tea in, "Milk, no sugar" he assured her, "though without the sweet stuff, it tastes horrible!" he wrinkled his nose slightly.

"Thank you," she replied with a smile, "But I'm sweet enough." He didn't dare argue with that comment, it just wasn't safe.

"Whatcha got?" he asked looking at the phone she had in front of her. It was connected to one of her devices, one he had only the vaguest idea what it did.

"I'm cloning it first," she replied matter-of-factly, " that way even if we screw things up, we've got a backup with all the settings in place, and I can play with the clone first, just in case there's encryption software on there."

"How long ya reckon?" Joey asked as he put the tea down in front of her. He headed back to the kitchen. A few seconds later, he reappeared with a plate of chocolate biscuits.

"About ten minutes," she replied, "that's if we've got everything right."

Cloning the phone only took a couple of minutes. Setting everything else up took the rest of the time. She'd used the laptop to run the cloning programme. As soon as it was finished, she disconnected the original phone, turned it off and put it into a Ziploc bag.

The laptop had software to override Gromatski's device. She was effectively turning it into a 'slave' that would do anything it was ordered to. The software told the phone to copy all its files onto the hard drive of the new device, and it gave access to all the passwords. Nothing was secure.

"Is it password protected?" Joey stared at the screen as Sandy worked.

"With this software" she tapped the laptop, "It won't matter, we go around the passwords, not through them." She clicked the mouse, a fresh screen came up, the message on the screen said that 'Poseidon', the decryption software, was ready to run.

Sandy hit a few keys. It didn't matter which one she hit; the password was already programmed in. She just 'executed' the command to open the files. Within seconds, the computer had dismantled the security software of the phone. They were ready to begin.

"How long is this going to take?" Joey asked. He sat down beside her and looked at the screen. He was genuinely interested in learning the process, but couldn't help a mischievous dig at her.

"Patience is a virtue you know!" Sandy replied smiling, "it'll take as long as it takes," she tapped a few more keys, "we won't get the phone conversations, but we'll have a good idea who called, and hopefully by matching it to the contact list in the phone we'll get some idea of who was talking to whom, as for the rest, we can give them to Sir Mike to decide on whether he wants to listen in to their conversations,"

One thing that the phone companies never tell their clients is that every phone conversation is actually recorded! It's usually deleted within a few hours of the recording taking place. But for an experienced operator, it's very easy to get them back from the servers they were recorded on. Even on the average laptop to truly destroy a file beyond being able to 'retrieve' it, your machine has to record over the same area of the hard drive at least half a dozen times. That's how the police catch so many criminals with incriminating evidence on their machines.

Every conversation is recorded by the servers the company uses, and not just one. But every server in the chain the conversation goes along gets a full copy. That means the server that the first phone connects to. Then the servers at each junction on the way (the exchange, then the relay stations. Even the satellites and finally the server of the phone receiving the call, and finally the destination phone itself). When the servers get full, all that happens is an electronic marker that 'tells' the server where the conversation is gets removed so that space can record a fresh conversation. But the first one is still there, and all it takes is someone with the right equipment to go looking for it, and it will be found. The question is always time. Who has the time to go sifting through all the data necessary?

Normally, that's where GCHQ in Britain would come in, or the NSA in the United States. Their computers can sort through the information they need to within seconds, and they do it regularly, looking for terrorists. They can even retrieve old conversations that the phone companies deleted years before.

Sandy had a list of phone numbers, some of whom she knew who they were, others she didn't. They took priority.

It took a few minutes, but things started to come together. Serkhov's number was the one called the most. There were a few calls from Sasha, all to be expected, but then came the ones that were not on their lists.

"Burners?" Joey pointed at the list she'd made, the ones they couldn't identify.

"Maybe," she replied, "I should still be able to get a location, though. Getting the record of the conversation might take a while, and tip our 'friend' off, but we can if we need to,"

"If there's a chance of tipping that swine off," Joey almost spat the words out, "then don't go there."

"No intention of" Sandy replied defensively frustrated that it seemed Joey thought she would, "I just meant it's there as an option if we need it"

"Duly noted" Joey was seemingly oblivious to her frustration. She was about to say something when a light started flashing on the screen. It was an alarm wired to the house security system.

"Someone just opened the front gate." She said as she tapped the keyboard. The screen came alive with the view from one of the outside cameras. Joey reached for the Browning in his shoulder holster. Checking that the safety was on, he cocked the weapon and went towards the front door. He propped himself up, back against the wall, both hands gripping the gun.

"It's okay" Sandy didn't shout, but was loud enough for Joey to hear in the lobby, "It's Jacko and Mac" he relaxed slightly, but not much, they still didn't want to give anything away, especially not how many they were at the house, he waited for one of them to open the door.

Jacko came through the door first. Jacko didn't even glance in Joey's direction. He went straight in. Mac was right behind him. He took one last look down the street, then closed the door. Making sure the door was closed, he turned to Joey. "Ya can stand down now"

"What have we got?" Jacko fired the question off in Sandy's general direction. He headed for the kitchen, knowing that like all good soldiers, Joey would have a kettle boiling. He wasn't disappointed.

The kettle was just over half full, and still hot from the drinks Joey had made. Jacko reached into the cupboard above the bench the kettle was on, took out two cups, plopped two tea bags from the jar next to the kettle into them. Two sugars in each cup, a splash of milk. Then add the water and they had 'NATO standard' as soldiers liked to call a steaming cup of hot sweet tea.

"How's your Russian?" Sandy asked with a smile on her face. She knew full well none of them spoke it. She swivelled the computer screen so that they could see what was there. "I'm into Gromatski's texts. This one was from a number I've traced to Serkov, and before you ask," she saw he was about to ask something. Sandy would lay money on knowing the question, "it's got Cyrillic script, from a Russian, doesn't take a rocket scientist to figure out it's in Russian, that and I used Google translate!"

They all chuckled, "you DID ask!" Sandy was laughing, "It just seemed the obvious thing to try, not perfect, but good enough,"

"What's that?" Jacko pointed to a piece of text on the screen. It looked strange, it had numbers in the midst, "looks like an"

"An address," Sandy replied, "and if he wasn't on his way to some unpleasant place, it would sign his death warrant. It's the address we picked the hacker up from."

"And you say," Mac asked, "this text came from Serkov?"

"Along with the time we said we'd be picking him up, " she replied, "They were expecting a soft target! You should see the texts after. He may work for Serkov, but he 'lets fly' with his opinion" she turned back to the screen, "by the way, heard from Smithy at the O.P."

An 'O.P.' is a military term for an observation post, a concealed hiding place snipers use to watch the enemy and report back what's going on. Smithy had insisted they needed to set one up across from Serkov's nightclub, "sound tactical move" he'd said. No one had argued. "He took the nifty fifty that Joey commandeered from the idiot lookout," Mac went on, "Just in case something happens"

Right at that moment, their phones buzzed. A message was coming in, it was from Smithy, it simply said, "Serkov on the move, am following" Jacko looked up at Mac, "Time to roll," he turned to Sandy and carried on, "send us what we need, the rest, you know what to do with."

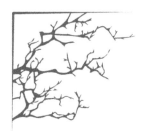

Chapter 33

The club was just a front for Serkhov's real business, but it was a profitable 'front' with the rich and famous enjoying the place. It was one of 'THE' places to be seen.

Chelsea might be the most expensive part of town, and where the billionaires live. But they all had to get their groceries from somewhere, and none of them liked to send their 'minions' far to get them. So right next door was Coleridge Gardens. Serkhov's 'club' was there, where it wouldn't attract too much unwanted attention, but he could still charge the exorbitant 'Chelsea' prices.

Smithy had been watching the place since the early morning. Not that anyone would have noticed. First, there were the delivery people. They came and went from 4 am onwards. All he needed to 'blend in' was a hi-vis vest. No one noticed the extra body unloading the trucks, and not once did his eyes leave the club entrance

They stopped at about 7 am, but the local cafe was open, and he was hungry. The hi-vis discarded (returned to the rightful owner, who never noticed it gone) and breakfast ordered.

Normally, on a 'stake out', the person watching would find a place 'out of the way' where they could see what was going on but not be seen. That wasn't possible. There wasn't anywhere to hide, except in plain sight, so that's what he did.

The traffic was getting busy. Delivery vans, couriers, taxis and buses, but nothing that stayed more than a few minutes. Yet he blended in.

The sun had passed the midway point in the sky when the door to Surkov's club flew open. A red Ferrari was parked out the front.

It couldn't have been more obvious, even if his name was written all over it. That's why Smithy had fitted a tracker as soon as he saw the car. All he had to do was activate it remotely.

Taking his phone out, Smithy tapped in a number. A slight beep told him the tracker was active. Next, he pressed the 'group message' to let them know.

Serkov was in a rush. His training forgotten. He jumped into the car, revved the engine and took off. Tyres squealing as he sped away. It would have looked good on a racetrack, but in urban London? He may as well have had a big red flashing light on the top.

"He's on the move," Smithy spoke into the phone. The programme transcribed it into text and sent the message. Meanwhile, he casually walked to where the moped was parked. It wasn't totally hidden, but out of the way enough to not be seen. He put his earpiece in and donned the helmet.

Flicking the bike off its stand he turned the key and pulled away. The moped had a holder for another tablet. An iPad fitted just below the speedometer. He took the iPad out of the bag he was carrying and clipped it into place, pressing the one switch the device came to life, already set to the tracking programme they were using the device showed a map of the area, a bright red dot showed that the 'target' Serkov was a hundred yards ahead and off to the left.

"Smithy," Jacko's voice came over the phone. The screen stayed on the map. "Where are we heading?" They were already mobile.

"Not sure yet boss," he replied, "he's only just left the club, heading south, possibly over the river. That's all I can tell ya,"

"Okay," the reply came back, "we'll head towards the Vauxhall Bridge and see where we are from there."

"Roger that, boss. Will keep you posted," he concentrated on riding the scooter.

'Bloody typical' he thought to himself, 'Joey and Sandy do this and they got a flamin' Commando and a Bonneville, all I effing well get is a bloody Vespa!' He chuckled to himself as he headed in the same direction as the Ferrari was showing to have gone.

"Smithy, Jacko, Mac Stand down, STAND DOWN" Sandy virtually shouted into their headsets. She sounded animated, almost frantic.

"Whoa, what? What are you on about Sandy?" Jacko cut in. "We're nearly at the bridge,"

"Stand down," she shouted again. "It's a ruse, a fake! He's not in the bloody car!" she sounded confident, but frantic for them to stop. "He's leading you on a wild goose chase with it,"

"But he's in the car" Smithy had pulled over to the side of the road, "I saw him going for"

"Did you actually see him climb into the car and take off?" Sandy shot back.

"I saw him climb in," Smithy shot back. He was watching the screen with the red dot showing the car was getting further and further away. Another couple of minutes and it would be out of range.

"But did you see him drive off in it?"

"Of course I flamin' well saw the car pull away" Smithy was getting angry.

"But did you see him in the car as it drove away?"

"I was getting the bloody bike," he shot back. "How could I? But he did. The sodding thing pulled away,"

"Yeah it did," Sandy replied over the phone, "but he wasn't in it, he was standing on the pavement, I just pinged his phone to confirm we had him, it's not in the bloody car, it was walking towards the tube!"

The 'Tube' is the nickname that Londoners affectionately call the London underground. Thirteen underground lines that connect every part of the vast city. At least there are thirteen of them that the public can use. There are others, ones that the public isn't told about.

There isn't a part of the city that doesn't have a 'tube station' within a couple of hundred yards of wherever you live.

"He just went into the station at Earls Court," Sandy went on, "looks like he's heading for the district or circle line. I'm sending Joey to intercept the eastbound, probably at the Embankment." She shooed Joey towards the door. He got the message and set off out the door at a sprint.

High street Kensington (the nearest tube station of the circle line to Earls Court) and Embankment are only two or three stops apart. But nearly a million people use that part of the line every day. Not just that, but both stations have other lines that intersect. It'll be like the proverbial needle in the haystack. The only advantage they had was that Sandy could 'ping' Surkov's phone even if it was turned off. They could use the technology against him.

The tube station was three hundred yards down the road. Joey covered it in less than a minute. He already had a season pass for the tube. He scanned the pass and sprinted for the platform. People moved to one side as he ran. They just thought he was late for work or a business meeting.

"Which way am I going?" Joey didn't even sound out of breath.

"He's on the train, about to arrive at the station," Sandy replied.

"Which bloody way?" Joey demanded.

"Eastbound if you'd let me finish," Sandy shot back.

"Thank you," Joey replied, "and sorry,"

"Should think so," she couldn't resist the dig. "Get visual confirmation, then back off. Since we know we're right, we'll track this bit with the GPS."

The Circle line first started operating when Victoria was Queen of England. First, as a line from Paddington to Kings Cross. They soon 'looped' it around the old city of London in the 1870s. It connects all the major tourist places including the famous Tower Bridge and the houses of parliament. A great way to get anywhere in the city, and perfect for losing any 'tail'. That's what Serkov was counting on.

"He's heading Eastbound," Joey spoke into his mike. He had a Bluetooth device in his ear. Joey looked just like any other commuter. "heading towards Tower Bridge, the third carriage from the front. I'm in the one behind,"

"Got that. Stay there in case he moves," Sandy instructed Joey as the doors closed. "we might lose comms in the tunnels, but should be good with the GPS,"

The train was about half full. Most of the seats were taken, but no one was standing. Everyone was doing their own thing. That made Joey's life easier.

Serkov was about two-thirds of the way towards the back of the carriage. He was sitting on the left-hand side facing the opposite side. The seat to his left was vacant. A blonde woman was already sitting on the right. She seemed not to pay any attention to the man sitting next to her, but something, a niggling feeling, told Joey to pay attention to her.

Joey took his phone out. He made as if he was checking emails. No one bothered him despite the fact that email would not work inside the tunnels, besides he only made it look that way. He was after the camera.

He got half a dozen photos of the two. They seemed not to know each other, but looks can deceive. He kept watching as he put the camera away.

In London, there's an underground station every three or four hundred yards. The trains travelling the routes take just over a minute to reach the station from the previous one. People getting on and off at each one. A few times Joey momentarily lost sight as people crossed his line of vision, but a second or so later, he confirmed Serkov was still there. The woman seemed not to even be aware of her neighbour. Joey was beginning to relax.

The train was just slowing for the next stop on the line. Pulling into Westminster. Literally right underneath some of the most important buildings in Britain.

The blonde got up and headed for the exit. Serkov was still sitting there. Joey couldn't help noticing he had a smile on his face.

'Like to wipe that sod off,' Joey thought about Serkov's smile, *'oh for the chance, still, it'll come.'* He thought to himself.

"Joey, where the hell are you?" Sandy screamed into his earpiece, @he's moving!" She yelled excitedly into the device.

"No, he's not!" Joey was emphatic.

"He IS," she came back, "the GPS picked up movement,"

"And the MK1 eyeball says he isn't. I'm bloody watching him. He must have slipped the phone into the blonde's bag," he replied.

"What bloody blonde?" She didn't give him time to explain.

"The one he sat next to" Joey replied, "and before you ask" he cut her off, "they didn't seem to know each other, that's why I said nothing, but sending you the pics as soon as you stop shouting in my ear!" He took the phone out, flicked the camera function on, selected the photos he needed and clicked send. As soon as the email address came up, he typed in the one Sandy was using. As soon as he'd finished he spoke again, "They're on their way, I'll stay with Serkov"

The next few minutes were filled with a tense silence. He wasn't sure if Sandy was annoyed with him, or simply that she was busy. Not that it mattered all that much. He'd probably have to apologise for the way he spoke. But she'd also understand it was in the heat of the moment, and besides, he'd been right not to trust the technology totally, not that it would go down that well.

Half an hour later, they were still on the circle line and Joey was thinking they'd missed something. They were approaching a famous London address.

"We're at the Baker Street station," Joey spoke up, "with any luck a friend from number 221B might get on the tube and take over."

"You know the stories are fictional, don't you?" Sandy replied, totally missing the joke, "and it's the Abbey National Bank address!"

"Yeah, he'd have this case solved in ten minutes while making the cops look like total idiots!" Joey replied. He caught movement. Serkov was getting out of his seat, "we might have movement," He watched closely.

"Jacko, Mac, where are you now?" Sandy called for the sitrep. "Be good if one of you can take over from Joey,"

"Just arrived at the station," Mac came over the radio, "Jacko's still in the car, Joey what platform?"

"Westbound," Joey replied. "Where are you?"

"Just at the turnstiles, stay on the train and search the seat,"

"Roger that," Joey said, but thought *'shit'* as he dived back into the train, just in time before the doors closed. He launched himself for the seat just as an elderly Jamaican lady was about to sit. She gave him a disgusted look. He pretended to have lost something as he searched the seat. He was checking for a 'dead drop'

The 'dead drop' is something you often see in the movies. It's an old trick the spies used to use, but it's far more elaborate than the movies make out. In a nutshell, it's a way for spies and their 'handlers' to pass messages along without being seen together.

The way it worked was when one of them had a message, they would notify the other. Either through an ad in the local papers or as is today a Facebook and where the recipient is certain to see it.

A seemingly innocent phrase like 'Blackberry picking at the farm at 2 pm' could have a double meaning. The average joker might wonder why a London newspaper with no farms would advertise such a thing, but then might think it's for those living in the suburbs. But the intended recipient would know exactly what it was talking about. Once the message was delivered to the intended location the sender would also put another signal out, this time in a place where the recipient would see it, usually on the way to the 'drop' showing that the message was there and with a means for the person to know that the message hadn't been tampered with, usually a mark they'd pre-agreed to. Joey wasn't sure what he'd be looking for, just that it would seem odd to be there. He found nothing. "Nothing here," he whispered into the mike as he stood and pointed for the lady to take his seat.

"No, thanks" she almost shouted, clearly annoyed at the first incident. Joey sort of ignored her and moved towards the door, anyway.

"I'm getting off at the next stop," he spoke into the mike, "where to now?"

"He took the Bakerloo line south," Mac spoke up. "Not sure where yet, but I'm on it as well. We just passed Waterloo station."

The 'Bakerloo' line was originally built as the connection between Baker street (half a mile from Euston and Kings Cross stations) and Waterloo stations effectively connecting the two main stations with trains to the North of England with the station that served the south-west of the country. Hence the name 'Bakerloo'

"Joey," Sandy spoke up again, "You and Jacko get back here PRONTO. We've had a development, Mac. You'll have to see it through on your own," she clicked the mike off.

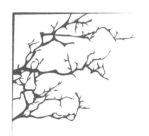

Chapter 34

"What gives boss?" Joey asked Jacko as soon as he climbed in the car. "Any ideas?"

"Not a clue" Jacko replied as he put the car into gear, checking behind he indicated and pulled into the traffic, it wasn't too bad, but they could barely do twenty miles an hour, he indicated to Joey to give Sandy a call.

"Whatcha got for us?" Joey spoke so quickly the accent came over strong.

"Got a bit of a situation in the West country. Needs a delicate touch," Sandy replied.

"Okay, I'll drop Joey off and pick up a sledgehammer," Jacko chuckled. "that's far more delicate than he is," they were both laughing.

"Maybe," Sandy replied, "but you might need his talents for,"

"Destruction?" Jacko couldn't resist. He may be the commander in the team, but everyone was equal in their eyes, and that meant making fun of each other.

"A message from Mildred," Sandy went on, "the car's gone active again. We think it's headed for its final resting place."

"Scrapyard?" Joey asked, his speciality was explosives, and by default of the fact they're often set using electronics. It included 'all things electrical'.

"Chopshop," Sandy replied, "recycle the parts, turn the scrap into profit,"

"It's a good vehicle though,"

"That the cops are looking for! Even if they change the chassis plate and numbers, there'll be telltale signs. Better to get rid of the vehicle. Anyway, it's on the move, and we need to get there before the cops find it."

"They don't know where it is, do they?"

"They will when we tell them, but we need those trackers back first," Sandy replied. "that's what the message was about. She wants the kit back, and not tied up as evidence in some court case," she finished. "I'm giving you a head start before we call the cavalry in. I'm sending you the location."

The location was in an industrial area just north of Cirencester. Not exactly known as a hive of criminal activity, just a quiet place in the suburbs. Being just off the M4 motorway meant it was easy getting to and from it, ideal if you want a car to disappear 'fast'

"Got the location, will be there in an hour," Joey spoke as Jacko gunned the engine. "that's if we survive the drive!" he couldn't resist a bit of payback. "What about Smithy?"

"Car did a circuit, went back to the garage. Smithy's on his way to you folks, should get there just before you do,"

"Have him set up an O.P. across the road," Jacko spoke. He was smiling. The thought of Smithy trying to navigate the motorway on a moped that struggles to go above thirty miles an hour would have Smithy 'cussing like a good un' as he would say, not that they would dare say anything to him.

"Figured that," Sandy said, "He's already got it sussed. Should be in position by the time you get there,"

It looked just like any other mechanic's garage, just bigger. Two roller doors at the front opened to reveal four hydraulic jacks. Each one capable of taking a large van or minibus, they each had a car 'on the jacks', half of the ten parking spaces out front was filled with vehicles patiently waiting their turn to get fixed, these were the 'legit' customers, the ones who did not know where the parts for their vehicles came from.

At first glance, it looked like that was all there was. What wasn't seen was that the workshop was only half the depth of the building, and the two doors didn't show what was in the corners.

The doors were just coming down as they turned into the street. Joey punched a number on the phone. A gruff Geordie voice came on.

"About bloody time you two got here," Smithy spoke up. From the sound of it he wasn't impressed. "I'm set up in the building across the street, there's an entrance at the back, use that one, the third window from the right, top floor," he stopped for a moment, then went on, "We need eye round the back, boss head down the end of the street, at the T junction take a right and the next right at the lights, that should bring up and the back of the building, that way we get a good idea where things are at"

"Roger that," Jacko replied, glancing over at Joey. It would be Joey going into the building. He knew where the trackers were. He'd been the one taking the shots. Joey was also the best of the three of them at disarming burglar alarms and the like, "What about Joey?"

"Looks like a standard burglar alarm from here," Smithy replied. "Place has cameras, wouldn't be surprised if they were connected to one of 'ems phone, not sure if there's a blind spot yet though" Joey was making a mental note of everything he was being told, "three cameras out front, one on each corner looking down each end of the street, and one over the door looking at whoever enters the building, the two on the corners are wide-angle, but the one over the door seems to be for recognition only"

"Thanks for that," Joey replied, "gives me an idea for if I find nothing out the back,"

"Any ideas where the car is?" Jacko asked. They couldn't see anything that resembled the Mondeo outside. Then again, it would have been pretty dumb to leave it there. They just hoped it wasn't in the back.

"Nah" Smithy replied, "not seen it. Must 'have arrived just afore I got 'ere" there was a slight pause before he went on, "Probably in the back, that could be a problem if they've already started work on it"

"Hopefully," Sandy cut in, she'd been listening, "they'll just think they're bullets that bounced off something soft before hitting the panel," but even she sounded doubtful.

"One look at 'em will show even the rank amateur that's not what they are, they're stainless steel casings," Joey went on, "even armour piercing don't use that, anyone who knows about this will know the casing is protecting something, we gotta get in before they find 'em,"

Bullets have two parts, there's the 'brass' part which is exactly that, a brass shell that holds the actual bullet in place, inside the brass 'casing' is an explosive charge, it used to be gunpowder, but in modern weapons, it's usually Cordite when the chemicals get 'mixed' they ignite and the force of the explosion causes whatever is there to get pushed out of the way, or in this case, pushed along a long narrow tube (a barrel) getting faster and faster as it goes.

The 'shell' itself used to be made of Lead simply because it was easy to shape into a ball and could be easily handled, today they're mostly made out of a mix of Lead and Nickel, hard enough to do serious damage at high speed, but as it slows down, it becomes soft enough to flatten causing more damage, armour piercing have a small Tungsten bolt in the middle that when the shell 'flattens out' is much harder and carries on straight through whatever stopped the first part causing devastation to whatever stopped the first. Stainless steel is harder than the Nickel and Lead compound. It wouldn't break. It would be a dead giveaway to someone who knew what they were looking for.

"Then let's hope they're thicker than we think they are," Jacko replied, "meanwhile let's work on a plan." He pulled the vehicle into a car park a few buildings down from the back of the garage. They were outside the range of the cameras. From here on in, they would be on foot.

Twenty minutes later, they were on the second floor of the building opposite the back of the garage. Downstairs was some kind of shop. Upstairs looked as if it hadn't been visited in years. There was dust everywhere, a table and a couple of chairs made up the total of the furniture.

There were still a couple of cars outside the garage. They could be clients, or workers. "Smithy, any idea if there are still folks inside working?"

"Still one or two," Smithy replied, @but I doubt they're working. I can see the canteen. Looks like there's four of 'em playing cards and drinking a few beers, kind of Happy hour." He replied.

That was frustrating, it was getting late, and the plan was to tell the cops overnight so that they'd raid the place first thing in the morning. Just as they were going to work, and hopefully before they got the chance to ship any parts out. Joey wasn't sure how long he'd need to disable the alarms and find the stuff. Still, it was what it was, *no use crying over what I can't change*, he thought. He was still working on a way in. It looked like there was a blind spot that led him to the window of what he thought would be one of the toilets in there, but he needed the place clear first.

"Looks like they're getting ready to leave" Smithy finally spoke up, Joey looked at his watch, a full forty-five minutes had passed since they got into the room, Joey had used every one of them to get ready and check his equipment, but still the wait had felt like an eternity. "One of them's just put the alarm on, they're heading for the door."

"We'll give 'em a half an hour," Jacko turned to Joey, who was checking his equipment, "any chance we can override the alarm?"

"Got it sussed boss," Joey replied making a final check on the device he was checking. It looked like a plastic lunchbox with wires sticking out of each end, one from each end, both had crocodile clips for connecting to a terminal, "clip this up to either side of the alarm box and I can put any code in I like. We just bypass the security code"

Thirty minutes later, it was going dark outside. The streetlights had come on, but there was still some daylight left.

Six cameras surrounded the building, covering every angle when you approached from the street. It looked almost impossible to approach without being seen. But looks can be deceiving.

Four of the cameras had wide-angle lenses, they were set on each corner looking diagonally across the street, with almost one hundred and eighty-degree arcs the interlocked in places, but not directly in front or behind the building, other buildings got in the way.

Over the two entrances (one front, one at the back) were two more cameras, but they had a narrow focus covering only the path to the door. Approach to an angle of ten degrees and you wouldn't be seen. That was the first thing Joey noticed.

The second was where the junction box serving the alarm pad was. It was on the outside, just left of the back door.

The control pad itself was inside at the front, but tap into the system and you can bypass the pad. That's what he intended to do.

One last check of everything and he was ready to go. As soon as that was done, he spoke into his lapel-mike.

"Are we good to go?"

"All good here" Smithy was first to reply.

"All go here," Sandy spoke next. She was monitoring everything electronically, even the building's phone system. Hopefully, if it detected Joey's approach, she'd be able to warn them even if she couldn't stop the signal being sent.

Joey looked at Jacko, who just gave him a 'thumbs up'. He opened the door and stepped through, "on my way"

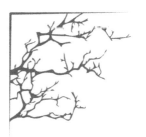

Chapter 35

Serkov was still on the train when it got to its terminus at the Elephant and Castle. As soon as it stopped, he went for the door, heading for the escalator.

Mac wasn't far away. Just close enough to see where he went. Yet far enough that Serkov didn't see him, hopefully giving the impression he wasn't being followed.

The escalators were between the north and southbound platforms. The train on the northbound platform just about to leave. Serkhov made it look as if he was going for the southbound platform.

"Shit" Mac cussed as Serkov ran and jumped onto the northbound train. The doors were closing.

Sprinting for the last door still open. A suitcase jammed in the door by a hapless traveller, the door released giving both the suitcase and Mac time to get on.

"Sandy, we're heading back into the city." He spoke into his lapel mike. "He's been trying to lose any tail, don't think he's aware of me though."

Serkov was in the middle car, Mac was in the one behind. The car was full, so that gave him a good excuse to stand. He could see into the next car from where he was.

"Regents Park" Mac spoke into the mike as Serkov disembarked, "heading upstairs"

"Roger that," Sandy replied, "stay with him."

One of the 'green areas' in the city. Regents Park takes its name from the only time when a King who was regarded as being insane ruled Britain.

King George III was declared insane, so his son, 'The Prince Regent', was appointed to rule as his representative.

To the north of the city of the day was a Royal hunting ground that had been owned by the crown since Henry VIII 'acquired' the land in the dissolution of the monasteries during the reformation.

In the sixteenth century, it was a good day's ride from the palace at Hampton Court. By the end of the eighteenth, the turn of the 19th century, it was on the outskirts of what was then London, and became the fashionable place to live. Huge Georgian mansions ringing the outside of the Park, giving way to botanical gardens and even a zoo which became famous as London Zoo.

Today it houses gardens, the Zoo and Europe's biggest mosque, a mecca for tourists. It was perfect for losing a tail, but the team still had one ace to play.

"Mac, I've got him on camera with the F.R.C," Sandy spoke for the first time since he got off the train, "back off a while, make a change and I'll tell you where to go."

"Roger that, keep me updated." He knew he didn't really need to. Sandy wasn't a novice at this, but it was a kind of automatic reaction.

There was a sign for public toilets to the right. He followed the sign and went into the Gents' toilets. The urinals were on the right, but a bank of five cubicles was on the left. Four were not in use, only the one in the far corner was in use. He slipped into the nearest one and undid the small holdall he was carrying. Two minutes later a jeans-wearing tourist stepped out, complete with sunglasses and camera, though even that couldn't totally hide the short haircut.

The stubble of the last few days might throw off anyone expecting a 'Military' look, but stubble was the norm for Special Forces. "Okay, I'm ready" Mac came back on the line, "where is he?"

Three hours later, the sun was beginning to disappear beneath the skyline of the buildings. They were still 'on the chase. Serkov had led them a merry dance through Regents Park. Then onto a bus and back into the centre of the city again, this time stopping at Battersea Park, literally a stone's throw from Vauxhall House, the home of MI6.

"Sandy," Mac spoke for the first time since they'd arrived at the park, "Northwest corner, a park bench, he might go for a dead letter drop!"

"Could be," Sandy confirmed, her fingers literally flying over the keyboards of the laptop she was using. She had two laptops working 'full bore' at her disposal. One was keeping track of what Joey and Jacko were up to. The other she'd used to hack into the mainframe of the Met's network of closed-circuit TV cameras. Every inch of London was covered with them. But in the public areas, it went much further. George Orwell, in his most frightening picture of the future, London never dreamed of how much surveillance there would be. And Sandy, if she didn't have the keys to unlock its potential, she knew where the keys were kept. She was watching every move.

A dead letter drop was a relic from the cold war when a spy needed to get information either into a place or out of it without being seen 'cavorting' with the enemy. Simple, yet effective, and all it called for was a bit of lateral thinking.

A spy who needed to send a message would simply write the message and hide it in 'plain sight', usually in a public place, but not one you'd think of normally. A park bench. Even a gutter at a famous building (maybe using a loose brick, etc.) Then they would place an ad in the local paper. Usually in code, telling the recipient exactly where to look.

Once the recipient got the message, they would go pick up the information and place another ad. Or even a notice in the obituaries that the first one would read and know that the message was passed, there wasn't any need to go back and check the hiding place, Serkov might be using this method to talk to his contact 'The mole' inside MI6.

"I'm downloading the footage for the last forty-eight hours," Sandy said. "I'll keep the cameras on so we see who turns up just in case." She began typing commands into the laptop, glancing over to the other laptop she saw Joey was about to enter the garage.

"Oh, shit" she let out a squeal, a hand going to her mouth in an automatic reaction when she realised she'd sworn out loud. Quickly recovering, she hit Mac's speed dial,

"Mac, I've got the footage, get back here pronto, the shit's about to hit the fan."

As soon as she was off the line, she clicked the laptop's email program open. Finding the address she needed, she typed a simple message in code. "Fish on the line, begin the reeling in."

Chapter 36

Joey came at the building from an oblique angle. Avoiding the cameras was vital. Joey didn't want to leave any trace of what he was about to do. He was carrying a holdall with the tools he was going to need for the job. As soon as he got to the door, he put the holdall down, unzipped it and took out a Stanley screwdriver. The screwdriver had multiple heads; he selected a Phillips screwdriver and got to work undoing the junction box.

The junction box for the alarm was just to the left of the door, but the camera looked directly at the path. There was a blind spot right at the door, but off to the left. The camera covered the alarm security pad, but not the junction box.

It took him about two minutes to bypass the alarm pad and disable the security alarm. Another minute and he had the lock picked. The door creaked slightly as he opened it, a clear sign the back door wasn't used very often.

As soon as he had the alarm sorted he carefully replaced the Junction box cover making sure that the screws all looked identical to when he first undid them, once that was done he did a quick check to make sure he hadn't missed a thing before putting the screwdriver back in the holdall and zipping the bag up. There would be no evidence.

Slipping in silently he waited a few moments for his eyesight to adjust to the darkness.

There was a second glass door. On the right was the office, on the left was the lunchroom. The office looked too small to go all the way to the edge of the building, but he couldn't see any door. *'Must be in the main workshop,*' he thought as he cautiously began trying the door. It was unlocked.

Four cars were in the workshop, not unusual for the size of the garage, but the security of the building was all wrong. *'Where's the sodding Rolls Royce?'* he thought to himself, *'with this security, the sodding place should be full of 'em, that or a Ferrari or two.'* Instead, they were two Japanese cars, a BMW and a Volvo, nice cars, but significantly below the price tag for the security.

In the next room was a different story, four more cars, two of which were high-end sports jobs. To Joey, they looked like a Ferrari and a Maserati. They were partly dismantled. The third one was just a chassis, possibly a car being rebuilt. The last one looked really odd because of its 'ordinariness'. It was the Mondeo.

The Mondeo was so 'ordinary it just looked like a green-skinned Alien on planet Earth. Something just wasn't right. He couldn't say what it was, but it just didn't seem right having an average car in the same garage as the two supercars! Also, the fact that they were half stripped down gave a strange feeling. There was something else going on here that he was sure of. *Better get my arse into gear, get the job done and get the hell out,'* was his immediate thought. 'after all, she said it was a chop-shop,'

He'd brought a torch, an Army issue one which had the light sitting at a right angle to the handle, the bottom of the battery pack (which was also the handle) was flat so soldiers could stand it up anywhere and still have two hands-free to work with whatever they needed to work on. He clipped the red filter on and turned the torch on; it gave him just enough light to do what he needed to.

A quick search of the back of the Mondeo showed where the projectiles had hit. They'd passed through the back panel. A couple of seconds later, he'd popped the boot or trunk open and searched inside. Both bullets were in the back panel, smashed into the back wall.

A pair of tweezers came in really handy, and a little gun oil. Dabbing a tiny amount of oil onto a rag he used the tweezers to push the rag into the crevasse the bullets had made. Slowly a tiny amount penetrated between the bullets and the car, eventually popping the round out.

The criminals would know that the car had been shot at, and the bullets were still in the car's boot if they saw the holes, but no rounds, they'd know something had been tampered with. He was prepared for that.

He'd take the cases off two rounds earlier in the day. Now he took the first one out, punched it between the tweezers, and pushed it into one of the holes. As soon as it was wedged in, he did the same to the second. As soon as both were in, away went the tweezers. Out came a rubber mallet and both were hit hard enough to knock them firmly into place.

'*Good use of a Manchester screwdriver*' he smiled to himself, remembering what his Dad used to call a Hammer. 'If only you could see me now, Dad.' he packed everything away.

"Joey," Smithy's voice sounded urgent, "Stay put. The security company is doing the rounds, driving down the street."

Joey was still by the car. He almost froze, then slowly crouched down, an automatic reaction. There were no windows in the room and very few in the entire building, but noise still carries, and that was the main concern, knock a spanner off, or anything over and the latter would be enough to 'wake the dead'.

'Two places in this street' the guard thought to herself as she wound the window of the car down. The security pad was right by the driver's window. Reaching out, she waved a small device over a pad. The gate opened.

"Just a security guard doing the rounds," Smithy whispered into the mike, "She'll drive around the yard, check all the vehicles are where they're supposed to be. Might get out and check a few doors at the office building or workshop, then she'll be out of our hair, standby," he reassured everyone.

Jacko couldn't see what was going on. It was on Smithy's side of the building. That didn't mean he could be careless, one wrong sound, or move, and that might trigger an alarm that would have the guard coming over for a look. He stayed perfectly still, then again, he was sitting down already.

The gates closed behind the car, but no one moved. They all knew the guard would only be a couple of minutes in the yard. She may be a security guard, but like everyone else, they had targets and deadlines to meet. Forty businesses a night, minimum of two visits 'at random' but at least an hour apart, she'd only be a few minutes zt the site, five at the max, and she'd be back later in the night.

Three minutes later, the car was heading out of the driveway and down the street. Unfortunately, towards where Joey was, he could hear the engine and tensed up. The car drove right past, then stopped at another place down the road, car wreckers. This time, the guard got out of the car and went in on foot. Ten minutes later, she was back and away.

"Street's clear," Smithy reported as soon as the car disappeared. "Guard shouldn't be back for at least an hour."

"Any chance we can track her?" Jacko asked. He really hated surprises.

"Are you serious?" Sandy cut in over the link. "I'm tracking you folks and following Mac through London. You think I'm Superwoman or something?"

"Guess it's a no to that then, boss," Joey chipped in, everyone knew he'd have a huge smile on his face "humour relaxes the tension," he'd tell them, and he was right, "I'll be out in a jiffy." He carried on, "Give me five, then call the cavalry, meanwhile you folks have a big day tomorrow, so get ready,"

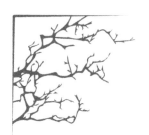

Chapter 37

" The car you and Sergeant Harris are interested in," the voice spoke. It was the same voice that had sent the first message, "is in a garage in Cirencester. A chop-shop I believe you call them, owned and run by the Russian Mafia. It was delivered this afternoon and they'll be dismantling it,"

"Now you've heard the message," BJ assured Harris, "I called you to set this up as soon as I got it, and yes, my source is first-rate." She assured him, "I'm pretty sure they're linked to the intelligence services, but can't confirm it."

"And you trust them?" Harris asked.

"It's the same one who gave me the information about Akbari, the stuff I was almost killed over," she assured him, "so yeah, I trust the source, but there's more that you need to pay attention to!"

"The garage is known to have weapons," the voice went on. "Consider them well armed and extremely dangerous. They have at least one Mac 10 and possibly AK47s, though we haven't confirmed how many. Exercise extreme caution."

"That's it?" He asked, slightly disappointed, "you want me to get a warrant with that information? We'd have no chance!"

"No," she replied, "What we need is a ruse to get in and check the building!" She looked slightly sheepish. She knew it was asking a lot. The whole thing was stretching the bounds of credibility, "what we need is to use this," she waved the phone screen in front of his face, "to get your boss to give us a bomb drill, we get that," she put the phone away, "we get in using the excuse of checking the building, no need for a warrant!"

"You want me to go with that?" he was incredulous. "you realise everything we find would be illegal. We'd be crucified in court." He assured her. "Not with that! I want a warrant, and I want a hard copy,"

"How about this then" she slammed a brown envelope about twelve inches long and eight inches wide down on the table, it was about an eighth of an inch thick, she slid some papers out, the top one was a signed warrant for searching the premises. He didn't know the Judge's name, but it was official, under it were ten or more photographs of cars and what looked like quantities of drugs, "This enough for yer" her Manchester accent coming through before he could say anything she went on, "and yes, it's the same garage, taken inside, don't ask me how, I've got no bloody idea, but it's a drug deal that went on apparently, inside the bloody place!"

How or when the photos were taken she did not know, but they didn't look 'faked' or at least not to her they didn't, she had no real idea if they were of the same place, all she knew was someone wanted them to raid the place, and they'd promised the car they were looking for was in there. The photos showed the car entering, and they were time-stamped as yesterday at 4 pm. Less than twelve hours before. Chances were, the car was still there.

Harris wasn't so convinced. He wasn't stupid, if they got this right it would be the biggest bust of their careers, but if the information was wrong, they'd be lucky to stay out of prison let alone still be on the force, he would not throw his career away, but at the same time, he would not let this chance get away.

"Look, it's three in the morning." He began.

"I know that," she shot back testily. "I only got the information last night at eleven, had to check a few things out on the way over. I've got a feed set up from the street cameras for us to watch, to see if the car really is there. It's on my laptop," she began pulling the machine out and setting up.

"Can I see the footage?" He asked. "If it's legit, I'll set things in motion as soon as it's daylight if everything pans out," he went on.

"It will, and can you be ready to roll by mid-morning?" She assured and asked at the same time.

"I get it," he spoke again, "It's a chop-shop,"

"Right," she cut back, "the car will not be whole for much longer, less than a day I'd say before they start shipping parts out, and it's an average family saloon." She turned the machine on. "Can you be ready by mid-morning?"

"One thing at once," he cut back, "but yes, if we need to."

"**A**re you two bloody serious?" It was Harris' immediate boss, the station 'super' short for 'superintendent' who was screaming at them. BJ tried to intervene, one handheld up silenced her. "Let me finish. Do you have any idea the panic it'll cause? And then when the press gets wind of this"

"That's why we want a drill boss," Harris began, "full bells and whistles, so we can get access,"

"You'll have them fawning over a major car theft ring broken," Harris cut him off, "besides,"

"Don't give me that crap," the super silenced him. "I know about the warrant. I've already checked. There's no such warrant logged in the flaming system. That's skating on thin ice. You get caught with that and not only kiss your career goodbye, you'll also be in jail,"

"And if we do nothing," Billie butted in. The super tried to cut her off, but she spoke even louder, "a bunch of thugs get away with murder, attempted murder, gunning people down in the streets for God's sake and who knows how many car thefts, YOU REALLY WANT THAT?"

"But,"

"If we go with a normal warrant and the shit hits the fan, who's going to explain the civilian casualties? Have you seen what an AK47 can do? My intel says they've got at least a couple!" She leaned right in. This may cost her career, she no longer gave a damn. "These pricks killed a man and dumped his body in the Thames, right under the bloody noses of all our bosses in Parliament. Then they tried to gun a man, no, make that three people down in broad daylight on your streets. You really want them to walk away?" She sounded disgusted. The fact was she was disgusted, not with the superintendent, but the entire system that has politicians and the like cowering in a corner because someone 'might not like,' what the police might have to do.

"If you want any more convincing," Bille took a brown manilla envelope out. She took a bundle of things out. They realised they were photographs. Even Harris hadn't seen them before. She spread them out. They were street camera pictures, some from London, others from the scene of the shooting, then following the car from where it was left to the garage. It was there! "How about this? Talk about the chain of custody!"

They arrived without sirens and lights. A Police Landrover at each end of the two streets blocked access off. Armed officers carrying standard-issue MP5s jumped down and started holding up traffic. More vehicles rolled in with Police going door to door evacuating the workers.

One vehicle, a Ford Transit, sides blacked out. The single back door had officers milling around it like bees around a honeypot. The Transit pulled into the curb at the north end of the street, about twenty yards from the barrier. It was the mobile command post or 'CP'

The rest of the officers, instructions given were steadily clearing the street

"What gives officer?" one guy asked.

"Suspect vehicle in the road sir," the cop ushering him out replied, "we're evacuating everyone, we've set up a perimeter just down the road."

"Must be a car bomb, then?" He asked. The cop didn't reply.

Everything was done with a minimum of fuss. Once the word of a bomb got out, no one argued.

Standard procedure in such things is instead of going to all the businesses at once and causing panic, the police quietly visit and evacuate each business one by one. That way, they didn't lose control of the situation. They just didn't tell people where the 'suspect vehicle' was.

Just then a Land Rover pulled up, a late model civilian looking vehicle. Three men and a woman in body armour clambered out. Each one carrying an automatic weapon slung across their shoulder and a pistol strapped to their sides. BJ didn't recognise the weapons at first. They weren't police issue, but looked similar to what she'd seen Special Forces carry, and the sidearms were in hip holsters like the old western gunslingers. Two of them went to the back of the vehicle and started unloading equipment. A third headed towards her and Harris, who were by the command post.

"Detective Sergeant Jones and Sergeant Harris, I presume?" The soldier put out his hand in greeting. There were four others at the 'CP' all four were senior officers. There for the glory if everything went well. If things went pear-shaped, they'd be scarce as hen's teeth. "Captain Jackson," He went on, "Army bomb disposal, heard you might have something you want us to deal with, that right?"

"What? er, who called you folks?" it was the station superintendent asking the questions he was a little 'flummoxed'

"Standard procedure," Jacko lied. "Anyone puts one of these things in. The computer gives us a heads up. We thought it would be good practice to get down here and get the lay of the land. Where's the suspect device?" his eyes were dancing between the people, watching to see what happened next. Everyone looked sheepish.

"Err, it's actually inside, but this is only,"

"A drill, we know. No matter," Jacko replied, "but I need to talk to whoever's in charge of the operation. Is that either of you by any chance?" He asked cheerfully, knowing what the reply would be..

"That'll be sergeant Harris," the most senior officer replied, passing the buck.

"In that case," Jacko replied, his face taking on a sterner look, "there's a cordon in place for onlookers." He pointed to the barrier set up and manned by uniformed officers. "Kindly move your arses behind it!" He escorted them to the cordon and made it clear the officers weren't welcome. Turning to the police officers manning the cordon, he simply said, "no one passes, and I mean NO ONE!"

"Sir" the two cops jumped to attention, 'Not arguing with this guy', they thought.

"Make sure of it. I don't care who they are!" Jacko turned to talk with Harris. "Sorry for seeming to take over sergeant, just needed to establish the cordon. As I said, you ARE in charge. It's just we know what, or rather whom, we're dealing with." He turned to one of the team. Sandy was heading to the CP, laptops slung in computer bags over her shoulder, "You know what to do Sandy?"

"Is the Pope a bloody catholic?" Sandy shot back, "course I do" she closed the door as soon as she was in the vehicle.

Two operators in the command post were coordinating the teams. One team at each end. Their job was to keep Joe public. Two other teams, each with two people, were slowly emptying each of the buildings of people and taking them to the barriers.

"Right, listen up," Sandy spoke loud enough to get their attention. "This is not a drill. I know you were told it was, but it's not. It's also not a bomb" she let that sink in for a moment. "What we have is a serious criminal gang responsible for at least one murder and numerous other violent incidents. They're well armed and extremely dangerous." She stopped to let that sink in. Everyone in the CP stopped and turned towards her. It was obvious who was taking control there. Besides the two operators, there were a couple of others. Mainly people working computer screens, digging out whatever information they could find for the men and women 'on the ground' it was vital everyone had whatever information they needed as soon as they needed it.

"Before you go looking," she turned to the researchers working with the keyboards, "The garage is owned by a front company. It's basically owned by the Russian mafia. They're using it as a chop-shop for whenever they need to get rid of a piece of machinery." She made the universal 'quote' sign with the two fingers on each hand, "Mostly it does legit business, but whenever they need something gotten rid of, these guys get the job, that and a great storehouse for weapons and the like." She added the last bit to get their attention. "Truth is, we know the vehicle is there. We made sure of that. What we don't know" every eye was on her, and she knew it, "is what else is there, so start searching, so be prepared for anything."

There was silence in the CP for a full ten seconds after she finished. It felt like ten hours as just what they were dealing with sank in. Then, slowly at first, each one turned back to their screens. The operators began relaying information to the teams and everyone began taking on the roles they were required to do.

"Charlie papa, this is the south barrier," a call came over the radio. "We have a bit of a situation here." The operator turned to Sandy, she covered her mike, "I think this might be serious she said quietly, then turning to the mike again, she called up, "Charlie papa to south barrier go ahead"

"We've got members of the press here wanting to know the situation. They want to know why they can't broadcast," the barrier team came back.

"Inform them we have a situation with an unexploded device" Sandy took the mike. "We are evacuating the area. Tell them there's a press blackout at the moment and all frequencies are disabled due to possible remote detonation. That's why they can't transmit." She lied, and she knew they would know it, but the fact was they were being jammed as well, the Police jammers used for preventing remote detonation of a device blocked every signal for up to half a mile, and they operated on every frequency available, not just the ones mobile phones used.

"Passed that message on," the team replied, "but they still want to know when they'll be able to broadcast, and is there a chance of an interview for being so patient?" From the tone it was obvious the press had been anything but that, but that went with the territory. She'd do the same in their shoes.

"Roger," she replied over the radio, "inform them we'll gladly oblige after the incident." She clicked the mike off, "Keep me apprised of that situation." Sandy told the operator. She had no intention of giving the interview herself, it would be set up for DS Jones and Sergeant Harris, if they wanted it, they just didn't know it yet, *'won't hurt their careers'* she thought knowing it would seriously embarrass their bosses who'd refused to look at the evidence.

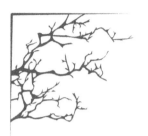

Chapter 38

"Okay, let's cut through the Bullshit shall we? Just what is really going on here?" BJ asked Jacko as soon as they were separated from the rest. Jacko had teamed her up with himself going to the front of the building. Mac and Sergeant Harris were teamed up together. Their job would be to segregate the people as they came out. No one had explained much at this point. A third member of the squad had taken two officers around the back of the building. It seemed really strange unless you were trying to prevent escape. That was all she could think of. The fourth member seemed to play with some kind of remote control robot on tracks. A very strange robot with a camera fitted to a long tube-like structure and a mechanical arm that looked like it had some kind of firearm fitted. She knew the arm usually had a high-pressure water cannon fitted, but this one didn't look right! "And just who are you?" she looked sideways at him as they prepared to approach the door.

"The last question first," Jacko began. "We're known as Scorpion One, and our job is taking down scumbags like these." She knew he was only telling part of the truth, but it would have to be enough. "These clowns are only part of the wider picture, but they're an important part, and they have the evidence you need to get the men behind Akbari's murder."

That stopped her literally in her tracks. So far, she hadn't mentioned the case. "What do you know about that?" She couldn't help the question.

"You know whom Akbari worked for, don't you?" He asked as they began picking up their equipment. She was uncomfortable around firearms, and it was strange that a supposed 'bomb disposal' guy was bristling with them. He wasn't carrying a weapon she recognised. The team had made sure their 'commandos' were ready for them, all that is except for Smithy. He had 'something special; as he put it. The captain was also carrying one sidearm she could see, and probably others she couldn't.

"He worked for MI6," she replied, then added, "Which is strange as they normally 'clean their own house' and we rarely get to hear much about it,"

"Except this time," Jacko cut her off, "we hoped a rottweiler would catch the case, and MI6 have tried to shut you down, but there are people inside who want this in the public domain."

"But isn't it national security and all that crap?" She protested slightly. "They usually fire off at us, they get us to back off, and all that!"

"Usually," He admitted, "but this one has too many rotten apples trying to hide, instead this time, we want to expose a few and watch the rest scurry for cover. Believe me, there'll be quite a few, anyway, enough of the chit-chat. Let's get on with this," he banged on the door. "POLICE, OPEN UP."

"Alexei, it's me, Sergei, we've got trouble down at the Garage," the voice on the other end of the phone sounded worried. Not frantic, but concerned, "The Police are here, banging on the door demanding to be let in."

"Why?" he demanded. "What for?"

"No idea," the reply came back. "I called you first. The others are making everything ready. Did you know anything about this?" the voice demanded.

"Don't be stupid," Alex replied. "No one told me anything about it. What do they want?"

"They're saying it's some kind of exercise, looking for bombs," Sergei replied. He sounded on edge and had good reason to be. The Mondeo used in the shooting a few days before was sat in the damn place, and he'd had no time to start work on it. It even had the 'VIN' number still attached to the Chassis. He indicated to another mechanic to get to work covering it up.

Everyone knows that cars have number plates to help track the ownership of a vehicle, and even a chassis number. But very few know of what's called the 'Vehicle Identification Number' or 'VIN' for short. That is also used for tracking when a vehicle is stolen.

The Number plate is on the back and front of the car. That's obvious to deal with. The chassis number is often riveted to the chassis in a place where the mechanics know. It's never removed, but because it's riveted there, they can be removed by clever thieves. The VIN is a whole different story. It's stamped into the frame. Usually in the door arch and into one of the main supports, you can't remove it without seriously affecting the safety of the vehicle because you have to cut the plate out, and that causes serious problems for all except the best of thieves, Alex and Sergei were the best at what they did.

"What are they looking for?" The question was automatic, out of his lips before he even realised, "is everything away?"

"Place is clean boss. As much as we can make it, just the car."

"Can you get it out, away from there?" the worry came through in his voice.

"What do you think?" Sergei hissed. "We got it last night. Mikhail started work on it, but it's in pieces. It still has the VIN number on it!"

English people wouldn't understand the words used in the reply, but Sandy spoke pretty good Russian. They just didn't know it, but even she was struggling with some phrases they used.

Sandy already had things set in motion. She had an extra tent. A nine-foot by nine-foot military-style tent they'd brought with them. Two officers had set the tent up. Then put a chair and desk in it. A flap connected it to the rest of the CP. She was monitoring the phones from her devices, though they could only see the two laptops.

"Smithy," Sandy spoke into the Bluetooth mike. The team were still all wearing them. They were on a separate frequency to the Police network. "You still got the two plods with you?"

"Affirmative" Smithy sounded businesslike, even though they were on separate frequencies to the cops. He was right there with his two, they'd still hear his half of the conversation, "What do you need?"

"Just confirmed one bird is not in the nest. Make sure the 'Eaglet' doesn't fly away," She replied, "we need a pickup, you take your two and do that. I'll get Mac and Sergeant Harris to enter through the back."

"Roger that," Smithy replied and clicked off. Turning to the cops he said, "come on boys, time for some real police work"

Smithy took his phone out, glanced at the screen, which had Google maps displayed, saw the markers and decided.

"Leave the car." He told the cops, "follow me" and started sprinting in the direction where the other marker was, "and move your bloody arses"

Sprinting in full body armour isn't easy at the best of times. Add weapons and ammo and you're pushing the limits for most people. Smithy wasn't even breaking a sweat.

Sprinting down the street he swerved left at the first junction. Using a parked car like a wall he planted a foot on the centre pillar between the doors and pushed off without slowing. Gaining speed and distance. The two cops did the same.

They went straight through the next junction. A car that had been coming down the street braked hard. The screech saying it all. The car behind wasn't so fortunate. Driving too fast and too close she swerved missing the car in front, but not the lamppost on the left.

"You two," Smithy turned and hissed. It was meant to be a whisper, but spoke a bit too loud. He made sure he was heard. "We need this prick detained under the investigation of Terrorism ACT, you're up for it". It wasn't a request.

The place was a small cafe, a 'greasy spoon' kind of place, with six tables. Two were occupied, one had two heavy-set men sat there, neither had anything in front of them, the other had one, also heavy-set but slightly younger looking, he was on the phone, they were getting ready to leave, the bulges under their armpits suggesting trouble.

"I'll take the back" Smithy took off like a steeplechaser in the Grand National, "Go" he shouted as he cleared the first wall, a six-foot leap.

"What do you think is going on, the boss?" One of the 'heavies' asked as they stood up. Each one reaching for their coats. They headed for the door as it opened. Two cops carrying weapons walked in, everyone stopped in their tracks, the Russians backed up, the 'heavies' moving in front of the boss.

"Just stay where you are!" the older of the two cops demanded, "and no funny stuff". His weapon was already in the shoulder and pointing in their direction. He checked the safety.

The two big guys were at least a hundred and thirty kilos. That's two hundred and fifty pounds each. Both of them put their heads down and barrelled into the cops trying to knock them flying. The two cops had expected something like it, and fast as lightning, they sidestepped neatly. Grabbing their opponents they deftly used a little Aikido and used the big guys weight against them. Slamming them both into the ground hard, "You're both under arrest" the older of the two screamed as they roughly wrenched hands behind backs, plasticuffs out and clipped into place they were secure.

Every operation has a plan for 'when the proverbial hits' and theirs was 'do whatever you need to buy time for Sergei to get away'. Once that happened, then he could do whatever was needed. Warn whoever needed to know and hopefully get you some legal help on the way. Brits loved to play everything 'by the rules' so a lawyer was a must, or just tell the big boss to make things like money or drugs disappear. They just followed protocol like they did this every week.

Sergei made for the back door. He knew there was a car, an old Ford parked out back. The owner wouldn't miss the car for a few hours. The old Ford was so easy to break into that one Ford key in five would fit any of them. He had that key with him all the time. He also knew there'd be enough petrol in the car to get him out of town. That was all he needed.

He slipped through the back door frame and turned. That's when the lights went out as he met a fist coming in the opposite direction. The thud was so loud the two cops stopped their cuffing the other two heavies momentarily and turned only to see Smithy dragging an unconscious Sergei back into the room. "Cuff this one too while you're at it!" He spoke to the two cops, "By the way, good job, we can read 'em their rights when he comes round." He then turned to the stunned cafe owner who'd been glued to the spot while all this was going on and asked. "Any chance of three cuppas for your hard-working security forces?"

"**S**corpion four, you ready?" Jacko's voice came over the intercom. They'd gone back to their callsigns so as not to give their real names away in the operation.

"Roger that," Joey replied. "Barrow will be ready in thirty seconds." He reached into the vehicle and lifted what looked like a small radio-controlled tracked vehicle with what seemed like a periscope out. Putting the vehicle down he picked up a remote control unit with a small joystick on it and pushed the stick forward. The vehicle lurched forward. They were in business.

The whole charade was that there was a bomb somewhere. That meant they had to be seen to be looking for the device, and if the job is hazardous to life and limb, then you never send a human to do a job that a machine can do, that was the 'Wheelbarrow's' job.

The little 'periscope' had two devices fitted. One was a remote camera so that the operator could see what he or she was looking at, and the other was Joey's adaptation. Instead of the normal water cannon, it had a single barrel 12-gauge shotgun.

Car bombs almost always use plastic explosive, but plastic explosive, no matter what kind is used, are all pretty safe to handle under normal circumstances. It won't catch fire. Won't explode if you drop it. You can even shoot the stuff and it won't explode. For an explosion to happen, you need an electrical current, and that means a detonator and an electrical source like a battery. Disconnect those and you stop the explosion, hence Joey's 'Wheelbarrow' having a water cannon to take out the detonator while the operator is still a safe distance away, Joey had fitted the shotgun that could do that, but he had another purpose for it.

"Scorpion four to one and two," Joey called back as the machine rolled forward, "We're on our way"

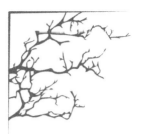

Chapter 39

"Police" the voice outside shouted above the banging on the door. "Open up." It wasn't a request. "NOW!"

"What the?" the mechanics, all three of them, nearly jumped through the roof. They looked at each other. No one knew what was going on. What they knew was there was a car in the shop that was so 'hot' it wasn't just going to burn anyone in the area, it was going to 'deep fry' everyone.

The roller door of the garage was partly open, one of them ran to push the button to close it, the button didn't respond, and a strange little-tracked vehicle, one that looked like a toy tank was slowly trundling towards the half-of the and door.

"We have a robot coming to the garage door," one of them yelled in Russian. "I break it" he reached for a wrench.

"No," one of the others yelled. He pointed to the third guy. "YOU," he pointed, "go check everything is hidden." Turning back to the first he carried on, "Igor, that robot is a device, the British use them a lot, see the periscope" he pointed to the top, "it has a special gun"

"So?" Igor shouted back, "big deal, I hit that first."

"And if it goes off," the first one cuts in. "Every cop out there will come in guns ready to shoot anything that moves. We'll have no chance!"

"OPEN THIS DOOR! YOU HAVE FIVE SECONDS" the voice out front demanded, then started counting down, "five, four"

"Okay! Okay," the first Russian spoke as he began unlocking the door. Why they wanted this one open when the garage main door was already up was beyond him. He opened it slightly, "what do you want?"

"We have reason to believe," BJ explained, "that an explosive device has been placed in your,"

"There's nothing here" he dismissed them and tried to shut the door. It bounced back hitting him on the nose.

"We'll be the judges of that sir" Jacko moved forward, straight into the big Russian who ended up in a heap on the floor. The Russian had a good four inches extra height, and thirty or so kilos, around sixty pounds, and Jacko didn't really push, more like bulldozed his way into the building, and the obstruction was simply flattened.

"Hey, what you?" the big Russian began getting to his feet. "You can't do that, it's a free country,"

"It's a bomb threat," BJ cut in. "When that happens, we can do what we need to in order to ensure public safety," she was in Jacko's wake, but just as strong, "Now stand aside and let us do our jobs,"

"Stupid bitch, I TELL YOU THERE'S,"

"CAN IT!!" She wheeled around and grabbed the Russian by the throat. Kids from Moss-side never take that kind of crap from anyone. It's the kind of talk that will get you a knife in the throat. "I don't give a shit what you said" she might have been a good deal shorter than the guy, but it was obvious who was in charge in this exchange."WE ARE checking the place, and you can either accept it, or we can talk down the local station, and I mean under the investigation of Terrorism act of two thousand and eight. That could take a few days, and by the way Lawyers aren't welcome, NOW WHICH IS IT TO BE?" she almost threw him down.

"Two and four" Jacko spoke into his radio, "begin the search" he walked back to the Russian, "Now sir, if you'll accompany us outside, we can arrange a place for you to wait while we check the place out.

"I told you," the big Russian began again. By now, the others from the Garage had gathered round. A couple of them had wrenches in their hands. Billie glanced at Jacko nervously. Jacko seemed to be totally relaxed, almost as if he was enjoying the whole affair. He was, immensely, but relaxed he wasn't. He was ready for anything. "There's nothing here!"

"In that case sir," Jacko began, "you won't mind us checking the place out, will you?" he seemed oblivious to the others in the garage, one of whom had come up behind him, Billie saw the wrench start to fall, she almost got a scream out, but not quite.

Jacko pivoted on his right leg, the left coming up and out in a Taekwondo kick that caught the would-be assailant in the side of the head. He went down. Two others began a swing, but stopped mid flight as fifty thousand volts jolted them. Tasers attached to their skin, Mac and Sgt. Harris didn't let go of their triggers until the men were unconscious on the floor. Others were trying to join in, but they were facing five drawn weapons, and they had none.

"Up against the wall, all of you, MOVE IT" Jacko screamed as Joey and Mac began manhandling them. No one was being gentle. Harris moved to cover them as Mac began a frisk search. As each was searched, they were handcuffed using the plastic ties called 'plasticuffs' and led away. Meanwhile, Joey went back to using the 'Wheelbarrow' to check out the building.

"Under the prevention and investigation of terrorism act of 2008 we are hereby detaining you folks for further questioning" Sgt Harris began, they'd run through this before the Op began with the team, Jacko had clarified that any detaining had to be done by Harris, and it had to be 'done right.' "You are not under arrest, therefore Lawyers are not required, but should you withhold information during the investigation it is likely to affect your residence permit and may result in you being deported as 'Persona non grata' he knew that part was a total fabrication, but they likely didn't and the last thing they wanted was to be sent back to mother Russia.

"That's screwed things up a bit" Billie was angry, she just wasn't sure who it was with, the idiot Russian for arguing, or Jacko for being 'pig-headed'.

"Why?" Jacko sounded surprised. He was heading for one of the rooms at the back. Joey had the robot in the building and was working through the first vehicle bay.

The standard 'Wheelbarrow' is normally only used to defuse explosive devices, and it does it by firing a small jet of water powerful enough to rip out any electrical wiring and soak any connection. But the one he was using, along with the modification that was the shotgun, had one other slight modification. It had an extra small box. Four inches by three, attached to the arm that the camera was on. It looked just like a camera, except where the lens should be something similar to a mesh face. It looked like a microphone, but the noise didn't affect it. Aromas did. It was an electronic sniffer.

The finest sniffing device is still the canine nose, but not far behind, and able to be programmed for specific aromas much quicker is the electronic sniffer, and Joey had programmed it for specific things.

"Boss," Joey spoke into his lapel radio. Everyone snapped back to attention. He wasn't in the room where the Mondeo was yet. "We've got a hit, sniffers reading GSR on this vehicle but no device, someone used a firearm from this vehicle" he pointed to one of the vehicles on the ramps, it was a Land Rover.

"Roger that," Jacko replied. "Sgt. Harris, you better get your people in here. This room is safe, but start tearing that vehicle apart," he started walking over to the Land Rover, then turning to Billie he carried on, "you were saying?"

"It's a bloody Landrover, with a rifle rack!" Billie replied frustrated, "probably some upper-class idiot who enjoys hunting!"

"In the middle of town?" Jacko shot back, not too impressed Billie was willing to overlook the obvious, "besides, this vehicle" he slapped the Lannie's tyres, "has never seen a dirt track, let alone the hunting country!"

"Holy crap," Joey whistled to himself as they went slowly through the room. He'd switched the camera to infrared when the sniffer unit picked something up in the door panel of the Mondeo he couldn't believe what he was seeing, "Jackpot boss, we got 'em, we've got the smoking gun, and I mean literally.

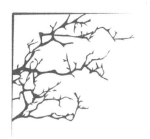

Chapter 40

"This is the news at one from the BBC, and I'm your host Alastair Burnet," the newsreader began the bulletin. The station was one of two dozen channels they were monitoring. It was amazing how much valuable intelligence came to light through commercial news channels.

"Earlier this morning, police raided a commercial property believed to be linked to the shooting last week on the outskirts of Bristol,"

That one sentence brought everything to a halt. No one in the operations centre at MI6 was even aware anything had been going on. Let alone anything linked to the shootings.

"TURN THAT UP!" a supervisor screamed at whoever had the controls. This was a major screw up and someone was going to pay heavily for it. She just didn't want it to be here. "And get me everything they effing well have NOW!!"

"Several firearms were found as well as a vehicle believed to be linked to both the shooting and the murder of a man in central London," the newsreader went on. But by that time, the phones were going crazy, and someone wasn't happy.

"My boss was at his club having lunch when a reporter called him asking about the situation" the voice, a female one whom the officer had heard of but never met. She was the one you didn't want to annoy. A brief career could be the result, and it was abundantly obvious he was probably going that way simply because he was on duty today. "So, kindly send me all the details on how our entire intelligence community, along with the most extensive surveillance operation on the planet, screwed up and got bloody blindsided so flaming badly. And I want it by the time he gets back from lunch. That is in about ten minutes" the voice had risen with each word until it reached a crescendo close to screaming, then the sound of a device, presumably the handset of a desk phone slamming down, was so loud it actually hurt the operator's ear.

"A fat lot of good that's gonna do!" He whispered to himself he was seriously considering redialling the caller and telling her just what she could do with the ridiculous demand, 'either way, I'm finished here' he thought, but it was really tempting.

The room had windows. Three were facing the wall on the left, three more on the right wall and a small walkway down the centre. Jill, the supervisor, was pacing up and down the middle.

The ops room was frantic. The handful of the staff were frantically trying to collect every piece of information they could find. Anything would do. Each one had their own responsibility. Police, MI5, GCHQ, local authorities and even local security companies. Anyone who had any way of tracking what might have gone on, they were all being monitored. Six of them were working frantically.

"I can't believe this!" She was young for the position. In her early thirties, slim build and blonde with blue eyes, but don't let the Scandinavian good looks fool, everyone in the room had at least a university education, usually in one or more languages. Jill was fluent in a couple, but that wasn't relevant. She also knew computers, that was why she was working there, "Does no one follow the bloody rules?" She threw her arms in the air, frustration was written all over her face, "we should have had some warning it was going down! How the hell do we explain the whole screw up?"

"It gets worse," the male operator chipped in, "that was 'the Princess Margaret' herself on the line. She wants details for the boss, like yesterday." He inverted the commas in sign language.

Margaret may have been Sir Mike's secretary, but she wasn't that well-liked. "Thinks she's too bloody good for us" was the feeling.

"Shit! What DO we have?" Jill was almost pleading, "give me anything!"

"I might have something to tell them," another of the operators chipped in, "but it'll cause more questions like how the whole thing was missed!"

"Speak," Jill demanded. She whipped around and faced the one who'd spoken.

"Well, it's kinda strange, they notified but" his specs were slipping down his face. Or at least that's what it felt like when he got nervous, and he was terrified. He just wanted to crawl into the nearest hole and hide. What he was about to say would not go down well with 'the Brass', "but they emailed the local cops HQ that they were running a keen wind exercise!"

"They did what?" Jill was furious. "Who the hell authorised that? And what the hell is a Keen Wind exercise?"

"Didn't need authorisation," the operator cut in, "it was local, the station superintendent signed off on it, called it a snap keen wind!" He shrugged, then went on, "It's what they call an anti-terrorist operation, bomb threat in particular! They used to use them for IRA threats in the eighties."

"No use arguing about this." Jill really wanted to argue with someone, but it would not get them anywhere. "Find the email and create a file. They're gonna want to see all that for the debrief. " She turned back to the other operators, "meanwhile someone get me the details on what a local keen wind is supposed to look like!"

'Keen wind' is the code name for the precautions taken to thwart a potential terrorist attack.

Intelligence networks do their best to listen in to anyone wanting to cause a problem. As soon as they get an idea of a threat to a place, the local security services in the area are brought to a higher

state of readiness, on military bases things like the guards at the gate
are doubled and issued live ammunition, extra searches of sensitive
areas.

For the civilian population, the cops also get extra powers and if
a place is suspected of being a target, then the Army can be called in
and bomb experts search for devices. This usually only happens when
someone in Whitehall decides, but occasionally the local station can
'pull' an exercise to test their own response times; that's what they'd
done, and now everyone was scrambling, dealing with the crap no
one knew was there.

"Thank you" Sir Michael was in a foul mood and rushing, but
that was no excuse for rudeness. He quickly turned without
waiting for an acknowledgement and was through the door.

Margaret waited until she heard the elevator close, then,
reaching for her bag, she stood up and headed for the door.

The elevators are quicker than the stairs, but more people use
them. Using the stairs means others are less likely to see you, and the
last thing she needed was to be seen.

The elevators open out into the main foyer on the ground floor,
complete with the security desk and guards. They might be busy, but
the cameras would catch everything.

But security is only ever as good as the weakest link, and every
system has them. Vauxhall house was no exception.

The stairwells had cameras that were monitored, but Margaret
knew the cameras wouldn't pick up the face of anyone heading
downward, and on the first floor they were down, maintenance was
booked, so anyone checking the system would see it arranged, but no
one 'cottoned on' to the fact that the dates for it kept changing.

Turning right out of the stairwell she headed down the corridor. There was a fire escape at the end that took her down the back of the building and into the car park.

Two minutes later, she was on the street and heading for the local underground station.

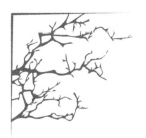

Chapter 41

"Look," she cut across his tirade. "We've been damn well blindsided by this, and we need to get it together!" Margaret was angry at this. A angry and scared. For the first time, she was beginning to see just how dangerous what she'd been doing really was. She wasn't a bad person, at least she didn't think she was. But she was trapped, trapped in a life she got through one of the seven 'deadly sins' her father, an Anglican priest had always harped on about, she turned her back on his teachings as soon as she'd left home, now she was paying for not listening, "and it's much worse than you think"

"But you were meant to warn us of anything like this!" Serkhov was angry. He was directing the anger at the little secretary sitting here on the park bench with him. But the truth was, his anger was more at himself for not having much of a contingency. "Instead, I've got a missing right-hand man, and now I learn from the TV that the police have hit the garage!" He stopped for a second to let the information sink in. She was there to stop them doing this, or at least give him some warning the raid was scheduled. She did neither. "What else haven't you told us?" the look he gave made her shiver inside.

"They're working outside of the system." She replied. "We've got a team at the moment that seems to be running amok in the country. Some of the divisional heads are saying they've 'gone rogue' and they're the ones creating the havoc," Margaret reached into her purse. "Here's what I can find on them. They were the ones sent to the West Country a couple of days ago, to protect the hacker." She slowly took out a plain brown A4 envelope. It was about an eighth of an inch thick. "They were also the ones in New Zealand a few weeks ago." She stopped giving him time to digest the information.

"And in Iran?" He asked. She nodded in reply. That answer told him volumes. He'd heard of what happened there, and the damage they'd done to the organisation. This was one job he was going to take great delight in carrying out, and he would destroy them even if it was the last thing he did on this earth. "What else is here?" He held the envelope up.

"Enough for you to set a trap," she came back, "they're onto us, but we can destroy a large part of their evidence, maybe not all, but enough to make them think twice."

"You think they'll back off?" He was surprised.

"The team won't!" She replied, "but they're already working outside the system, but a string of bodies littering the countryside will make anyone else think twice. And MI6 are crapping themselves that word of a rogue team might get out, so you can guarantee they'll back off for a while."

He thought for a moment. He'd come here angry and frustrated, but the beginnings of a plan was forming in his head. It wouldn't stop them hunting him, but it might just buy enough time for him to go to ground, but the operative word was 'might'. He glanced over at the woman. She was showing no emotion, something that surprised and yet didn't surprise. They were people she'd worked with for years. Okay, she'd worked against them for a lot of that time. Slowly climbing the ranks, waiting until she could be of some use to her real allies, and by that time, her original bosses in the Kremlin had been replaced with. Well, let's just say 'same people, different agenda'.

"Look," she began again, "I'm giving you the information. It's up to you what you do with it. You can cause enough carnage to maybe slip away in the night. Or you can do nothing and hope, but rest assured, now they have the garage, the car and the weapons. They're coming for you and me. As for me, I'm hoping it'll buy me enough time to get out while I still can. I really don't fancy the rest of my life in Holloway or Dartmoor!" She stood up and walked away, leaving the thoughts of a long stay in either of the two of the most notorious prisons in the United Kingdom as a parting unpleasant thought.

Serkhov didn't leave immediately. He waited a good fifteen minutes. It looked like he was reading the news on his tablet, but he was reading a note that had been on the envelope. It simply said, "all communication devices are tapped." Whatever he arranged would have to be done the old way.

He looked as if he was watching the other park benches and pedestrians walking past. But he wasn't paying much attention to the trees and such. He didn't see the slight rustling of the trees a few dozen feet away.

Less than a dozen feet away, Chambers had watched everything. He'd also recorded most of the conversation. Best of all, he could confirm the mole had just betrayed themself.

"Let her go, at least for now," he whispered to himself. He hated the idea, but sometimes a little 'evil' is necessary for the greater good. At least that's what he kept telling himself.

There was one thing he could do though, and that he set about doing. Taking a small plastic piece of equipment out of his pocket. He pressed a button on the side and waited as the small phone came to life. It went straight to the email programme. Typing in an email address he sent a simple two-word message. It read "Bait taken"

As soon as the message showed up as being sent, he got up from the bench, checked there was no one watching and began walking off in the same direction Margaret had taken.

"Listen" Jacko turned to talk to Sgt Harris as they neared the Land Rover, Smithy and Mac were stowing their weapons in the back of the Land Rover. Checking each one and carefully making sure they were locked away in the lockbox, Joey and Sandy were packing the equipment away at the CP, they had another vehicle for transport. "It's vital that no one finds out about us. WE WEREN'T HERE RIGHT!" he was emphatic.

"Yeah, we got that Harris replied, Billie was with Joey and Sandy. She was getting the same brief, except probably stronger. "How do I explain it, though?" He meant how did he explain the Army turning up and taking over, then disappearing, "you made a pretty big impression"

"Just tell the truth." Jacko opened the vehicle's door and pulled himself in behind the steering wheel. "You were running a practice drill when you saw something that just wasn't right." He closed the door and reached for the starter button. "But don't mention us, and if anyone else asks, deny any outside help, and that includes Billie's too!"

That was weird! A bust this big and he was being told to take all the credit. This was a career-making bust. One that any cop would give almost anything to be associated with, and he was being told to hog all the credit? It was Billie who had brought him the information; She would not like being shut out. He had ambition, but trampling over fellow officers on the way up just didn't sit right.

"Listen," Jacko read his thoughts. "This is vital! The people we're chasing are very good at disappearing. They're also bloody well connected. They know every move the authorities make. The only way to beat 'em is if they don't know who's chasing 'em, and for that, we need to stay in the shadows, so." He stopped momentarily, made eye contact and went on, "you ran a practice and found things GOT IT!" he pushed the starter button and went to release the handbrake.

"What about BJ?" Harris still didn't like the idea of 'stitching another officer up' and it still felt that way. He could accept they wanted the shadows, but Billie had taken a lot of flak for this bust. She deserved some credit.

"Don't worry" Jacko assured him, "We've got something bigger lined up for her" and with that, he pulled away, leaving the copper there scratching his head trying to get the vaguest idea of what he was going to say.

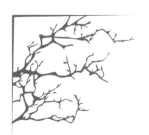

Chapter 42

"You ready?" Joey shouted to Sandy as he ran towards the CP. She was coming out with the two laptops. Both were in their cases. She opened the back of the Land Rover and lifted the back carpet. Two recesses about the size of small padlocks were the only hints to the false floor the vehicle had. She reached in and pulled the catch over the pin where the padlock normally went. Up came a lid revealing a space just big enough to take the two bags that the laptops were in. She put them in making sure that both sat snugly in the space.

Closing the lid she took out a small padlock and inserted it into the pin. Clicking the arm of the lock into place, she ran her fingers over the four-barrel combination lock securing the laptops into place, only she had the combination to the laptops.

"Yeah, ready for phase two, we just got the go-ahead from London." She replied making eye contact with Joey. This was the most dangerous part of the mission. It was also the most important, and there was still someone they needed to explain it to. She was vital to the whole thing.

"Phase two?" BJ had followed Joey, who was making his weapon safe. He'd flicked open the lockbox on the other side and was putting his weapon, a colt commando, in. He stopped and turned towards Billie, hand outstretched as if saying, 'Give me your weapon. She was reluctant, as it was a police issue MP5, or at least she thought it was!

"Yeah, phase two," Joey replied, "this was just the start, there's more to do,"

"But these are the people who killed Akbari, right?" BJ stopped, wanting an answer. *'don't tell me I've been suckered into this!'* She was thinking.

"Sort of," Sandy replied. She indicated for Billie to give Joey the weapon. Billie began checking the safety and removing the magazine. "They were involved, and that WAS the vehicle seen in the area, but as for the man who actually did it? No, he's not in England anymore, but his boss, the man who gave the order, that's who we're going to pay a visit to next, and it will not be a social call!"

"Hence the artillery" BJ nodded in Mac and Jacko's direction.

"Nah," Joey replied, "they've got another job to do, just as important, but not the same. This one we'll be on our own for, but having a copper around is going to prove vital,"

"What? How the hell did that happen?" She was angry. She'd so wanted to make sure that the creep who'd murdered Akbari paid for it with jail time. Now she was being told that would not happen. She wasn't impressed. "How in God's name did that happen? And where the hell did you send him?"

Sandy stopped momentarily. She slowly looked up and over in Joey's direction. The look said 'do you want to, or should I?'

Joey caught Sandy's look, and took the initiative, "British jails are way too soft for that piece of shit!" He began, "Don't get me wrong, they're pretty rough for some, but for this guy, they would have been like a five-star hotel. The guy was a Russian mobster with a string of countries wanting him. We just facilitated one of the less pleasant places getting their hands on him. Along with a promise that he'd get a lot of pain thrown in well before anything ever gets to trial,"

"Jeez" Billie was frozen to the spot, "where did you send him?"

Joey had taken her weapon out of her hands, checked the safety, removed the mag, then worked the bolt three times before holding it open and putting his finger physically in the breach to make sure nothing was in there. Once he was satisfied everything was clear, he closed the bolt, flicked the safety off, took aim at the sky and squeezed the trigger. The metallic click told him the firing mechanism had released the firing pin. All that was left to do was reapply the safety and stow the weapon in the lockbox. He did that and closed the box up. Pointing to the rear passenger door, he said, "Let's carry the conversation on while on the move, shall we?"

Both of them climbed into the vehicle. Sandy was in the driving seat. Joey in the front passenger seat and BJ behind. She still wanted to know. "Okay, who was he and where is the creep?"

"Who he was isn't so important as what he was?" Sandy replied as she turned the engine over. "He was a lieutenant in the Russian mafia or 'Bratva', as they call it, have you heard of it?" She put the vehicle into gear and pulled away.

"Yeah" Billie replied, "not exactly familiar with it, but I've come across some" she was feeling just that little nervous, if these guys were taking on the 'Bratva' then they were in serious trouble, this didn't sound good.

"He was also wanted in a few places, one of which was for a triple murder in Kyiv. One of the people killed was a daughter of a police chief," Joey added, "They were very glad to have him back and made the offer that he'd go through a lot of pain before facing trial, if he ever lives that long. They have a three-year waiting list for trials and wanted to add a few more things to the list. You know, war crimes and the like!"

"You mean fitting the guy up for stuff" BJ was a good cop. The thought of doing something like that was abhorrent to her and hearing these two talking that way really shocked her.

"He killed Akbari in cold blood, and for no other reason than that, he was told to." Sandy's voice rose slightly. "Farid was a friend. He didn't deserve that, and besides, from what the Ukrainians told us, he was pretty brutal with the little girl, don't lose any sleep over it!" By now, they were on the outskirts of the city. BJ noticed they took the slip road for the motorway, heading back to London. She didn't see the other Land Rover take the other road and head North.

"You said he was told to. Who by?"

"His boss," Joey replied, "the one pulling the strings here in London, and the one who controls the mole we're after."

"A mole?"

"Yep," Sandy answered as the Land Rover sped up. Most 'Lannies' have the acceleration of a dead snail! They have lots of power, but it's all for hauling heavy loads over uneven ground. This one was different. It had plenty of 'get up and go'. They were flying along at just over the seventy miles an hour speed limit. "Ever heard of a guy by the name of Alexei Serkhov?"

Chapter 43

There was silence for the rest of the trip. BJ sat there wondering just what the hell it was these people were doing? Serkhov was one of the most 'connected' people in London, sure he was suspected of several things. But nothing was ever proved, and anything that seemed to link him with anything just 'disappeared' with no trace or record.

"How d'you folks come across Serkhov?" She asked as they slowed to merge into the inner city traffic.

"Bit of a story, really," Sandy replied, "and we can't tell you all of it. Let's just say his phone number keeps coming up in the wrong places." She slowed down for a roundabout, watching the traffic from the right she merged into it, Joey pointed to the second exit. They were heading for the centre of the city. Sandy went on, "but we can tell you he's the one who ordered the hit on Akbari and tried to make something unpleasant happen to the hacker who stopped the virus a couple of days ago." She said it as if it was a matter of public record.

"And you know this because?" ever the copper, she wanted hard facts.

"Want to listen to the conversation?" Joey asked as he reached forward, tapping the something on the dashboard the CD player came to life. The voice was Serkhov's, but she couldn't really tell what he was saying. It was in a foreign language. "That's Russian, here's the English translation." He flicked a switch. "We've got both recorded, compliments of Google by the way"

"You TAPPED HIS PHONE?" BJ was incredulous. She saw any chance they ever had of a prosecution disappearing in the mist almost as fast as it had presented itself.

"For your information, Cheltenham records all phone conversations within the UK," Sandy replied, "so relax, and no it wasn't them, that WOULD be illegal, but they farm it out to a friend, and it was them that told us.Not that it's going to come out in court, anyway!"

"But you had his bloody phone tapped" BJ's voice wasn't quite shouting, but wasn't far off it. "Do you have any idea how many laws you've broken?"

"Not a single one!" Joey replied. He turned to face Bille. "Look, we got the number when we took a drug ring in New Zealand apart a few weeks ago. Serkhov thought he was being smart, switching SIM cards and the like, even using a frequency hopper. But we identified him, and he's since confirmed it with what he's been doing,"

"But how?" Billie began again, "I mean, how come?"

"How come he hasn't been caught?" Sandy asked, "Simple really, he's got someone on the inside. A mole within the intelligence community. Someone at MI6 is how!"

They arrived at their destination; it was a nightclub, but as it was still daylight, there wasn't much going on at the moment. Just a couple of men working the door. From the looks of them, they were heavyweight boxers or the like, and they were the kind of people always ready for trouble, which was coming right at them. They just didn't know it yet.

"So what's the plan now?" She was dubious that any plan was going to have much traction. "What hair-brained scheme do you have in mind? Whatever it is, it's probably going to finish our careers!"

"In case you haven't noticed," Joey replied as he got out of the car. He turned and leaned back in. "We're officially 'gone rogue' and yours went into the proverbial toilet the moment you went down the West Country. Actually, it was probably already in the toilet the moment your boss gave you the case. Now we can argue about this all bloody day, or we can get some real work done? Which one is it?" he didn't wait for an answer.

"So, what's your plan?"

"You walk up and tell them you want to speak to Serkhov." Sandy replied as she got out of the car. All three had taken their flak jackets and body armour off before starting the trip. Both Billie and Sandy looked like professional businesspeople. Joey looked casually dressed. "Leave the rest to Joey, and by the way, I'm Sandy. You may as well know that much about us"

"You're honestly expecting them to show us in?" she couldn't help asking.

"No," Joey replied, "if they do, I'll be really disappointed. I need a good workout. Now let's get on with it."

"Are you bloody serious?" BJ spurted out. Joey was half out of the car. "I've heard of hair-brained schemes, but this is bloody ridiculous! We need backup!"

"Go ahead," Joey replied. "give your boss a call. Tell him what's gone on, and see what happens. My guess is 'jack shit' is what'll transpire!" He sounded angry.

"He's right" Sandy was also climbing out of the car. "Townsend is a career climber." She turned and looked directly at BJ. There was a look that said 'you know we're right' that she couldn't deny. They were right. Detective Chief Inspector Townsend had only ever taken on cases he knew he could solve, and ones that would enhance his career. All the others, the real police work, ended up with those he didn't like.

"Actually, call the local nick. Tell them, "officer needs assistance, armed thugs in Chelsea" Joey came back, "this is going to get violent, and the sooner we get armed cops here the better" he walked towards the two men. That's when she noticed he was carrying a sidearm. It was in a holster, but the holster was unclipped.

Billie hit the speed dial on her phone. It went straight through to the Police emergency response team; they were on standby twenty-four hours a day, seven days a week for if a copper got into trouble. She didn't even have to speak. It activated a beacon that told them a copper was in trouble, and it was likely firearms were in play.

British Police are still mostly unarmed, but that doesn't mean there isn't back up. Punch in a certain code and the response team will text back for verification. Punch in the wrong one, or none at all, and the nearest armed units are sent straight to you. Billie knew that as soon as she punched the number, at least three squad cars of armed police would be on their way. She also knew that doing it for the wrong reasons would see her out of the force, and maybe even in jail. Not a prospect she relished, but better than getting shot.

"I need to talk with Alexei Serkhov," BJ shouted as she trotted past Joey. The two thugs slowly turned to face her, "I'm with the Metropolitan pol"

"So what?" The nearest one sneered as he faced her. He was about four inches taller and a foot wider than she was. It was all gristle, but he liked to think of it as muscle. "You have an appointment?"

"I'm with the Metropolitan police," she replied. "I don't need an,"

"Piss off," he cut her off, "make an appointment" he turned to watch the rest of the street, ignoring her and Sandy.

"Stand aside," Sandy spoke for the first time in the exchange, "we're going to see Mr Serkhov."

"Piss off, bitch," the first one moved to block her. He stood there, seemingly immovable. The second guy had moved into a position to back up his mate. He'd also drawn his jacket back slightly, not quite exposing the pistol he had, but making it easier to get to.

"Police business," Bille began again, "stand aside, we want to,"

"I told you to piss off," the big guy went to grab Billie's arm as she pushed past.

BJ didn't see the move. All she saw was a flash as Joey reached out, grabbed the arm, twisted almost to breaking point and lifted him straight up. As soon as he was six inches off the ground, Joey pushed hard, sending the guy flying into his mate, who had his pistol half out of the holster. The weapon went off harmlessly. The bullet embedded itself in the garden just behind him. Joey deliberately didn't draw his weapon.

"Armed police, stay right where you are!" a voice from the street screamed. They looked round to see two squad cars already in the street, *'bit quick off the mark, boys and girls'* Joey thought, but he wasn't arguing. Another voice, one Billie knew well, said, "I was told you'd be here soon, and to have backup, but I didn't think you'd try to take on the whole bloody Russian mafia!" It was Jimmy.

"Thanks, Jimmy." BJ was more confused than ever. *'How the hell did he know to be here, and to bring armed cops?'* but she wasn't complaining.

Sandy and Joey were already moving inside. But they were only a couple of steps ahead of her. They were heading into the main entrance, a couple more thugs were making their way towards them.

"Police" she held up her badge for the goons to see. "Where's Mr Serkhov?" She dangled the badge right in front of their noses. Neither of them seemed too impressed. Then two of the armed police came through the door, alert, but not menacing. "I said where's Serkhov?" BJ raised her voice slightly, a slight twitch from one of the men gave his location away.

Joey ran towards what looked like a locked door. He didn't even try to open it. A flying kick and the door flew open. The door jamb splintering as it gave way to nearly one hundred and ten kilograms or two hundred and forty pounds of muscle.

Serkhov was sitting at his desk, phone in hand. He was pushing keys on the phone. "Put the phone down NOW" Joey screamed as he drew his weapon from it's a holster. He aimed at Serkhov. A click told them the safety catch was off. "PUT the phone down NOW"

"It's a phone" Serkhov began gently lowering the phone, "not a gun" he was shocked. "Who the F"

"It could also be a remote detonator," Joey replied, still in the position to shoot. "Now put it down before I blow your sodding arm off!"

Chapter 44

Life at the cottage was tedious. All they'd done so far was just look after an ungrateful asshole who really didn't get just how much trouble he'd been in. All he'd done was moan and bitch about not having the Xbox or PlayStation. Sam was getting fed up with the moaning.

Hene had a chess set which they'd used, that was, until they both got frustrated with Paul beating them. One time, he did it in six moves. He almost ended up wearing the board, and it wasn't Hene that was going to do it. Sam hated to lose at the best of times. It made things even worse when the guy was a geek trying to chat her up and failing miserably.

"You sure you don't want a game?" He couldn't help smiling as he sat in front of the board. There were no computers or a board game, so the entertainment either had to be cards or a board game. No matter what they played, the TV was on in the background, but neither was paying too much attention to it.

"Nah," Sam replied, "got a few things I need to do. Maybe Hene will when he gets back." She enjoyed the fact she was 'volunteering him,' for it.

"Where's he gone?" Paul looked up. He hadn't realised Hene wasn't there.

"Out checking the grounds," Sam replied, "just making sure everything's okay. He'll be back soon." It felt like she was promising a child that someone would *come and play* soon.

The farmhouse was in a secluded spot. Woodland at the back and on both sides gave the feeling of isolation. The trees stopped about a hundred yards from the buildings creating the perfect 'kill zone' for any intruders trying to get to them. Tripwires and sensors in the woods made it virtually impossible for people to slip past without being noticed, or that was the theory.

Reality's nearly always something different when one of your own is actually working for the other side! They'd improvised a few things, but everyone knew there were gaps in the defences at the farm. Hene was out checking what had been done, as well as trying to figure out what else could be done. They'd managed to put a few extra tripwires out, but most of them were just empty bean tins filled with rocks and attached to a piece of string.

"Hene," the little handheld radio crackled to life, " how far away are you?" Sam asked. It sounded urgent.

"Just finishing up," Hene replied.

"Roger, see you then" the radio went quiet again.

Everything looked quiet, *that has to be good'* he thought to himself as he walked towards the door, one more scan around especially out front, where there was a clear line of sight to the bridge over the stream before the road disappeared around a bend and began twisting up the hill opposite. There were a couple of dry stone walls about chest height. They marked off farmer's fields that ran either side of the road, and two more on each side that went from the first wall to the trees. Hene estimated there was about a hundred and fifty yards or a hundred metres between the two.

Opening the door, he could smell a fresh pot of coffee brewing, *'hazelnut mocha'* he thought to himself, *'Brits just don't appreciate some of the finer things in life.* Walking in he made his way down the hall, past the second door, which should have been closed, but they'd gotten a bit too blasé with security. He secured the Yale lock and made sure the door was locked.

"What's up?" He walked into the kitchen. Sam handed him a mug of the brown nectar, he took a sip.

"All good outside?" Sam asked, seemingly ignoring his query. As the senior officer, she was still technically in charge, though things had gotten somewhat blurred over the last few days.

"Yeah, all good," he replied, taking another sip of the coffee. There were four chairs around the kitchen table, high-backed pine kitchen chairs. He pulled one out and sat down. "I've put a couple more cameras linked to motion sensors. Should help us pick up any unwelcome visitors".

"How do we get the signal?" Sam asked, "And where'd you get the stuff from?" No one had said anything about putting extra stuff in.

"Compliments of Joey!" He replied, taking a swig of the coffee. It had cooled down some. "He told me not to ask too many questions, but said he figured we might benefit from them as the mole will know nothing about 'em!"

Same gave a bit of a worried look. After all, she was still a copper, and old habits 'die-hard'. She figured they might just have 'fallen off the back of a truck' knowing Joey. "Okay," she said, "just how does it work?"

"Basically," he began, "as soon as it picks up an intruder, it emails us a link for the live feed,"

"Whoa, stop there, emails who? and what live feed?"

"At the moment, me," Hene replied, "Paul only set me up with it, but he can."

"Wait a minute!" She wasn't impressed. "You told Paul about the security here?"

"Actually, he didn't" Paul was standing in the doorway between the kitchen and lounge, "I'm a security consultant, remember!" He moved further into the kitchen. There were a couple of English muffins on the table, part of a pack Sam had opened earlier, he took one, split it and popped the two halves in the toaster next to the cooker which was on the right of the door to the lounge. "It's what I do. Advise people on their security," he added.

"Yeah, internet security" she replied, the last thing they needed was a rank amateur screwing things up, "not the kind of"

"And how do you think we keep the servers safe? Not just the software, but the machines themselves?" He let that sink in for a moment, "we design the whole system, and besides, it's only clicking a few icons."

"You make it sound pretty simple." Sam wasn't so sure, "but I'm not so sure we should mess with stuff we can't control,"

"Too late," Hene interjected, "we've got four of 'em set up, all we need do is put your email address in here," he pointed to the screen, "and anything the sensors pick up will send a live feed to your phone, Paul can put an override in so only the nearest one to the house will broadcast,"

"Actually," Paul butted in, "that might not work, but I can set it up so you get an email from each and choose which one you're going to watch. How does that sound?"

Sam nearly threw the phone at him. "make it so"

Paul caught the phone and swiped the screen to open it, the 'password' icon came up, "here, you better open it, I'll talk you through what to do" he moved to her side, a little too close for her comfort. She stepped away slightly. Just then, it rang. She looked at Hene, a flicker of alarm registering, "It's Jacko" was all she needed to say.

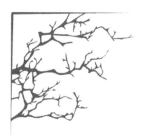

Chapter 45

The Colt Commandos were stored in the lockbox in the back of the Land Rover, along with something special Smithy had brought along. Something both Jacko and Mac thought belonged in a museum. Neither of them had the courage to tell him that, and he didn't have the courage to tell them that's where he got the .303 Lee Enfield from! They kept the Glocks handy. The Glocks were in the door pockets, *'could be an issue if we stop for a piss'* they all thought, but that wasn't the intention.

Jacko was driving. Mac in the passenger seat was monitoring their comms. Smithy was in the back plotting the topography and likely ambush points around the farm. They were going to be as prepared as possible for whatever lay ahead.

"I'd say we're gonna be three hours, maybe four" Jacko glanced at the speedometer. They were doing sixty-five miles an hour. A pretty respectable speed for a Land Rover, but still not fast enough for their liking. The Lannie (as they affectionately called them) would do eighty, even though they weren't exactly built for speed. Then again, the last ten miles might just be 'cross country' regardless of what might be in the way. That's what they were good at. "But we need to do it in a lot less!"

"What about Joey and Sandy?" Smithy asked. He didn't look up from what he was doing, but that didn't mean a thing. He could seem totally focused on what he was doing and still take in everything going on.

"About an hour and a half," Mac replied, "they called in with an ETA about half an hour ago."

Even though they were on a four-lane highway. It wasn't the motorway, and the car in front seemed to think it was a scenic tour doing about half the sixty miles an hour they were supposed to be doing, and severely pissing Jacko off. They were already in the fast lane.

"What the hell?" Mac grabbed the door handle as Jacko pulled violently to the left. The vehicle swerved between two other slower ones, narrowly missing the front vehicle and causing loud horn blasts from the one behind as the driver slammed the brakes on. They hit the service lane as Jacko gunned the engine. A momentary pause before the vehicle lurched forward, clearing the traffic. As soon as they were in the clear, Jacko pulled back onto the road and into the right hand 'fast lane' again, just missing the front of a fully laden semi. "Boss, we've got enough people trying to kill us," Smithy added, "yer didna need to add pissed off truckers to it!"

"Quit your whining," Jacko shot back, almost laughing, "we've got three hours to make a four-hour drive!"

The news reports would hit the airwaves about now. That meant every second counted. Serkhov wasn't dumb. As soon as he realised what was going on, anything could happen, and that was the plan.

Sam and Hene had Paul at the safe house, but nowhere was safe. They would be compromised, that was certain, and Serkhov would want revenge. He would want blood! He'd regard the hacker as the reason the scheme failed. It wouldn't go well with his bosses, and even less so if he told them the reason their money wasn't recovered was still 'upright and sucking air'

They would try to make the hit, *just hopefully not in the next three hours'* Jacko, Mac, Smithy, Joey and Sandy were all silently praying.

"Yer could have picked a faster ride boss" Mac couldn't resist a jibe at Jacko's expense.

"Yeah well, have you ever seen the luggage space in a Ferrari?" Jacko quipped back, "wouldn't even get you in, never mind the gear!"

"Be prepared" was the Boy Scout motto, "it was also the creed the SAS lived by, and that meant they had as many scenarios prepped for as they could carry, and then some!

"You reckon Serkhov's worked things out yet?" Smithy asked.

"Possibly," Mac replied. "Suppose I better give Sam and gang the heads up." He reached for the phone and began tapping out a message.

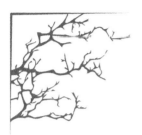

Chapter 46

"Yer got the location yet?" The Irish brogue was strong. He was frustrated, and when he got frustrated, the Irish brogue showed itself as a calling card.

"Da," the Russian replied, "it's not far, about fifteen miles, in a forest" he pulled his phone out, tapped in an address and up came Google maps a few more taps and a route from their present position appeared. " See" he showed the Irishman.

"Do ya think I've got a bloody magnifying vision or something?" Pat O'Flanagan let fly verbally, "bloody well put it on something I can see." He moved back to his vehicle, one of the others in the van passed him a laptop, "here" he thrust it at the Russian, "put it on this"

"Here," the Russian finished tapping the screen. "Fifteen miles away. There are two ways in, one to the north, and one to the east. Maybe we take them from both directions. What do you think?"

O'Flanagan couldn't quite believe his ears. 'Jeez, if brains were dynamite, these bloody Russians wouldn't have enough to blow their frigging noses!' He managed to keep that thought to himself, though. "We do that and we're likely to kill each other in a crossfire, ya bloody idiot!!" He adjusted the laptop for topography. "See here, to the east," he tapped the tablet, the Russian followed his direction, "there's a bit of a dip in the road, enough to keep you hidden, park your vehicle blocking the road and wait in the trees."

"What for?"

"Friggin Christmas, what do ya think?" He was getting really annoyed. Working with Gromatski had been hard enough, but at least he'd known what he was doing. These clowns had no idea, "ya there the stop any help to get through ya numbskull!!"

"What you talk about?" The Russian's name was Stefan. This wasn't the brief he'd been given by Serkhov over the phone earlier. Granted, Serkhov had said to help this stupid Irish 'Mick' but he'd been told to make sure the kid didn't carry on breathing beyond sundown, and preferably that he stopped well before it.

"Do yer have any idea who's guarding the kid?" O'Flanagan was beginning to lose the plot. "A flaming team o' the best, that's who! Trust me, I've dealt with these pricks afore! They're gonna come at us from all bloody angles. And I want your boys to stop 'em coming in from the east." He stopped for a moment to let that sink in, "let me deal with the kid, and if it gets too bloody hot, you hit 'em from the east, but we don't let 'em know you're there until we bloody well have to, have you got it?"

Stefan didn't like the plan. It meant he wouldn't be able to confirm whether 'the mick' had done the job. "Serkhov wants confirmation" was all he said.

"Then I'll make sure to post him a bloody picture!" The Irishman quipped back. "Look, your boys seal off that road. I'll leave a couple of lads to seal off the other, and the rest of us will go in and finish the bloody job. Got it?" He paused again to make sure the Russian understood. He could see the anger in Stefan's face, but he also knew the Russians were outnumbered in this one. They had four guys where O'Flanagan had brought his whole cell, six of them, more than enough for the average hit. But this was no average hit. "Now, what did you bring?"

"Boss," Mac spoke up, they'd been driving for a while, "I reckon we're about forty-five minutes out, the roads get narrow from here on in." He glanced nervously over at the speedometer. He couldn't tell the speed, but the needle was well over on the right-hand side. The dial went up to 90 mph, but it looked as if the needle was well off the dial, and in a Land Rover, that wasn't crazy, it was suicidal!

"Boss" Mac spoke up again, his knuckles were white with holding on, but Jacko, in fact, all of them had done the police pursuit driving course. It was part of the training, "message from Sandy. " He looked over at Jacko, who glanced back. Jacko didn't like what he saw.

"What?"

"Says at least two teams, one Russian, one Irish," Mac put the tablet back in the recess and grabbed hold tightly, "Ya better stop playing around and get a move on boss."

"Looks like two entry points boss," Smithy added to the conversation.

"Yeah" Jacko was concentrating. They were fast approaching a car doing the speed limit, but he had no intention of slowing down. There was a slow lane just in front of the car. He was plotting the best way forward.

The car wasn't moving over. Jacko blew the horn, but all he got back was a 'one-fingered salute. He swerved left and gunned the engine. Considering he hadn't slowed in the first place the Lannie flew past the car. Smithy obliged with a return 'salute' and was serenaded with a long blast of the other car's horn, something that other motorists would normally take as an insult. For Jacko, it was just normal.

There was a crossroads ahead with a set of traffic lights on it. They were yellow or 'amber' heading for red. A car was pretty close to them coming from the left. The driver had expected the change and was cruising up. The lights changed, and he started to go as Jacko flew into the junction literally 'drifting' the Lannie round the other vehicle. No horn came on, but seconds later a police siren came on as well as red and blue lights receding but pursuing them.

"Boss," Mac joked, "I know we're gonna need the cops later, but bringing 'em with us, that's bloody ridiculous!"

"Shut up, " Jacko responded, "and get on the blower, get someone to call this idiot off "

"Roger that" Mac reached for the phone.

"Smithy, directions, now please," Jacko barked

The difference between map reading and high-speed map reading is for high speeds. You have to read the map a couple of miles ahead of where you actually are. At ninety miles an hour you're travelling at three hundred feet per second, identifying an object, recognising what it is from the map and relaying the information might only take five seconds but you're already nearly twelve hundred feet or a third of a mile past the object. Then you've got to break, turn round and get back, all of it time lost if you got the map reading wrong.

"Half a mile, turn left, then four hundred yards, at the crossroads turn right boss."

"Got it, hang on" Jacko braked and yanked the wheel in a hard left turn. Halfway round, he gunned the big V6. She growled in delight at finally being able to lose some traction. Smithy tried to throw himself as much as he could onto Mac's side of the vehicle as the two wheels on that side left the ground. They came back down with a thud. Dust spraying everywhere as they left the tarmac road and entered a gravel one. The 'Lannie' was doing what she was made for, and it was as if she was trying them how much she loved it.

The cop had been slowly gaining, that was until they hit the gravel, then they seemed to back right off. Stone chips were flying off the back tyres like bullets. Anything behind them was going to get pelted with them.

"Ya got through yet?" Jacko shouted at Mac over the engine noise, "or am I gonna get a roadblock?"

"Chambers is trying now," Mac replied, "Smithy, alternatives?"

"Four hundred yards on the left, dirt track boss, should avoid any roadblocks, brings us out three miles south of the farm, but she's pretty rough."

"It'll have to do," Jacko replied, "hang on." This time, he yanked the handbrake and turned. All four wheels locked as she slid sideways around the corner, gravel flying in all directions. Halfway around, Jacko let go of the handbrake and floored the accelerator. All four wheels spat gravel as they searched for traction. As soon as they got it, the vehicle jumped forward, pushing them back into their seats with a force that slammed their heads against the headrests.

The Lannie made the turn but fishtailed coming out of it. She went on fishtailing a few times before Jacko finally got her under control. "Guess she didn't like that much then?" Mac shouted above the engine.

"I'd say she loved it," Jacko replied as she straightened up. He had a smile as wide as the famous Cheshire cat, "Didn't even hit anything!" he smiled as they took off like a bat out of hell. "Any sign of the cops?"

"Nah" Smithy replied looking backwards, "he's got more respect for his life than to follow you!" he couldn't resist a dig at the boss.

They were less than ten miles away now if they had to, they could ditch the vehicle and 'hoof it' in, but that would take about two hours, and they just didn't know how much time they had, it could be minutes, but then it could be hours, they just didn't know.

Jacko's phone was mounted in a cradle on the dashboard. So far, the phone had been silent, and that was a good sign. That was the number Sam and Hene had for emergencies. Right at that moment, it came to life with Queen's 'Another one bites the dust. That wasn't good.

"Go," Jacko shouted, just after pressing the answer button. It was already on speaker. Pleasantries would have to wait. He barked out one word "Report?"

"Jacko," it was Sam on the phone, "Bozos got round the security MI6 put out, but Hene got four cameras on the north and eastern routes. We've got three pax north with two vehicles and four with another to the east, not sure how many are coming our way yet but the cans just went off!" She stopped, then came back on and added, "Vehicles look like SUVs, possibly seven-seaters."

"Thanks, Sam," Jacko replied, "Now get Paul to the bolt hole. I want you and Hene to do a token only. Three each, then into the hole yourselves GOT IT!" he was emphatic.

"Got it," Sam replied, "Paul's already there, we'll do as you say," the line went dead.

"Shit," Mac cussed, "that isn't good, no bloody good at all, we're ten miles away, even at this speed it's gonna take seven minutes at least, then we gotta close in,"

"Gimme options people" Jacko had the foot to the floor, but they were racing into something. They just didn't know how it would go, and they did not know how many there were. There were three vehicles, possibly seven-seaters, that meant potentially twenty-one bad guys, against three! That meant serious trouble, and the only weapon they might have was taken away from them as the mole had gotten the location. They could be driving straight into an ambush!

"Boss, three miles ahead there's a clearing, drop me and 'Lee' off there" Smithy waved the rifle he had in the case in the rearview mirror. It was his own personal .303 Lee Enfield. Classed as a 'hunting rifle', the fact is the .303 Lee Enfield is just about the best sniper rifle ever made, bar none.

"What the? How the hell did you get one of those?" Jacko shouted. They're regarded as a dangerous weapon, and there are strict regulations on who can hold them. Smithy had never let on that he had one.

"Ask no questions boss" Smithy replied, "and I'll tell yer no lies, and no you don't have to check the armoury logs" he knew that's the first thing that would be thought if word got out, that he'd stolen it from the armoury/.

"Okay," Jacko replied slowing down for the clearing, "what's your plan?"

"The eastern vehicle is four hundred yards that way," he pointed to the right, "And I'm loaded with tracer, ten minutes and I put two into their tank, should give a nice little fireball. It'll give a bit of a distraction."

Both of them knew better than to point out that a full fuel tank doesn't really burn that well. Especially when the fuel is Diesel, but they also knew that out here, the tanks wouldn't be full, and Smithy knew exactly where to aim to ignite the fumes. That would heat the fuel up causing more fumes that would ignite causing more, etc, until the whole thing just exploded.

They were now five miles away, and it was time for Smithy to leave.

"Go," Mac shouted as the vehicle slowed to less than ten miles an hour. The back door flew open and Smithy forward rolled out of the vehicle. As soon as he touched the floorboards with the accelerator the wheels spun as the Lannie sped up.

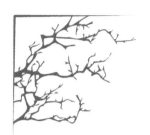

Chapter 47

"Alexei Serkhov, in accordance with the prevention and investigation of terrorism act of 2008, I'm taking you into custody." Billie went to handcuff him. Joey stopped her and launched a kick into Serkhov's groin. He dropped the knife he'd secretly pulled.

"Spread 'em" Joey screamed as he grabbed the Russian's head and went to drive it into the desk. Serkhov reacted by grabbing the desk with both hands as Joey kicked his left foot away from the right. "Assume the position"

A quick and not very gentle pat-down had Serkhov spread-eagled, with fingertips only touching the desk. His feet off the floor with only the tips of his toes touching. Every time he tried to move, he was rewarded with a kick to the offending part by Joey. "I'll kill you for this, you" Serkhov began.

"You're not capable," Joey screamed into his ear, "and you can forget your lackeys. They're bundled up in the back of a black Moriah. Or you call it a 'paddywagon' waiting to be shipped to wherever wants to give them the longest prison term!"

By now, two armed uniformed officers had entered the room. They went to stop the abuse, only to be physically blocked by both Sandy and Billie. Somehow Billie just knew Joey wouldn't be stopped and would break Serkhov. This boy only ever understood terror, and Joey was good at that.

"You'll never get away with this," Serkhov replied, "I have friends, I'll,"

"You mean the Judges and lawyers you think are going to help you? you know, those you've been blackmailing all these years?" Sandy reached for an electronic device that was on the desk. "Don't worry, we'll be talking to them as well. Those that don't go to jail will be glad to see the back of you, so I wouldn't count on help." She indicated for Billie to continue with the handcuffing. Joey pulled the man to his feet. Then wrenched his hands behind his back.

"You have no proof," Serkhov began again, "I'll be out in an hour, then I'll come hunting for you. After I've had your jobs, and ruined your families, that is!"

"Dream on," Joey replied as he threw the Russian towards the two coppers who were still standing there, open-mouthed.

"Stop," Billie stepped forward. "Mr Serkhov, under the act, I don't need proof to send you into custody. I can do it indefinitely while we investigate, and there is no right to appeal. So good luck with that," she indicated to the cops to lead the man away, then stopped them again, "Oh and let me add, all your accounts are frozen as of this moment, so any funds you do try to use will only complicate things more for you."

Serkhov stumbled into the two cops as soon as he regained his feet. He slowly turned, his face as white as a Russian winter snow. It was dawning on him just how royally screwed he really was. "You'll never get away with this. We will track you down, we will kill you."

Sandy had been busy with the electronic devices they'd found in Serkhov's office. Almost as if she was there, but concentrating so hard that she was missing everything. She wasn't. Sandy missed nothing, but only now she stopped what she was doing. She signalled the two cops to wait a moment. "We know who you are, Mr Serkhov, we know who your friends are, " she let that sink in for a whole ten seconds. Then went on, "we know the death and destruction you've dished out since you went freelance. We know and we're finally doing something about it. We're getting our vengeance, Mr Serkhov,

Scorpion's Vengeance!" She stopped, then looked directly at the two coppers, waved them off, and said. "Take him away."

"Not to the local nick," Billie added as they frogmarched Serkhov out. They stopped and turned around, confusion written on both faces, "take him to Scotland Yard, and I want one of you with him in the cell until I get there"

"Yes, ma'am," the older of the two cops replied.

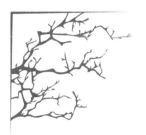

Chapter 48

Sandy was still working on the devices. A lot of it was encrypted, but there was a huge amount that wasn't. It was in Russian, which was almost as bad. She was struggling with some of it.

"Joey" Sandy looked up from the device she'd been working on. They were still in Serkhov's office. She was at the desk. "Send Jacko a message now, " there was some urgency in her voice, "oh give me the tablet, it'll be quicker if I do it, I can put all the relevant information in" she reached for the tablet Joey was handing her.

"Any problems?" Joey asked, not sure if he should be worried. He came round to her side of the desk to see what she was working on. Billie was still in the room waiting for the crime scene people to arrive. She looked curious. "Anything we can help with?"

"Not at this stage," Sandy looked up, then thought again. "Second thoughts, do you know anyone in the Cheshire Police force?"

"Not really," BJ replied, "but I could make a few calls. Why?"

Sandy finished typing the message, "cos I think there's gonna be a bloodbath in Eastern Cheshire, around a place called Macclesfield forest in about half an hour, that's why!"

That set alarm bells off in BJ's head. She grabbed her phone and began punching numbers. As soon as someone came on the line, she started barking orders. "Put me through to the North-West operations centre NOW!" turning to Sandy, she asked, "What do you need and where?"

"There's a cop car following our team now. He's got the sirens and lights on," Sandy began. "Tell the maniac to back off. We also need a five-mile perimeter set around this grid, nothing in or out. Our people are outnumbered four to one and will not be asking questions if you get the drift!"

"But,"

"Too many bodies cause mayhem," Sandy replied, "and these boys don't need any help to cause that, but we should try to keep it to a minimum."

"Okay," Billie turned as the phone came back to life, "this is DS Jones of the Metropolitan police. We've got a situation developing in East Cheshire, in the Macclesfield forest. One of your squad cars needs to back off the chase they're involved with." It took a full ten minutes and raising her voice at a few people, but eventually, she put the phone down. Looking at Sandy, she said, "you've got it, but they're not happy,"

"They'll be even less happy when they see the result," Joey muttered under his breath. Thankfully, only Sandy heard him. She gave him a filthy look. "What?" Joey asked, "you ever tried to follow Jacko? That cop's got real balls and I mean big brass ones!" He totally changed the subject.

"SHIT, I DON'T BELIEVE IT!" Sandy stared at the screen, her mouth open. "Shit, blast the bloody swine!"

Both Billie and Joey stopped what they were doing and focused on her. "What?"

" That's not Serkhov!" she pointed to the man the cops were putting into the back of the police can. "We've been duped!"

"What? How?" Billie demanded. She held up the picture they'd pulled off the police database earlier. "That says he is?" She was emphatic.

"I'm tracking calls from Serkhov's number at the moment," Sandy cut her off, "and we just got a video call to his private plane. Take a bloody look," she swung the small device she'd been using round so that both of them could see. "Look familiar?"

The face on the screen was the spitting image of the man they'd just had taken away. It had them stumped.

"A double?" Joey asked, confused.

"No idea," Sandy replied, "but he just told a pilot to get his plane ready. He'll be there in half an hour. Any idea where that plane is?" She began searching for information.

"Half an hour, you say?" Billie was on her phone again, hoping the people at Lloyds could help. "five airports in London. Where did the call originate?"

"Pinged cell towers inside the M25 Sandy replied. "Half an hour from there has to be Docklands, I'll see who's got a private plane at Docklands and where they are."

"Screw that" Joey shouted as he ran for the door, "yer can get that info as we go, let's haul ass, COME ON" as he bounded down the steps.

"JOEY" Sandy shouted as she bounded down the steps after him. It was the first name Billie had heard for any of the team. "Joey, where the hell are you going?" She caught up with him as he climbed into the vehicle. She climbed into the passenger side. BJ was only two steps behind and was half in the vehicle as he started the engine.

"You just said the pilot was told to be ready in half an hour, right?" Joey explained as he put the Land Rover into gear. " The only airfield, let alone airport that close, is Docklands. That's where most of London's billionaires keep their flying toys. So that's where I'm going" he was just about to pull away. He stopped, then threw the driver's door open causing total confusion. Looking back towards BJ he said "second thoughts you drive, we need to get ready." It sounded ominous. That and the fact he went round the back, opened the back door and took the commando assault rifle out of the lockbox, along with magazines and grenades.

Billie jumped out of the vehicle. Running round to the driver's door she unclipped a small cylinder out of the glove box. It had two lights on the top. One had a red filter, the other blue. On the bottom, a small wire about twelve inches long leading to an electrical jack.

Slamming it down on the roof there was a metallic thud as the magnets gripped. Next, she pushed the jack into a socket at the end of a wire that exited the driver's doorpost at the top.

Flicking a switch on the side, the lights came on along with a police siren sound. She looked over at the two, who were a little surprised. "You're meant to be bomb disposal, remember!" She almost smiled, "they all have this kit!"

As soon as the vehicle took off, both Sandy and Joey went to work checking their equipment. That meant weapons. Joey loaded both the normal magazine and the grenade launcher. He had a feeling they were going to need it. Sandy just prayed he didn't do too much damage.

"What's that?" Billie glanced curiously at Sandy, "doesn't look standard issue!"

"It's not," Sandy replied, "at least not here, one of the perks of the government department we work for." She smiled back. "We get to choose our own weapons. Mine's a Makarov, Russian made, pretty reliable, Buffalo Bill back there," she pointed with her thumb to Joey in the back seat. "He's got the Colt commando with a forty-millimetre grenade launcher. Though what the hell he's loading that for? I have no idea," she turned to Joey. "So how are we going to play this?"

"Who exactly are you people?" Billie was driving fast, threading her way through the traffic, but that didn't stop the detective's mind asking questions.

"You mean you haven't figured it out?" Joey acted surprised. He knew she knew, but she wanted confirmation.

"I figured the security services, but even they."

"Good enough. Now let's get moving," Joey cut in. "just say nothing more okay,"

They were on the A13. The slip road to the left took them onto the East India dock road. The old docks that used to trade with the East, now long gone except for the names, names from an era long passed but not forgotten.

"Sandy sitrep?" Joey's request sounded like he was barking an order.

"Plane's a Cessna," Sandy replied, "and I don't mean a poxy little trainer. It's a Citation, with a range of about two thousand miles. It can take two or three passengers. The pilot was told to expect two, no prizes for guessing the guest list!"

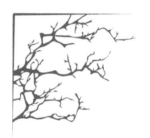

Chapter 49

"You" Sam pointed to Paul, "In here NOW!" She opened the door to what he'd thought was the pantry. It was in the kitchen. To him, it looked like a pantry. It had been in the kitchen, so he'd just assumed that's what it was.

"What, the bloody pantry?" Paul was surprised. Pantries don't have windows, so they're good for keeping food cool, and the stone walls would protect from bullets, but he was claustrophobic, and that looked a pretty small space, "You gotta be"

"Kidding you?" Sam asked, "Not a chance, and no, it's not a pantry, it's a stairwell! One that leads to a safe room." She pushed some sacks of food out of the way revealing a trapdoor in the floor. It had what looked like a barcode reader in the middle of the right-hand side of the door. Hene took out a small device and swiped it over the reader. A faint click was heard as the door raised itself five millimetres. Just enough for a fingertip to get the edge of the door. "Remember why you were brought here?"

"That was what you claimed," Paul spat back. "All I know is someone was shooting. That's all I know!"

"Yeah, well, they're here," Sam replied as Paul's face turned to one of absolute terror. "Look, get down here and follow the path to the room at the end. Get into the room and close the door. You'll be safe there," she assured him. He looked down into what seemed like a black hole, with stone steps leading down into the blackness.

He looked around frantically. He was really hoping that this wasn't really happening. That he saw Hene strapping body armour on. He knew that's what it was from the games he played, it was amazing how like the games it really looked, the guns though were a different story, they looked puny compared to the armour they were wearing, "what about you?" was all he could say as he disappeared down the steps. He was still looking up at Sam, hoping for some reassurance.

"We're just here to observe," Sam assured him. "Help is on the way. They just want us to tell them how many and where the bad guys are." They both knew she was lying. "Now get a move on!"

As soon as he was 'down the hole', Sam replaced the floor tile that was the trap door they'd lifted. She hit the 'lock' button. A slight click and the door slid back into place. You couldn't see the joint where it slid in. They were going to put the spuds back but thought better of it. They'd need the extra time it took if they had to make a quick getaway. Their brief was to keep Paul alive and get out with him. Hene was in the kitchen checking their comms link as she ran in. "How far away?" She didn't need to mention which group she was asking about.

"They're here," Hene replied as he stood up. Reaching for the binoculars on the table, he moved towards the stairs that led to the tower in the attic. He turned and carried on, "the team's about ten miles away. They want to know the lay of the land. See you later" he climbed the stairs.

The farmhouse was from the fourteenth century. A time when this part was pretty wild, and possessions had to be guarded. What better way than a stone watchtower that gave you a good view of what your enemies were doing as they approached. It wasn't a high one, but just enough to clear the tops of the trees so they could see down the road. Not perfect, but better than nothing.

Sam got to work. She was monitoring the security equipment they had. Right at this moment, she was regretting rejecting Joey's idea of landmines! He'd wanted to put mines and tripwires among the trees, but they'd rejected the idea as they didn't want animals tripping them and causing false alarms. Not to mention the panic it would cause any forestry workers who accidentally came across one!

"We're in position," the message came across their radios. They had the earpieces in, so no noise carried, it went straight to them. "Sitrep?"

"Four vehicles," Sandy replied, "One three klicks north, two, three klicks East and one mobile from the North to here, not sure how many occupants but six others following on foot and four on foot closing from the East,"

"How many are at the vehicles?" Smithy's voice came on the line.

"Four in the East, three in the North," was the reply. It was Hene, "and the other stopped half a klick short of us, north of the boundary wall."

"Hang on a minute," Mac spoke to both Jacko and Smithy, "Sam and Hene are both Kiwis right, that means they."

"I know" Smithy didn't give him a chance to finish, "They think in metric, and that's different to our imperial, a mile is about one and a half 'klicks' so three klicks is just under two miles, got it, no worries."

Timing would be everything. They were up against at least five to one against. If their plan was going to work, then everything had to be done at exactly the right time. Start too early and they'd lose the edge of surprise. Start too late and they'd be killed in a blast of gunfire as the distraction wouldn't be working!

"Smithy," Jacko said as he slowed down, "Mile and a half, seven minutes?" He asked as the back door flung open. They were still doing about fifteen miles an hour. "AND REMEMBER, AS MANY AS POSSIBLE ALIVE!" he shouted after the Sniper.

"Make it six boss, see ya," he flung himself out and rolled at the same time. The door closed under its own momentum. Holding the rifle firmly at a right angle across the chest prevented anything from going into the barrel. But all the while he was thinking about the command Jacko had just given and thinking 'you gotta be kidding me!' but he had no intention of disobeying. There was too much respect for the man.

Paratroopers are used to hitting things at speed, unlike when a skydiver comes to ground and has controls to slow his or her rate of descent down. A paratrooper doesn't have that luxury. The 'chute' slows them down enough that the jump will not kill them, but if you don't know how to control the landing, you're going to get a bone or two broken on landing, Smithy was ex 'paras' and knew just how to do it.

As soon as Smithy was clear, Jacko hit the accelerator again. Gravel flew as the wheels spun and the vehicle sped away. "Two miles to our debus point" Mac readied his weapon, as the passenger he would exit first and cover Jacko as he sought to hide the vehicle.

They were on a track that ran parallel with the road but didn't go all the way to the farmhouse. About a mile further up it veered off to the left. Skirting the forest. Far enough away that they wouldn't be heard approaching, yet near enough to get in close without too much trouble.

The .303 is an old bolt-action rifle. But it's one that's absolutely loved by hunters! First developed at the turn of the twentieth century, the ten-round bolt-action rifle was one of the most accurate rifles ever made, and using the MkVII .303 round gave the thing an effective killing range of up to two miles. In the right hands it's a lethal weapon with few equals. The beauty is that up to a thousand yards, if your 'Mk1' eyeball is that good, you don't need telescopic sights. Or as Smithy would say, "Yer can shoot the pimples of a gnat's arse"

'**B**loody typical,' Smithy thought as he took a first look at the position, 'no sodding sentries, no bloody clue!'

All eight were in the vehicles. That just made his job a lot easier, it did, however, mean that there would be a lot more who wouldn't live out the day, that couldn't be avoided and there wasn't room for complacency, he needed to get things right.

He had ten rounds in the magazine and fifty more in clips where they came from. One of the great things about the .303 is the ease with which you reload. The ammunition comes in five-round clips. All you do when you run out is open the bolt, grab a clip, slide into the slot just behind the sights, and push. All five will slide in smoothly. Then take the second clip and do the same. No need for changing mags and losing pieces as you fumble in the dark. Less than a second later and you're blasting away again. And the rate of fire is so good you can easily get 30 rounds a minute down accurately. All from a bolt action that's supposed to be obsolete!

'Fuel cap's facing me!' He couldn't believe his luck, *'makes it so sodding easy. It's almost an insult to my abilities!'* He aimed and let the first round off.

Not all ammunition is made equal. If you cut the end of a bullet with a file, you create what's known as a 'Dum-Dum' bullet that literally flattens out as it hits a target and rips a body to shreds. Get hit with a Dum Dum and you're as good as dead. The blood loss will be so great, that's why they're illegal under the Geneva convention, but there are others that are legal, and just as deadly in certain situations.

Back in the days of the world wars. There wasn't any such thing as night vision equipment, so they did something different. How about a bullet that shines a big red light all the way to the target? That 'light' is actually a small gunpowder charge that burns all the way. Result, anything flammable that it touches ignites, and that can make a pretty magnificent spectacle.

Most Land Rovers aren't Diesel! They don't need the extra grunt of a Diesel motor. Not when you've got four and a half litres of pure strength under the bonnet, not that it would matter much.

They were less than two hundred yards away, and he had a clear line of sight. Four rounds would cause mayhem. Actually, he was confident he could do it in two, but didn't want to miss an opportunity for some target practice.

It was time. He'd been down behind a log getting ready. He swivelled up and lined the shot, took it and was back down before he heard the explosion. No one would want to get caught in the blast of a fuel tank exploding. The three men in the vehicle didn't stand a chance. But the men in the second one were already running for cover.

One man had survived the first shot. That was because he'd just gotten out of the vehicle on the opposite side to go talk with someone in the back vehicle when the explosion happened. He was blown five feet into the trees. The others were all gone, burned to a crisp.

Half a second later, Smithy was up again and took the second shot, diving back down just as the first rounds of return fire began. They'd seen the flash of the rifle. It's the one drawback of the .303. No flame eliminator like the modern assault rifles. If an enemy was half expecting fire, they'd probably see you, and considering the carnage he caused with the first, that wasn't surprising.

Smithy was already slithering along the ground in a snake-like manner as the second explosion went off. He heard another scream, that meant another was down, only 'God knows' how many more to go.

Bullets were pinging into and off the log now. A collection of small arms fire. Three or four separate weapons. He only needed to move a couple of yards for his next part to work.

Ten whole seconds later, something like a voice of authority began giving commands. Smithy knew what was coming, and he was ready. More importantly, he wasn't where they thought he was.

Two machine guns opened up. From the way they were stopping and starting Smithy guessed they were AKs, he'd have to deal with them, but later, if two were firing, that meant three were coming his way!

Jacko and Mac heard the mayhem from two miles away. It was the signal.

Chapter 50

The tower wasn't huge, but the top resembled the battlements seen in mediaeval castles. It had a parapet and stone wall for archers back then to shoot from behind. It might only be ten feet above the roof of the house. But was perfect for giving a splendid view of the area and preventing anyone getting too close without being seen. Hene was up in the tower when things kicked off.

"Will ya listen to that" Hene spoke softly into the mike he was wearing, a throat mike. It picked up every syllable he uttered, no matter how low his voice was. He slowly moved so he could see the direction he'd heard the noise from. There was a pall of smoke rising from the east, and it wasn't a dying fire. This was burning furiously.

"Just a wee intro," he recognised the Scottish accent. Mac and Jacko can't have been far away. "Thought we'd let you know we're here. Smithy's enjoying himself at their expense. Now, where are those arseholes?" ever direct, he brought them back to reality.

"Seven of 'em approaching from the north." Hene replied as he ran for the stairs. He'd just reached it when he heard the 'whoosh' and explosion.

"And three more coming from the east. They're seriously considering turning back, I'd say," Sam butted in. She was watching the video feed. "If you can get word to Smithy, tell him the two machine guns are about fifty feet in front of the second vehicle he hit, but they're staying put for the moment,"

"Roger that," Mac replied, "but I'm pretty sure he's got it under control." There was a couple of seconds' pause, then came back on the line, "you two get to the bolt hole, we'll take it from here"

No one needed any encouragement. Hene was halfway there anyway, and Sam wasn't far behind. Whoever was coming for them was close, less than a couple of hundred yards. They weren't on the cameras anymore. That meant it was time to leave.

"On my way" Hene reached for the trapdoor to the stone stairs. He got it open and was halfway down when the first pings of metal started hitting the stone walls. "Shit, we're taking fire!" he shouted into the mike as he cleared the last step. Sam was already in the kitchen, trapdoor to the cellar open and ready to go. The gunfire was increasing.

Hene almost jumped the entire length of the kitchen. He wasn't even using the steps, but just seemed to dive right down, slamming the door shut as he landed halfway down. Reaching up, he slid the bolts across that would hold the trapdoor closed. It wouldn't deny whoever it was coming for long. Just long enough for them to make it to the 'bolt hole'

Sam went back up to make sure the trapdoor was closed properly. It wasn't "the dam trap won't seal!" She shouted into the mike as she tried to pull the stones down to seal the entrance.

"Don't worry about that!" Jacko responded harshly into the mike. "Get your arses moving into that room NOW! We'll deal with the rats chasing you!" it was all part of the plan, he just didn't want to tell them that.

Most of the 'pings' were coming from the door. NThere was no chance of it giving way. Not too small arms fire, it was two inches of solid English oak followed by half an inch of armour. It wasn't giving way easily. Then there was an eruption as the door shook on its hinges. It seemed to buckle and bend yet didn't give way.

"What the hell was that?" Sam shouted as Hene ran across the kitchen to her. She descended the steps two at a time. Hene would have to secure the trapdoor.

"I think they've got an RPG or something." He sang out as he slid the last bolt into place, "didn't penetrate the door with the first one, but the next will!"

"They know they haven't got much time before we get there!" Jacko's voice came on the line, "I'm guessing they don't think we've made it here yet, but they know we aren't far away, they're coming in hard and fast, but RELAX we have this under control!"

'If this is under control' Sam was thinking, *'I'd hate to see what you think out of control looks like!'* she reached out to her right, there was a small ledge there with a standard Army issue torch. Nothing else was in the tunnel. No lights, nothing that could be used to light the way, just the torch. Flicking the switch the torch came to life with a dull red glow. Just enough for them to fumble their way into the tunnel to find the safe room.

"What the hell was this place?" Hene asked as they moved along. Instead of the neat if somewhat damp concrete walls, maybe even with mould on them, they were feeling rough crumbling what almost felt like bricks. It felt like the tunnel was about to fall down.

"Sandstone" Sam replied, "same as the house, I'd guess this place was built about the same time, maybe as an escape route, all 'six' did was to block the tunnel and shove a concrete bunker down here!" they got to the steel door of the bunker, it was shut and locked, not a problem as it was a combination lock, Sam found the pad and tapped in the six-digit combination. There was a faint click as the lock disengaged and the door slid open.

"I know what the damn stone is!" Hene replied, "But what's with the tunnel and rooms underground?"

"It's an old house," Sam replied, not really sure why the house would have the tunnel. "I think it's from the middle ages. You know!

When it wasn't all that healthy to be Catholic," she stopped for a moment, "if I remember my history, some people wanted to stay Catholic, and help hide the priests. So they built tunnels into their houses along with hiding places. Joey said this place was a rich man's house back then. Maybe he had a place like that, it wouldn't take much to upgrade the place, just a new door and lock!"

After the dim tunnel, the light inside was almost painful to look at. The room was little more than a broom closet, but the door had six inches of steel that stopped anything coming at them from the tunnel. At the other end, it looked like a concrete wall with the Sandstone tunnel walls running in between. It was barely wide enough for two to pass. There was a ledge with a bed of sorts running down the length of the space. Then again, it wasn't meant for long stays!

Jacko and Mac reached the edge of the wood just in time to see the second shot from the RPG rip the door clean from its hinges. They knew what the plan was, and they knew they only had seconds to get ready for it. Two men headed around the back, and two others got ready for the front. Three were heading inside while the front and back were guarded.

"I'll take the back" Mac slowly moved from the crouch position, he turned and made eye contact, "you've got the door boss, that okay?" he was ready for a sprint

"See you inside" was all Jacko said as he crept forward, "One minute"

There are times when the most important weapon you have is stealth. This wasn't one of those. It was important, but much more so was speed. More importantly, now that Sam and Hene were in the tunnel they were effectively 'blind' and that meant that things had to happen super fast so that O'Flanagan and the Russians didn't get too far from where they'd been known to be.

Mac was still inside the treeline, and the Russians weren't paying attention to it. He could see them, but they weren't even looking for him, as soon as they got to the rear door he could see them preparing to go in, He guessed they were timing it with the team at the front, just as Jacko and he were using the entry to time their move.

The Russians were wearing body armour. It looked as if it was top of the line gear. The stuff would stop a bullet from even a high-powered weapon at close range. He was just weighing up the options when Jacko came on air. "Remember, we need prisoners"

Normal SAS procedure was a thing called the 'double-tap', where they shot for the torso first and then went in with a headshot to make sure the target was dead. That worked for 90% of operations, but sometimes the double-tap wasn't a good idea, that was the 'suicide bomber'.

The thing with the suicide bomber is you have to stop them pressing the detonator button, and even a jerk reaction from a kill shot can set them off. The only way is to make sure the spine is snapped before it has a chance to give the command. And that means a 'headshot' and in particular one to the base of the skull. Right where the spine connects with the brain.

Jacko had just ruled all that out. They'd have to improvise, and that meant using the Russian's body armour against them. That was when he realised the challenge they had.

The speed with which a bullet or round travels when it leaves the barrel is called the velocity of the weapon. They can be anything from two hundred yards per second for low-velocity weapons to the fastest at over one thousand yards per second. Literally twice the speed of sound for the highest velocity weapons.

Body armour stops most weapons from penetrating the body, but you'll never stop the velocity and something that hits you at even two hundred yards a second is going to literally 'kick the crap' out of you, and the Commando was about halfway at 700 yards a second, it would feel as if you'd been hit with a sledgehammer at full swing.

He waited for the bang of the flashbangs.

O'Flanagan's men entered the house, firing in both directions. They didn't have time for trying to identify where the targets might be, not that it mattered as Serkhov wanted everyone here killed. Three seconds later, the shots stopped as they ran out of ammunition in those mags.

"There's no one here," the voice to his right shouted as he slapped a fresh magazine on. They'd half expected that and had both exits they knew of covered. There was no escape.

"You" he pointed to the man on his right, "you take the back room, I'll take the stairs" he headed for the stairs to the next floor.

"I'll check for exits," the third man, the youngest in the group, said as he began checking for windows. The ones they saw weren't large and sealed. No one had gotten out of them.

"Igor, come in," O'Flanagan called into the radio as he moved up the stairs. There was no reply. 'don't tell me the stupid bastard's gone and left us!' was his first thought. "Igor, WERE ARE YOU?" he demanded as he reached the top of the stairs. Reaching down, he took a stun grenade, pulled the pin and tossed the grenade onto the landing and ducked, waiting for the bang.

As soon as the bang went off, he was up and firing, coming over the top of the landing spraying bullets everywhere, ricochets flying in all directions. Two actually hit the body armour and damn well hurt, but nothing else. No one there, just furniture with holes in where the bullets had gone clean through. 'But where the hell was Igor? He should have called back. O'Flanagan didn't like that. He might just have to teach the stupid prick a lesson he will not forget in a hurry. All hell was about to break loose. He just wasn't aware he'd be on the receiving end!

Chapter 51

Three men were running to where Smithy had been. He was only ten feet to the side, but he was far enough that they couldn't see where he was. They were grouped pretty close together, but the .303 would be too slow to take all of them. He laid it down and reached for the Glock.

The Glock pistol has a conventional magazine of seventeen rounds. Powerful enough to do serious damage at close range, On fully automatic, it fires just as fast as he could pull the trigger. He just couldn't keep the trigger pressed as it would only fire one single shot.

The two AK47s had moved slightly so that they could give covering fire as the men approached. The men had been steadily approaching using 'fire and manoeuvre' to keep Smithy's head down. Normally he'd be returning fire to 'win the firefight', but they outnumbered him. Straightforward tactics would not win this fight.

'Wait until you see the colour of their eyes' was his thought as they charged forward. He waited until they were right on the position then sprang out Glock at the ready, fired the first shot which missed, but wasn't even noticed. The second caught the lead man in the neck. He went down and stayed down. Shot three was at the second man. It hit square in the chest knocking him off his feet, shot four, hit the next man in the leg. He was crippled, but not out of the fight.

Smithy raced forward. The Glock still had eleven rounds in the mag. He got to the one with the injured leg and shot him in the shoulder. The screams were unnerving for even him, and that was the intention, but he ignored it. He was here to take them down, but preferably with the maximum pain. The other guy was slowly climbing up and reaching for a weapon. One shot to the shoulder stopped that, but just to make sure Smithy kicked him on the other arm. He heard bone splinter. This guy was out of the fight. The screams from the two would unnerve the other shooters. There'd be time to sort them out later. He still had some stuff to deal with.

He was in the line of sight for the shooters, but they were so shocked it took them three seconds to respond.

In that time, he'd stripped the three men of their weapons and gotten back to the safety of his original position. From now on, it was a game of 'hunter and hunted' and he had no intention of being the latter. The men were shouting instructions at the shooters. They were giving his position away, but he was already on the move. They were getting false information.

Snipers aren't just good at shooting. The sniper also has to be an expert at stealth. They have to be able to move about the battlefield without being seen or heard. They have to be able to do it with speed.

"About fifty feet from the vehicles" was what Smithy'd been told, but which way? He was pretty sure they were to the left, but that can have changed. "Where are they?" was the crucial question.

"What the hell?" He could hear a voice, but that was only a guess at what was being said as it was speaking Russian. He got some bearings from it. One of them, at least, was still where Sam had said they were.

Replacing the Glock in its holster, Smithy reached for the .303. Sliding the bolt back, he reached into the pouch on his right-hand side and took a clip out. Five rounds in the clip. He placed it in the slot just behind the breach and, using his right thumb, slid all five rounds into the magazine. Then he did exactly the same with the next clip before sliding the bolt back home. He didn't even check the safety. There was no need, as the rifle wouldn't go off unless he pulled the trigger. And the pressure at five pounds was pretty substantial for any rifle. Another reason he loved the rifle so much.

M ac had gotten to the door and duct-taped the two men's mouths shut. The last thing they needed was a warning given to the men inside. It was going to be hard enough.

"Scorpion two and three, this is Scorpion one, sitrep?" Jacko's voice came over the radio.

"Scorpion two, door secured, two bandits down," Mac replied.

"Scorpion three, seven bandits eliminated. Three down, two to go" Smithy's report was brief, yet graphic. They'd all heard the explosions, but he's got seven of them in it.

"Roger, three carry on," Jacko replied, "two standby for breach. Sam, are you still in the hole?" Jacko's voice came over on the radio. It sounded worried. "Are you still secure?"

"Affirmative," she replied simply, "we're still down here, and the door is secure, though I think your friend is on the other side by the sounds of things."

"Roger that," Jacko replied. "Make sure the doors are secure and remain so for until we inform you otherwise," he broke off. She looked over at Hene. They both knew what was coming next, and neither had any desire to get in the way.

Jacko came back on the radio. "Scorpion two, breach on three, one, two, three,"

"W hat's going on?" Paul asked. He was scared, but at least he was doing what they told him. He wasn't hyperventilating anymore. That was a good sign.

"The help we told you about," Hene began. "They're dealing with the people who came to kill you, but we need to stay here a bit longer." They couldn't hear much. The room was almost totally soundproof, almost, but not fully. They could still hear some things, and they'd heard pings against the door that Sam had told Paul were bullets being fired. She'd also assured him that the steel was thick enough to take the bullets. She didn't tell him there was another entrance, one they'd kept quiet about.

"They're arresting them then?" Paul asked, "are the police here?"

"I said they're dealing with the situation, but no," Hene cut him off, "they're not the police. They're a special unit from the Army called in with situations like this. Ever hear of the Special Air Service?"

The blank face said it wasn't registering. Then a light went on. "The SAS, aren't they some ultra-special forces, kinda like Ninja SEALs on steroids?" He replied.

"Yeah," Sam chuckled at the reply. "Sorta like that, but don't let them hear you say it! To them, the SAS can't be compared with others. They're in a league of their own," she joked, then looked at Hene and added, "then again, with this mob. That might just be true. They are in a league of their own!"

Mac and Jacko came in from different directions. They were methodical but quick and silent. Every room was checked, making sure no nasty surprises were waiting for them. Then they got to the trapdoor. It was up.

Jacko looked at Mac and pointed. They could hear O'Flanagan in the hole lecturing the two others. They were prepping a C4 charge for the door. Mac took a flashbang from his pouch, struck the wick and waited.

Two seconds after striking the wick, he rolled it down the steps and dived back around the corner of the pantry. Almost the instant it hit the floor, the device went off, blinding and deafening anyone who wasn't protected.

O'Flanagan was still cussing the friggin' Russkies, as he called them. Where the hell were they? They were supposed to secure the perimeter and prevent any cops or anyone else getting through. The whole friggin thing had turned to crap, and he just wanted the job finished. He was focusing so much on getting the job done he missed the things going on around him, including the fact his men were seemingly disappearing.

"We'll blow this friggin thing, kill 'em inside and get the hell out of here!" He spoke to the other two, who were still with him. "Then we'll sort those stupid," he never finished the rest of the sentence.

The light was blinding; the noise knocked his hearing out. Being in the confined space amplified the effect. Two of their five senses ceased to work. They were blind and deaf to anything going on. All three knew what was coming next. They may be blind and deaf, but their spatial awareness was still working and as fast as their bodies would function, all three went for their weapons and turned to face the entrance. They were going to blast anything that came through it. They didn't get the chance.

Jacko was at the top of the steps leaning over literally hung upside down. He was shooting. His first two rounds caught the first guy in the chest knocking him back into the second. The force of the fall sent both weapons flying. They'd forgotten to take their safeties off and were using old Sten guns, and the safety was never that reliable. One of them went off and spewed all thirty rounds at head height.

"Pull me up," he screamed as soon as he'd fired the first burst. Mac was holding his legs. He pulled as hard and fast as he could. They could hear screams in the tunnel.

"What gives boss?" Mac asked as soon as Jacko was clear.

"Bloody idiots were using SMGs" Jacko shouted. He was deafened by the noise, even after using ear defenders. "One dropped the damned thing. The whole mag went off" he scrambled to his feet, they knew the guys downstairs would have broken bones and the like, it might not have penetrated the body armour, but the velocity would have 'knocked 'em around a bit"

They reached the bottom to see only two were moving. O'Flanagan had been hit in the face with a bullet. It had smashed his goggles and gone into the eye. He was dead. The other two were moaning, and neither Jacko nor Mac wanted to be gentle. "Shut up and spread 'em" Mac kicked the first guy into the position for a body search, he screamed.

"Ya damned English Bastard," the Irishman spat out as he tried to fight back, only to scream as Mac forced him back into the position.

"I didnae tell ya to move!" Mac screamed into his ear. "And quit insulting me if ya wanna live. I'M A SCOTTISH BASTARD AND DINNAE FORGET IT LADDIE!" he began a brutal body search.

Jacko was giving the same treatment to the other Irishman. They also both made sure that the two prisoners could see O'Flanagan's face, what was left of it. Blood was pooling around the head. It wasn't a pretty sight, but for Jacko, it was very satisfying. A major player in the terror networks was dead, and their people were alive. That had to be good. "House secured," he reported, "Scorpion three, sitrep?" they hadn't forgotten Smithy.

"All accounted for here, boss," Smithy replied, "Seven casualties. The rest are injured, but not life-threatening."

"Roger that," Jacko replied, "Time to call the cavalry,"

It was Sir Michael who answered. "They're on their way, will inform of possible hostiles in the area, they can earn their keep with the three to the north!"

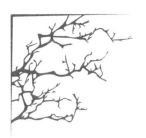

Chapter 52

"What the?" The first officer through the farmhouse door couldn't believe what he was seeing. They knew the situation was all over, and they were there for the 'clean up' but having them all sitting drinking tea as if nothing had happened was bloody ridiculous. There were bodies and injured criminals everywhere and they were drinking tea? "What the hell is going on?" was all he could say.

"Evening officer" there was a young lady, a blonde and not unattractive by the look of her. She was the one that spoke. "I'm detective sergeant Sam"

"She's attached to MI6 at the moment," one of the heavily armed men said, "and it's best you don't know our names. Just call us 'A, B or C or whatever you like, but no names. I'm soldier A." He stood up to greet the officers, "and the tea helps with stress relief" he carried on. "Now to business. We've been tracking this gang for a while. All we can say is it's linked to the ransomware that happened a few weeks ago, apparently someone was really pissed off that young Paul here" he pointed the young hacker out, "his name you can have, but it doesn't go in any reports or news-feeds, GOT IT?" He carried on, "Young Paul here really pissed some people off who tried to kill him. We knew they would, so we set a trap for 'em"

"Sir" one of the cops who'd followed the first officer on the scene shouted from the Pantry. "Sir, we have something here!" He poked his head around the door beckoning for the senior officer to come and look, "looks like a."

"An entrance to a tunnel" Jacko hadn't given his name. He was 'Soldier A', but he went on. "Down there you'll find a body, one Patrick O'Flanigan, a man the world has been after for a while if I'm not mistaken, and you won't say anything about whatever else is down there WILL YOU?" He knew they'd had strict orders not to reveal anything they found. Everyone knew the cops were only here for cosmetic reasons. MI6 has no powers of arrest. Neither does its sister organisation MI5, although '5' is supposed to be the one dealing with internal stuff.

Just then, another cop walked in. This one was different. He had the six-pointed star and pip on the shoulder said he was a Chief Superintendent, the look of disgust on his face said it all, he was having to play 'second fiddle' and clear up a mess that was every senior officer's nightmare.

"Captain," he looked straight at Jacko, *use the man's rank,'* he thought to himself, *'show him he's not the only one who can find things out'* he walked straight up to Jacko, "Care to tell me what this is all about?"

Jacko didn't even flinch, "I believe you'll already have been told sir, and don't use my or any of our ranks again, IS THAT CLEAR?" Jacko shot back, establishing the real control "Russians and ex-IRA terrorists working together, but otherwise no sir, I'm bound by the official secrets act."

"Don't come that with me, boy," the cop glared at him. "I can have your career in an instant,"

"You'd be welcome to it sir," Jacko replied raising the mug of tea, clearly enjoying baiting the cop, "but no, unless you get a briefing from your people, I'm not at liberty to tell you anything, other than to thank you for cleaning up here, oh and you can look after Paul now the danger is over." He put the mug down, turned to the others, and indicated it was time to leave. They got ready.

The cop wasn't done. He turned to Hene and faced off, "and who are you?"

Before Hene could reply, Mac stepped in. "These two lovely folks are seconded to us from overseas. Mess with them and you'll have the foreign office, not to mention us in your case. Now be a good boy and do yer job." He helped Hene grab his gear.

Their Landrover appeared as soon as they left the house. Smithy was behind the wheel. Jacko went around the back of the vehicle and opened the back door. Next, he opened the lockbox at the back and indicated for the weapons to be given to him. Each cleared his weapon, checked the breach and handed it to Jacko, who did the same and stowed it away in the lockbox. Not even sidearms were kept out. Then each got into the vehicle. Smithy gave the driver's seat up for Jacko. Mac offered the front seat to Sam, who was slightly puzzled but took it anyway, and Hene climbed in the back. Only when they were all in and on the way did the conversation start again.

"It's better for them if they don't know" Jacko was the first to speak as they turned onto the main road.

"But they're cops," Sam replied. She knew what Jacko was saying was right in some ways, but she knew she'd never been satisfied with the answers the cops had. "They'll keep digging"

"Let 'em," Mac chipped in. "Sir Mike only needs a few days to make good on what we have. After that, it won't matter!"

"Why?" Hene asked as Sam turned to face Mac, the same question written all over her face.

"Look, we got the mole," Jacko answered the question, "That was the goal, but I'm guessing in Serkhov's files is much more than the mole. I'm betting he has dirt on just about every part of our system, and he's been using it for years. Now we have it!"

"And now they go to jail?" Sam asked. She already knew the answer, but wanted to hear it.

"Not all," Jacko replied. "Serkhov had a lot of friends, and they're going to pay for that friendship, but that's not for us to deal with."

"So we just walk away?" it was more a statement than a question. To the coppers in Sam and Hene, it just felt wrong. They would, as that was what they were told to do, but that didn't make it feel right.

"For now," Jacko replied, "yes we walk away, and let the system do what it can!"

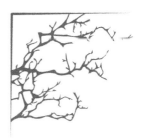

Chapter 53

"There it is!" Joey screamed as they came into sight of the airport. They were running along the wire that separated the airport from the rest of London. The runway was to their left and about four hundred yards away over the grass. The plane was a twin-engined Cessna jet. Four portholes down the side told them it was an executive jet. And it was Serkhov's own personal one.

"We're too late!" Billie shouted in frustration. The plane was taxiing out from the terminal. They'd already loaded passengers and were getting ready for takeoff. "They've already left the terminal" the anger was dripping from every word.

"Like hell we are!" Joey shouted back. He pressed the button on the electric windows. "Head for the fence, get us through there, and head for the plane. Leave the rest to me."

"What?" Billie spun round momentarily, just as Joey lined up the Commando he had in the back and fired the grenade launcher. The fence disintegrated. "Where the hell did that come from?" She was screaming.

'That explains why he was loading it!' Sandy thought. "Just do as he says," she shouted at the woman. "Even planes don't get away when he's doing this stuff, believe me! He's taken 'em out before." She also had her window down and was getting ready to use the Makarov. "Move it, bring us alongside the plane!"

Joey's shot blew a ten-foot hole in the fence. But it was now past them, so Billie yanked the handbrake and waited until she was lined up with the gap before releasing the brake and flooring the accelerator. The vehicle lurched forward, tires throwing dirt and gravel everywhere as they picked up speed.

The plane was still taxiing to the position. Every aircraft had to wait for permission from air traffic control before they could start their run for takeoff. The pilot hadn't seen what was happening, but air traffic control had.

"Cessna 200 hold your position," the voice came into the pilot's ear. "We have an obstacle on the runway, at your two o'clock. Security is on the way,"

"Roger that control. Please advise the delay," the pilot replied before turning to inform the passengers. "Sorry folks, we're going to be a little delayed. Some idiot just got onto the runway. Should be clear soon," he smiled as he turned back towards the controls.

"Get us airborne now" Serkhov shouted, he began climbing out of his seat.

"I have to wait for clearance," the pilot replied.

"You want a job after this?" Serkhov shouted back, "Or better yet you want to live?" The pilot looked back. Serkhov was holding a pistol. "Get us airborne NOW!"

There were two of them in the cockpit. The co-pilot had listened to everything. She didn't even argue. The copilot, a young female pilot, just pushed the throttles to their take-off speed. The increase in engine power told the pilot to get on with the job. "Docklands air traffic. Negative. We cannot wait. My passenger has advised me they need to leave now. The obstacle won't affect us." He clicked the radio off, turning to the passengers. He simply said, "Stand by" as the engines came up to speed. Then he threw the brakes off and she was away like the fast jet she was.

J oey was hanging half out of the window. One hand holding on for dear life. The other he was trying to steady the weapon with. Sandy was also half out of the other side of the car. She knew that at this distance she had no chance of hitting the plane with the Makarov. "Joey we need them alive, remember!" She shouted into the mike. They were still on their local network. He switched from the grenade launcher to the rifle and selected automatic fire.

"You two are bloody bonkers," Billie shouted at both of them. She had her foot to the floor and was speeding up as fast as the car would go. But the jet was closing the distance much faster and would get to the take-off point, or V1, as it was known long before the car would be there to stop it.

"Head towards the sodding thing," Joey screamed, "We have to stop them reaching takeoff velocity,"

"They're almost there," Billie shouted back, "How the hell are you going to do that?"

"Don't worry," Sandy sounded almost as if she was trying to assure someone. Billie wasn't sure if it was her she was trying to assure, or herself, "Joey's King when it comes to hair-brained schemes, and he hasn't had one for an entire week, JUST GO WITH THE FLOW"

"You asked for it!" Billie realised that right at this point, if they didn't pull this off, her career wasn't just 'in the toilet. It had been flushed down the drain and disappeared out of sight. She yanked the wheel hard left and straightened up. The car was doing nearly ninety miles an hour, the plane doing closer to two hundred, and they had less than a quarter of a mile to cover.

"Sandy inside, NOW" Joey screamed as they sped towards each other.

Sandy had a sense of what Joey was going to try, and she didn't want to be anywhere near what was about to happen. She scrambled back inside. Then reached across and back, grabbing Joey's chest. She pulled as hard as she could. He would need the extra stability.

The car was less than a hundred yards from the plane when he pulled the trigger. He wasn't aiming for the aircraft itself. He was aiming for a point in front and letting the bullets 'drift' onto the target. They were closing at nearly three hundred miles an hour. The Commando can fire at a rate of 800 rounds a minute on automatic. That meant they were closing at around one hundred and forty-six feet per second. In one second, the machine gun would discharge maybe fifteen rounds. The chances of hitting anything were so small he just couldn't think of it. He didn't dare think of it. Joey held on and began blasting away, firing just in front of where he expected the tyres to roll.

Four seconds later, he was out of ammo. Unclipping the mag he swivelled it around. He'd taped another to it, clipped back in, and began blasting. Even though the plane was already past them.

Security was closing in from both sides, sirens wailing, lights flashing.

The plane was hurtling down the runway when the pilot felt a massive pull to the right. Warnings started going off in the cockpit as the plane slewed engine warning lights came on. Something wasn't right.

"What the hell just happened?" Serkhov demanded. He could feel the plane was almost in a skid. He'd got his harness back on and was strapped in for takeoff. Two other men with them were strapping in, faces ashen.

"I think the undercarriage just blew out," the pilot yelled above the noise. He was doing his best to control the skid.

"Can we still get airborne?"

"Not a chance," the pilot replied. "I'll be lucky to stop her bursting into flames, brace yourselves,

***"

"Turn us around and give chase." Joey shouted down to Billie. The other security vehicles were closing fast, but there was still room for the manoeuvre. "Bring us up behind, but make sure they don't see us"

"This better be worth it!" She shouted as she swung the wheel and the car careered round, not quite on two wheels, but not far off. Gunning the engine, they were off again, just in time to see the right wheel blow out. The whole side of the plane dipped dangerously towards the runway and the struts gouged a trench in the tarmac.

"Too bloody late for that!" Sandy shouted back over the noise of the engine as Billie raced forward, "we either pull this off or all our careers are finished, not that he's worried about that, bloody adrenaline junkie. He's having a great time," she nodded in Joey's direction.

The plane was slowing dramatically as the pilot fought to control the skid. They were coming up fast, but the airport police were also closing fast, and they weren't heading for the plane. A new set of sirens began, along with lights and the full paraphernalia. The fire brigade was heading for what it saw as a potential air disaster. Bille had to do something, and fast.

"We are the police." Billie was speaking urgently into the radio in the car. She'd been patched through to airport security. "this is a joint operation with the Metropolitan Police and MI6 DO NOT INTERFERE!" She hoped that worked as they came level with the slowing plane. Joey was inside the car and swapping magazines.

Sandy was doing the same. They both had their seatbelts undone and doors half-open.

"Come up behind the plane," Joey spoke instead of shouting, "I don't want them to see us."

Security surrounded both the car and the plane, not sure who to arrest. If anyone that was, BJ was on the radio giving them the information that she had. Someone told them to hold off, but they did not know who.

"What do we do now?" Margaret was feeling trapped. She'd only ever been in it for the money, and there had been lots of it, but field experience? She had none. Consequently, she had no idea what to do, but she was armed, they all were.

Joey and Sandy had got out of the plane without being seen. They were by the tail of the plane where all the action was taking place up the front. They needed it to stay that way.

The rear of the plane was open. Serkhov was getting ready to jump and make a run for it. Margaret was right there with him, both carrying weapons, both concentrating on the vehicles in front. The fence was less than fifty yards away. Neither of them had seen Joey or Sandy.

Sandy looked over at Joey. It was almost like she could read his thoughts. They were telling her to wait, "let Serkhov make his move." She heard his voice, but saw his lips weren't even moving. They were communicating directly, yet without talking. He looked her way, but the look said, "get my drift?" She knew exactly what was coming.

"You," Serkhov pointed to one of his bodyguards. They were on the plane with him. "Keep an eye out at the front. I want to know where every cop is, especially the maniac who shot at us!"

"Da" the guard went into the cockpit and started watching. Both the pilot and co-pilot were unbuckling themselves. The guard pushed them back into their seats. "The cop is talking to the other cops" he shouted back, "I keep watch"

"Good," Serkhov opened the back hatch, "Get the pilot and co-pilot to the front hatch, but don't let them off until I say. If the cops move, throw the pilot and co-pilot off. That'll cause confusion, then start shooting."

"Okay boss" the guards grabbed one each and held them near the door. All it would take was one wrench on the handle and it would fly open. They didn't open it. One guard tied the two pilots up while the other watched from the window. They knew exactly what the boss was about to do.

Serkhov opened the rear hatch and peered out. He couldn't see anyone there. Leaning back in the plane he looked directly at Margaret and asked. "Want to find out what a British jail is like? Or want to be free?" then turned, jumped onto the tarmac and ran. The turncoat spy was right behind him.

Joey'd holstered his weapon and was waiting. Serkhov came first. Joey glanced at Sandy and gave her a 'wait' signal. Then the turncoat came out. Sandy leapt and flattened Margaret as her feet touched the floor. Joey was off like a greyhound chasing the 'rabbit' on the racetrack.

Serkhov was fit. He was old, but he was fit and very fast. The distance to the fence was about a hundred and fifty yards. For an Olympic sprinter that would take about fifteen seconds, but fit as he was, Serkhov was no Olympic sprinter. For him, it would take more like thirty-five to forty seconds. He did, however, have a twenty-yard start on Joey.

Joey was closing the distance when the first shots pinged around his feet. *'No prizes for guessing where that came from!'* He thought to himself, but otherwise ignored what was going on. He didn't have time to zigzag, he just hoped for poor aim, then he heard a familiar sound, the bark of a weapon he was familiar with hearing. All shots stopped after that.

Serkhov was less than thirty feet from the fence when Joey launched himself into a flying tackle. He hit the man around the waist and took him down.

Serkhov had seen the dive and tried to sidestep, but Joey's outstretched arms wrapped around him and they tumbled sideways. He knew he was going down, but that wasn't without a fight. As he twisted, he reached out and grabbed the arm that had wrapped around his waist and accelerated the twist, wrenching the arm at an unnatural angle. He wanted to break it.

Joey went with it. Flowing with every move. He followed the twist and launched a classic scissor kick at the same time. Looking like a ballerina performing a ballet move, except instead of ballet shoes, making contact. They were Army combat boots, and it was full body contact that was aimed for. The first foot landed and broke Serkhov's hold on Joey's wrist. The second one, literally two-tenths of a second later, should have knocked him senseless. He went down on all fours, but came up brandishing a knife.

Joey landed on his knees, almost in a squat position facing his opponent. As soon as he saw the knife, he curled up into a ball and launched himself, hitting the man right in the chest before he'd had time to use the knife. He still had hold of it and was trying to raise the weapon, but Joey lashed out with a leg and kicked the hand so hard the knife went flying, at the same time he punched the man in the face, he heard the nose splinter. Serkhov was fighting for all he was worth.

"That's enough" he heard an English voice shout. Not one Joey recognised, but the click of a weapon being cocked made him stop. Right there next to him were two airport police, weapons drawn and ready. BJ also stood alongside them, her weapon in her hand. They were all pointing at Serkhov.

"What's the meaning of this?" Serkhov was trying a bluff. "Do you have any idea who I am? I'll have your jobs for this, and after that, I'll,"

"Save it," BJ stopped him, "Alexei Serkhov, I'm arresting you on suspicion of conspiracy to commit murder, espionage, drug trafficking and money laundering. You don't have to say anything, but should you later rely on evidence that you withheld from the police, you will be charged with perverting the course of justice? Am I making myself clear?`` She was already securing the handcuffs on the man as soon as they were on the two officers frogmarched him away.

Sandy had Margaret secure. The handcuffs were on and two other cops were leading her away. She slowly walked over and joined the other two. As soon as she was there, she simply reached up and kissed Joey. He responded by hugging her tight while Billie looked on slightly embarrassed. After a good minute, they relaxed and both of them reached out to give her a hug.

Chapter 54
Three days later.

"Yes, she's expected," the voice on the other end of the line assured the security guard. "We don't give visitors passes, so I'd like one of you to escort DS Jones up to my conference room. We're waiting for her there" the guard hit the button to end the connection, they were both slightly confused but for seemingly different reasons, the guard because visitors just weren't allowed into the building, and BJ because of who was asking to see her, worried was a major understatement!

It turned out that the woman on the plane was none other than the secretary of the 'DG' or Director-General of MI6! The most secretive man in the whole of the UK, the very man tasked with making sure all Britain's secrets stayed just that, secret.

Townsend had actually been giving her the biggest bollocking she'd ever had. She wasn't even sure she still had a job when he got the call, and it was a very unpleasant one, but not for her. Not from the 'super' or even the district commander. It had been somewhere much higher up the government food chain.

Whatever was said in the conversation obviously hadn't been pleasant for the Detective Chief Inspector, but he'd simply said. "You obviously have friends, Jones, and one of them wants to see you over at Vauxhall house. Get out of my sight," and virtually threw her through the door.

The elevator looked just like any other elevator in any other office block in the country. Six floors, six buttons. Plain steel interior, two cameras in the elevator, along with cameras in the entrance. The security guard looked like any other in the country. She was even wearing a uniform, except for the 9mm Beretta in a shoulder holster, that is. Both smiled at each other, but neither really spoke as they waited to reach the top floor.

As soon as the doors opened, the guard stepped out and turned left. They reached the end of the corridor and faced another door. This one required an intercom. The guard spoke into the intercom and the door opened. "there you are, ma'am" the guard indicated for her to go through.

"Aren't you coming up? He said to escort me all the way?" Billie replied, slightly confused. She was halfway through the door.

"The conference area starts here, ma'am," the guard assured her. "Top of the stairs, turn right and walk down, you can't miss it, there'll be another guard to show you the way, I don't have clearance for that area." and with that, the guard gently closed the door.

As soon as she was at the top of the steps, there was another guard, this one was also armed, Beretta in a shoulder holster, and just as businesslike, "If you'll follow me ma'am" he started walking down the corridor.

She didn't really like being called 'ma'am'. It reminded her of a spinster schoolmistress from the St Trinians comedy she used to watch growing up, but she managed to say nothing.

They came to a door, and the guard knocked before pushing the door open.

"Come in," a familiar voice spoke. The voice didn't have the metallic ring of the phone, but there was no mistaking the voice. It was the one from the phone calls. "Glad you could join us, everyone this is Detective Sergeant Jones, who was the one heading up the investigation into Farid Akbari's murder." The man speaking was slightly older than all the others in the room. Very 'distinguished' with short white hair, modern but metal-rimmed glasses. They looked like progressive lenses. He was the only one wearing a three-piece suit, and it wasn't a cheap one. "Oh, I forgot. Where are my manners? I'm"

"Thank you, Sir Michael, I recognise you from photos," Billie stammered out. She was in the presence of the 'DG' himself, and that took a few moments to get used to.

"Yes, well" Sir Michael stopped momentarily, "I believe you've met most of the people here" he began again, "Please, take a seat" he indicated to the one spare seat in the room, right next to Sandy and flanked on the other side by another female, a blonde who had a guy with a dark complexion and strange tattoos on his arm, they looked like coppers, they just had that look!

As soon as she was sitting down, Sir Michael pressed a button in front of him. "Yes, you can bring the drinks in now, as well as snacks for everyone" he leaned back as the guard came through the door with a trolley full of beverages. As soon as the server left the room, Sir Michael began.

"I just wanted to take the time to say a big thank you to all you folks here for your part in what we called Operation Scorpion." He gave a very brief pause, then went on, "Our aim was to hinder the flow of drugs into Britain, but what we've achieved goes much further than that, and it's only been possible because of what you folks in the field did,"

No one said anything, Billie did not know what they were talking about, neither did Hene nor Sam, or the Scorpion One, the only ones who really knew what was being hinted at were Chambers and. Sandy, it was Chambers, took over next.

"At first, it was simply diverting their funds into bank accounts they couldn't access." He reached down and took up the clicker on the table. A screen came alive down the end of the conference room. Figures started popping up. "That revealed money all over the globe when we started doing that. They got nervous, so they did something about that, and I was kidnapped."

"We couldn't let the Intel fall into enemy hands," Sir Michael took over again, "so you four were called on," he waved towards Jacko and the team, "You were sent into Iran to get him out!"

"We know all this," Jacko replied. "Where are you going with it?"

"You do," said Sir Michael, "but these folks don't, and they had their lives on the line more than once. I felt we owed them some form of explanation, and besides, this drug ring, the Phoenix group has been damaged, but we're not sure it's totally destroyed, they'll need to watch their backs from this time onwards, best they know who it might be!"

"They'll be joining a long list," Sam quipped. "Just about every villain in New Zealand would like a piece of me" that drew a few smiles, but the only one she reacted to was Hene, who got thumped on the arm. He rubbed it at the same time as smiling. Sam leaned over and whispered, "I'll deal with you later," but the smile on her face said he was going to enjoy it. Everyone except Billie missed it.

"New Zealand wasn't meant to happen, was it, boss?" Joey asked. He was still a little uncomfortable with what he felt they'd caused for Sam and Hene to go through, especially the near execution.

"You're right there Joey," Sir Michael used Joey's nickname instead of his real one, or even his rank, that didn't go unnoticed. "It was only after the fact we started turning things up, and you folks began to pretty much run your own operation. We wanted the mole, but that's where the lead came from. Care to explain how you knew?"

It was Jacko's turn to reply, "There was a call placed, just before we stormed the positions on the Island." He replied. "We weren't able to hear all the conversation as it was using a frequency hopper, but we got a location, and gender from it!"

"And from that, you deduced who the mole was?" Sir Michael was surprised. "You gave me a tape. I heard a full conversation!"

"Yes, you did Sir, but not THAT conversation. Once they had it, the people in New Zealand went back into the call logs. Found another from the same voice and played with it. That's why we couldn't just go in and arrest her sir, it was faked! But we had a location and gender!"

"You faked it?" Sir Michael's voice went icy cold.

"We knew the call came from the third floor of this building. It was female and had detailed knowledge of us, sir."

"What do you mean?" This was the first time he'd heard any of this, "detailed knowledge"

"Next to the phone was a list of five names. Our names sir, that's what I mean by detailed knowledge. Only three people had that knowledge." Jacko replied, "and only one was female. Nothing was ever recorded about our op in Iran. No names were ever recorded. The cameras were off that night as no one was to see us arrive or leave, yet the dealers had our names, they knew it was us, that can only have come from one source, but we needed to catch her in the act!" Jacko looked over at BJ it was almost as if he was trying to apologise for what happened. "We had a plan, but they acted first, so we had to run with what we had!"

"And that meant what exactly?" Sam couldn't help herself. It seemed they'd glossed over what happened to her and Hene.

"Same as in New Zealand," Joey replied. "When they took you, they thought they were getting me and Sandy. They were going to get what information they could out of us, and then it was bye-bye when they realised you weren't us. They moved it up. We weren't going to let that happen!"

Normally, at this point, the debate should have been at the level of a farce, but it wasn't. Yes, everyone was 'letting go' but Billie was amazed that it actually seemed to be 'therapeutic' in that each one was letting go of the stress in a way they hadn't been able to during the whole thing. Even the two people she didn't know, okay she'd worked out they were Kiwis. That meant the guy's tattoos were probably Maori. She filed that away in her brain, and by the sounds of it, they'd been cops who ended up with this crowd. That meant she'd figured out who everyone really was, and that made her feel a little happier.

"Sorry about all this sergeant," Sir Michael was looking directly at her, the noise had abated and everyone was looking in her direction, "but I felt that some explanation was in order, so you could see a little of how complicated things are going to get with the prosecutions."

"So I gathered," Billie replied with a trace of sarcasm in her voice, "Just how many will actually make it to court, though?" She didn't really believe they would want their dirty laundry airing in public.

"There are some that won't," Sir Michael replied.

"Dirty laundry?" Billie asked.

"On the contrary," Sir Michael assured her, "extradition. Serkhov is wanted in the Ukraine, as are a couple of his henchmen. We've decided to make it happen, naturally that means we can't charge our mole with any crimes as there's no evidence. But there is a thing called 'detained at Her Majesty's pleasure' that's what she'll get," he looked pleased. "As for the rest, the drug ring, the chop shop, taking down the terrorist. You get all the credit, except for what's been already given to Sergeant Harris, that is!"

The meeting went on for another half hour, not that she heard much of it after. Justice had been done, each had received some form of punishment, yet it still left a hollow feeling inside. But it was the best she was going to get, and she knew it.

Chapter 55
Somewhere in the United Kingdom

The lights came on. She did not know the time. They hadn't given her any means of measuring the passage of time, but that was part of the technique she knew they would use to 'disorient' her. Make her think weeks had passed when it might only have been days, but then again, it might have been months! It was all part of the game.

Next, a small trap would be opened at the foot of the cell door, and a metal tray with food would be pushed through. That was good. She felt hungry.

She guessed it had been a week or so since she was taken at the airport, but there'd been no contact with the outside world since being brought here that day. She was allowed no contact, not even sunlight!

There was a routine of sorts. The lights would go on, and would stay on regardless of whether or not she tried to sleep. A metal tray of food would be slid through the small flap at the bottom of the door. They would be watching, of which she was certain.

The cell, that's what it was, had no cameras. That would be too obvious, and too easy to break. No, this one had the old Victorian one-way keyhole spyglass. They could see everything in the cell, and she could see nothing of the outside.

Breakfast came through. Lukewarm porridge, nothing else with it, it looked like wet cement, and tasted almost as bad as that. She longed for a bagel and coffee, but that would not happen.

Proof that she was being watched always came when she finished breakfast. As soon as the bowl was back on the metal tray, it was withdrawn. That was usually the end of her contact with the outside world until just before the lights would go out, then more food would come through, usually with a cup of nearly lukewarm tea.

The rest of the day was spent in mind-numbing boredom. This day was shaping up to be the same.

Footsteps outside the cell. A rattling of keys, keys turning in the lock. No, she wasn't asleep. She pinched herself to make sure it wasn't a dream it was, but it was one in which she was conscious and never-ending, a living nightmare.

The door swung open, and the first human face she'd seen in who knows how long stood here. They showed zero emotion. Instead, the woman walked into the cell, clasped her on the shoulder and spun her around, grabbing her arms, first the right, then the left. She was handcuffed, with the arms behind her back. Then spun around again. Two more uniformed people, guards, marched her down the corridor.

Less than fifty feet away, she was wheeled into a room. There was a table there with two chairs. One was filled with a man she didn't know, the other was empty. She was forced into that chair; the handcuffs were not removed.

On the desk was a file, brown plain and not very thick. She knew it contained her life, at least what they knew of her life! And he was here to find out more.

"Hello Margaret," the man looked at her for the first time, a slight smile on his lips, "First welcome to the secure psychiatric facility at Broadmoor." He waved his arms, "Sir Michael said I should have a word with you, what do you want to tell me?"

"Nothing," she spat out.

"Really?" the man asked again, "so you like it here then?"

She stayed silent. The sullen look said it all, but she would give nothing away.

"Because until you tell me what you know, this is where you'll stay, with no contact with the outside world." He was almost gloating, "not even sunlight!"

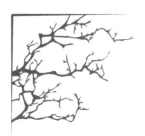

The End

If you enjoyed this novel then why not take a quick peek at the next one in the series, there's an excerpt right here. I'll be back afterwards to let you know about some things.

Before you go

T here's one thing I'd like to ask of you, it'll only take a couple of minutes, but it'll mean a world of difference for me.

As a self-published author, It's really important to me how well the books are received, and one way that both myself and Amazon use for this is the star rating and reviews. It would be awesome if you could give the book a star rating and leave a couple of sentences saying what you thought of the book.

You'll be offered the chance on the next page

Thank you, and hopefully see you soon

One last thing. Would you like a free book?

T he only thing I ask is would you also be interested in joining my
monthly newsletter?

If the answer to both is yes then head on over to the link below and
sign up and you'll hear from me soon.

Regards

Lawrence

Here's the link

**https://storyoriginapp.com/giveaways/e9d0321c-ea7a-11ea-
9cee-af527d115268**

Don't miss out!

Visit the website below and you can sign up to receive emails whenever Lawrence Hebb publishes a new book. There's no charge and no obligation.

https://books2read.com/r/B-A-YORP-QDEKC

BOOKS 2 READ

Connecting independent readers to independent writers.

Did you love *Scorpion's Vengeance*? Then you should read *Phoenix Rising*[1] by Lawrence Hebb!

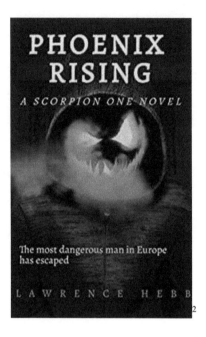

The most dangerous man in Europe is behind bars. Alexei Serkhov is on his way to a 'Black site' somewhere in Eastern Europe. MI6 can breathe a sigh of relief, the traitor has been caught, and the drugs are gone from the streets, or so they think!But the Phoenix is a mythical bird that dies in a ball of fire and is reborn.The ball of fire is accompanied by a hail of bullets leaving agents dead, and Scorpion One back at the start with a terrorist on the loose and hunting them.Joey and Sandy had been sent to oversee the transfer. But the tables are turned as the hunter becomes the hunted. And they try to figure out what his next move will be. Then the bombs start to go off, and the hunt becomes a race against time.

---

1. https://books2read.com/u/boqdkL

2. https://books2read.com/u/boqdkL

Read more at https://app.mailerlite.com/sites/preview/ 2515877.

Also by Lawrence Hebb

Scorpion One
Sting of the Scorpion
Scorpion's Reach
Scorpion's Vengeance
Phoenix Rising
Revenge of the Phoenix

The Saxon Chronicles
The Last Centurion

Standalone
Scorpion One First Strike
Safe Haven

Watch for more at https://app.mailerlite.com/sites/preview/
2515877.

About the Author

Hi there! Lawrence Here. Just taking a moment to say a big hello and that I hope you enjoy the book.

I love a good yarn, and I think this is a great one. A lot of the book is based around my experience as both a Soldier in the British Army and my experience in Iraq as an aid worker in the nineties, and I'll let you into a secret, this nearly did happen (but don't tell the wife PLEASE!)

Read more at https://app.mailerlite.com/sites/preview/ 2515877.